About the Author

MJ Fothe spent the last eleven years working for a sealing solutions distributor, and service center in Surrey British Columbia. She is a mother of two and grandmother of two based in Surrey British Columbia. After spending many years as a single mother with limited time to write, she became determined to relocate from her home in Edmonton Alberta to the Lower Mainland in British Columbia to break out of the demanding oil and gas industry, and into a more diverse field while continuing to work on her erotic novel series 'A Rockstar & A Runner'. MJ Fothe continues to write, as she juggles her time between her career and her personal life. Currently, she has completed seven rough draft books in the erotic genre and a children's book inspired by the arrival of her second grandchild, which she is looking to have illustrated then turning into an entire collection based on the characters.

Heart's Desire: A Rockstar & A Runner

MJ Fothe

Heart's Desire: A Rockstar & A Runner

Vanguard Press

VANGUARD PAPERBACK

© Copyright 2024
MJ Fothe

The right of MJ Fothe to be identified as author of
this work has been asserted by her in accordance with the
Copyright, Designs and Patents Act 1988.

All Rights Reserved

No reproduction, copy or transmission of this publication
may be made without written permission.
No paragraph of this publication may be reproduced,
copied or transmitted save with the written permission of the publisher, or in accordance with the
provisions
of the Copyright Act 1956 (as amended).

Any person who commits any unauthorized act in relation to this publication may be liable to
criminal prosecution and civil claims for damages.

A CIP catalogue record for this title is available from the British Library.

ISBN 978-1-83794-260-2

This is a work of fiction. Names, characters, businesses, places, events and incidents are either the
products of the author's imagination or used in a fictitious manner. Any resemblance to actual
persons, living or dead, or actual events is purely coincidental.

Vanguard Press is an imprint of
Pegasus Elliot Mackenzie Publishers Ltd.
www.pegasuspublishers.com

First Published in 2024

Vanguard Press
Sheraton House Castle Park
Cambridge England

Printed & Bound in Great Britain

Dedication

There's only one person I can dedicate this book to and that's one of my dearest friends, Katherine. Without your comments after reading the first book, I never would have written any of the other books. Thank you for telling me that the story couldn't be over yet. You were right. It wasn't. Not by a long shot. For this I owe you…

Other Titles by MJ Fothe

A Rockstar & A Runner Series
Book 1 Fate's Hand
Book 3 Kindred Souls
Book 4 One's Promised
Book 5 Love Everlasting
Book 6 Till the End of Time

Chapter 1

The morning after their wedding, Ryder woke to the sunlight streaming through the windows of their hotel suite and found Tana was still sound asleep beside him. Carefully he reached up and brushed the hair away from her face. Tana took a deep breath in through her nose and yawned. When she opened her eyes, she was a little surprised to see that Ryder was awake and smiling at her.

"Good morning my beautiful wife," Ryder said to her as he leaned in to give her a kiss.

After she kissed her husband, Tana stretched smiling.

Ryder smiled back at her then glanced at the clock on the bedside table. "Shit! We're supposed to meet my mom in an hour." Ryder hopped off the bed pulling Tana up with him.

"Sorry Baby, but we gotta move," he said as he planted another quick kiss on her full lips.

It was almost eleven, and they planned to meet Grace for brunch in the restaurant downstairs at noon. Ryder stepped into the bathroom, got the shower going then shaved and brushed his teeth. Tana brushed her teeth then got in the shower. They washed quickly then got dressed before they packed up their belongings.

Carefully Ryder hung Tana's dress and his tux in her garment bag while Tana dried her hair. The hotel was sending someone up to retrieve their bags and had arranged to hold them down at the front desk until they were ready to leave.

Grace was scheduled to leave on a flight at five that afternoon. Both Tana and Ryder were going to ride in the limo with her to the airport where they would see her off, then continue back home to Langley. The kids had been taken back to the house in their own limo late last night after the reception and were waiting for them there. Ryder had arranged for his housekeeper to be there for the night, so he and Tana could enjoy their wedding night without having to worry about them.

At quarter to twelve, Ryder set the last of their bags by the door just as Tana appeared from the bathroom. Opening the door, he ushered his new wife out into the hall taking her hand in his as they walked down the hall to the elevators.

While they were waiting for the elevator to arrive, Tana was absent-mindedly playing with Ryder's newly acquired wedding band with her fingertips. Glancing down at her out of the corner of his eyes, he smiled.

The car arrived and they stepped into the elevator. As the doors slid closed and the car began to descend, Ryder pulled Tana to him kissing her hard, slipping a hand down the back of her jeans to cup her bottom. Tana pulled back and arched an eyebrow at him. "Your mom is probably already waiting for us," she said hooking a leg over his hip and pressing her body against his.

The elevator stopped to let more people on and Tana put her leg back down. Ryder stepped off to one side to give the new arrivals more space but did not remove his hand from the back of Tana's jeans. He kept her close to him and weaved the fingers of his other hand through her hair. The look in his hazel eyes was pure sin.

All Tana could do was look up at him smirking, so he kissed her once more before the elevator reached the lobby. As the other passengers exited the elevator, Ryder released Tana. She turned to walk out the doors and he smacked her denim-clad ass.

Tana looked over her shoulder at him kissing the air then sauntered out of the elevator. Ryder caught up to her taking her hand in his again as they informed the front desk that their bags were ready to be brought down. Ryder turned in the room key then the two crossed the lobby to the restaurant.

Grace was indeed waiting at a table already sipping her coffee when she looked up to see her son and new daughter-in-law approaching.

"Morning Mom." Ryder sat down beside Grace and leaned over to kiss her cheek.

Tana leaned down and gave her a hug then sat down beside Ryder.

"My, you two sure look well rested," Grace commented as a server came around offering coffee and Tana requested a green tea.

Both Tana and Ryder looked at each other and smiled as they decided on what to order.

Grace congratulated them on a beautiful wedding saying it was a lovely representation of the two of them and she really enjoyed herself. Then she brought up their upcoming honeymoon in August, asking why they were waiting so long before leaving. Tana filled Grace in on why they made the decision to delay leaving on a honeymoon and Grace agreed that with the two graduations plus the move it was a wise decision.

By the time they were done brunch and visiting, it was after two in the afternoon and time to take Grace to the airport. Ryder excused himself to go to the front desk to check on their bags and limo. He watched as his mother and his new wife made their way from the restaurant to the lobby sofas arm in arm, where they sat and continued talking.

Tana suddenly burst into laughter while Grace spoke chuckling to her. It made Ryder wonder what his mother was saying that was so funny, but he was also slightly distracted by how well Grace and Tana were getting along.

When he had married Amanda, the two women had never gotten along. Right from the first moment they met, Grace wanted nothing to do with Amanda. It really warmed his heart now to see how well Grace and Tana enjoyed each other's company.

Their limo arrived and their bags were still being loaded in the trunk when Ryder came up behind his wife sitting down on the arm of the sofa that she was seated on.

"And do I dare ask what you two are laughing about?" Ryder asked as he took Tana's hand in his, lifting it to his lips and pressing a kiss into her palm.

Trying to keep a straight face Tana looked up at him. "Oh, nothing you need to worry about."

"Bullshit. I know that look."

"Ryder! Must you swear?" Grace chastised him.

Ryder closed his eyes and tried not to snicker. "You know me, Mom. Swearing is just part of what makes me who I am."

Grace crossed her arms in front of her chest. "Well, I wish you would refrain from it. Especially when addressing your wife."

"She swears worse than I do!" Ryder laughed trying to defend himself.

Grace looked from Ryder to Tana. When Tana admitted that she had quite the potty mouth, Grace just shook her head, smiling. "Well, at least she's respectful and doesn't swear around me."

Tana stuck the tip of her tongue out at Ryder. He leaned down to whisper in her ear. "I can think of a better use for that tongue of yours."

Tana's eyes lit up and she couldn't hold back her smile as the desk clerk came up to let them know their limo was ready. Ryder stood up and pulled Tana up with him.

"Are you two ready to go?" Ryder asked as he took Grace's elbow with one hand and his wife by the waist with the other, leading them out to the limo.

The trip out to the airport was quiet. Tana was leaning against Ryder's shoulder and he had his arm around her while Grace watched Vancouver pass by through the window.

When they pulled up in front of the airport all three of them got out. The driver got Grace's bag out of the trunk and discretely went back into the car as Ryder pulled his mother into a big hug. "Thank you Mom, for coming and for everything. I love you."

Grace wiped tears from her eyes as she kissed her son goodbye. "I love you too Ryder. Be sure to take good care of Tana."

Then she turned to face Tana and put her arms out for a hug. Tana smiled warmly and went to Grace. As the two women embraced Tana whispered, "Maybe we can all come out to see you for Christmas this year."

"That would be nice. You could see Ryder's home town and his baby pictures." Grace whispered back.

Tana laughed and nodded. "That I definitely want to see."

Wishing Grace a safe trip home, they all said one last goodbye while the newlyweds waved as she walked through the terminal doors. Once Grace was out of sight, Tana and Ryder got back in the limo to head home.

"Okay, not that it's a bad thing for my wife and my mother to get along, but I'm starting to get worried here." Ryder sat half turned, so he could face Tana better.

"You and Mom laughing in the hotel lobby then she whispers something to you just now and you laugh again saying that you definitely want to see something." Ryder raised his eyebrows at Tana wanting to know what was going on.

"Spill it Mrs. Evans. What are you and my mother up to?" Ryder leaned right over to Tana nuzzling her neck to entice her to come clean.

Tana slid over to Ryder's lap and straddled him nipping along his jaw. "Oh, nothing."

"Bullshit." Ryder's voice was deepening. Something Tana recognized as a sign that he was becoming aroused.

"She was just telling me some stories of when you were a baby and said maybe we could make it out to see her for Christmas this year." Tana continued to kiss Ryder's neck and collarbone as she spoke.

Ryder groaned and tried to stay focused. "You left out what you want to see." He buried his face between her breasts, inhaling her scent as his hands worked their way across her back and up to her neck.

Tana gasped and writhed at Ryder's attention on her back and neck. Her skin broke out in goose bumps all over and she arched her back leaning into his touch, dying for more.

"Tell me Tana." He growled at her from her chest.

"Or what?" She dared reaching under herself to caress his erection through his jeans.

Ryder grabbed her by the arms and tossed her to the seat lying on top of her. His eyes burned with desire as he quickly unzipped his wife's jeans and shoved them down to her ankles. Tana's eyes were wide with surprise, and she was utterly turned on with his sudden show of aggression. Panting, she met Ryder's eyes with her own sporting a look that told him she was not intimidated.

"Tell me, or I won't give you what we both want." He said rocking his hips forward and pressing his erection against her pelvis.

Tana raked her teeth down Ryder's neck making him hiss in reaction to her returned aggression.

"You really think you can hold off any more than I can?" She taunted him by lifting her hips to him.

"Probably not." Ryder admitted as he quickly undid his belt and jeans, shoving them down far enough to free himself.

"I know what you want. Tell me and I'll give it to you." Ryder positioned himself at her entrance and flexed forward enough to tease but not far enough to penetrate her.

"No." Tana narrowed her eyes at him grinning like the little vixen he loved so much. She lifted her hips to him so fast Ryder couldn't pull back in time. The head of his penis slid into her, parting her folds. He could feel her searing heat, how wet she was for him and lost his will.

"Fuck it." Ryder growled and slammed into her, his eyes rolling back at the feeling of her enveloping him.

Tana cried out through clenched teeth as Ryder pounded into her. His pace was controlled and powerful as the limo rolled down the highway.

"Ryder!" Tana breathed as her muscles locked and her back arched. She came fast and hard biting down on Ryder's chest to help contain her cries.

Ryder gave a few more long strokes before he emptied into her with one last forceful thrust and a deep guttural growl. As his spasms calmed and his breathing slowed, he looked down at Tana lying beneath him.

"Definitely not." He kissed her and sat up, pulling his jeans back up, zipping his fly and buckling his belt.

Tana pulled her own jeans back up and once her zipper was done, she turned to Ryder. "Baby pictures."

"What?" Ryder looked at her clearly confused.

"What I definitely want to see. Grace told me she would show me your baby pictures if we're able to make it out for Christmas." Tana admitted to her husband.

Ryder groaned and rolled his eyes. "Great. But I'm warning you. I was a dorky looking kid. All arms and legs, really scrawny and just a total mess." Ryder scowled at the memory.

Tana laced her fingers with his and looked at his wedding band. She wiggled it on his finger and looked at him. "Don't worry about it. We all have dorky or embarrassing pictures."

"You were a cute kid from the pictures you showed me not awkward and tall like I was."

Tana kissed his fingers. "No, but I was overweight and you saw those pictures. Either way, I love your height just like you love mine."

The driver was pulling up to the gates and Ryder lowered the window to enter the code.

"True. I guess seeing you openly showed me pictures of that embarrass you I should be more relaxed about you seeing mine." He took her left hand, raised it to his lips and kissed her wedding rings.

Chapter 2

It was spring break for Nikki and Ian the week after the wedding, so everyone decided to stay in Langley. The weather was on and off rain, but it was still better than the ten below and snow in Edmonton.

Ryder spent a good majority of his spare time during the first week after getting married teaching Ian how to drive. He had gotten his learner's permit the week after his fifteenth birthday but with all the commotion about getting ready for the wedding and staying on top both grads, Ian decided not to pester his mother about taking him out for driving lessons.

A few days after the wedding he brought it up and when Tana balked at teaching him on one of Ryder's vehicles, Ryder stepped in offering to teach him. Ian jumped at the idea and begged his mother to agree.

Ryder said he didn't mind in the least bit using his truck to teach Ian and he even voiced his opinion to Tana trying to help Ian's case.

"Look Baby, Ian handles the quads just fine. I can start him out here on the driveway and around the back of the house before we venture out onto the roads. It'll be better than starting him in Sherwood Park where there's cars parked on both sides of the road. But I won't do it unless you're okay with it."

Ryder said his piece and left it up to Tana. She thought about it for a few minutes and agreed to it provided Ian made a promise to listen and be extremely careful in Ryder's truck. Ian promised and gave his mother a big hug, picking her up and squeezing her tight as he thanked her.

Within minutes, Ryder and Ian were in the garage going over some general vehicle information and safety. He wanted to teach Ian right and do his part to help keep the boy safe when he was behind the wheel. Ian's attention was completely riveted to Ryder and if a question came to him, he didn't hesitate to ask it.

Ryder was impressed with Ian's drive and dedication. He saw so much of Tana in him at that moment. He was as focused and driven as she was.

Tana left the guys alone and went to check on Nikki. She had been studying pretty hard for her mid-term exams. In a few more months, she would be studying for her diploma exams then shortly after that, she would be done with high school. Nikki had already decided she wanted to go into graphic design and web technologies but before she started university, she wanted to take a semester off to work and have a little fun.

Tana walked into the living room where Nikki was sprawled out on the couch with her textbooks and binders. Her laptop was on, her headphones were plugged into her iPhone with the buds in her ears. She was still studying, so Tana decided to leave her be and went to go change into her running clothes.

Even though she had already gone for her usual morning run and workout, she had nothing else to do so she figured another run would kill some time for her. As soon as the dogs saw her getting changed, they started going crazy with excitement. Tana grabbed her cell and her running belt, getting that along with the running leash situated around her hips then connected the dogs.

Stepping out the front door, she was getting her iPod cord run when she noticed the truck had been pulled out of the garage and Ian was seated in the driver's seat. Ryder was in the passenger's seat waiting patiently while Ian adjusted the seat and the mirrors.

Ryder lowered the window and called out to Tana, "I thought you went for a run already."

"I did, but I'm bored, so I figured I'd go for another one." Tana called back.

Opening the door, Ryder hopped out of the truck and came over to her. The dogs were getting anxious to get moving and when Ryder put his arms around Tana, they started wrapping their leashes around his legs as well. Clapping his hands sharply at them to get their attention he got them untangled, putting them in a sit/stay.

"I love those dogs, but they can be such a pain in the ass at times." He chuckled as he put his arms back around his wife. "Tell you what.

When you come back, I should be done with Ian then I promise I'll entertain you." Ryder leaned down and kissed his wife deeply.

Tana could feel her insides stir with the never-ending longing she had for him and raised her arms from his lean hips up to encircle his neck. He broke away from the kiss and swatted her backside.

"Later Baby. I promise." He winked at her and headed back to the truck.

"Get that ass of yours moving, so I can watch you go." Ryder called out of the passenger window.

Tana stuck her tongue out at him and took off up the driveway with the dogs trotting happily at her side.

Ryder watched her go, enjoying the view for a moment then he focused his full attention back on Ian, double checking that he could reach the gas and brake pedals comfortably as well as see properly out of his mirrors.

When Ryder was satisfied, he looked over at Ian. "Okay. Start the truck."

"Now?" Ian looked at Ryder surprised.

"Why not. You'll never learn to drive unless you start the truck." Ryder encouraged him.

Ian turned the key in the ignition and the truck engine rumbled, ready to go. Ryder coached Ian on getting the truck into drive and slowly they got moving. As Ian pulled forward, Ryder continued to give him instructions on either needing more gas or on his braking as well as his steering.

Ian maneuvered the truck around the house to the back storage shed then back out to the main driveway. All the while Ryder encouraged him along giving him a few hints at looking where he wanted the truck to go and not just looking at the road in front of the hood.

By the time Ian drove up the driveway, he was more confident and in better control of the truck. Ryder got him to turn around and head back to the house.

"So how was that?" he asked and Ian was grinning back at him.

"A lot easier than I thought once I got the hang of where to look." Ian was thrilled to be learning how to drive and even more so to have Ryder teaching him.

"Do you want to try going out on the road?" Ryder thought Ian could handle it so when he offered and Ian's face lit up, he couldn't help but laugh.

"Seriously? Out on the road? Can we?" It was the most excited Ryder had ever seen the boy.

"Yes, seriously. Driving along my driveway isn't going to get you to pass your driver's test. If I didn't think you could handle it, I wouldn't offer." Ryder looked at Ian showing absolute confidence in the young man. "Ready?"

Ian shifted back into drive. "Hell yeah, I am."

He carefully turned the truck around and headed back up the driveway to the gates.

"Pull right up and use this." Ryder handed him a key-fob to open the gate. "The code to open the gate is 1-9-8-4 if you don't have this." Ryder instructed and Ian did as he was told.

The gates swung open and Ian waited until they cleared the truck before he pulled ahead. As the gates closed behind them, Ryder got Ian to turn left out of the entrance onto the road.

"Remember to look where you want to go, check your mirrors regularly and watch your speed. Your mother will kick my ass if you get caught speeding."

Ian agreed they would both be in deep shit if that happened and was careful to keep the truck at the posted speed limit.

Ryder directed Ian around all the roads surrounding his acreage for over an hour, getting him to do some right and left turns. A few times he had to remind Ian to watch his lane position, especially on his first left hand turn but overall Ian was a natural and was doing great. Even his acceleration and braking were becoming smooth and well controlled.

"I think we should head back. Your mom is probably back by now and wondering where we are." Not wanting Ian distracted by a phone, both Ian and Ryder had left their phones behind.

Ian drove back up the road that lead to Ryder's place and when he reached the gates again, he pulled up and used the fob. As he pulled through the gates, Ian looked ahead further up the driveway and saw his mom not quite half way to the house.

"Mom's right there." Ian pointed as he headed toward the house.

"I see her. Give her some space. She has no clue we're behind her and you don't want to spook her or the dogs." Ryder said.

Ian backed off a bit keeping a good twenty yards between the truck and Tana. Chloe and Kordie kept trying to turn around to see what was behind them but every time they tried, Tana would clap her hands and pull their leashes to get their attention back up front.

When they reached the split in the driveway where Ian could safely move off in the direction to the garage and Tana could continue to the front door of the house, that's when she realized the truck was behind her. She stopped suddenly and looked at Ryder waving to her from the passenger seat. She watched as Ian pulled into the open bay in the garage, parking the truck.

Tana pulled the ear buds out of her ears and as she stretched her arms, she walked the distance to the garage.

"You guys went out on the road already?" She looked a little surprised as Ian hopped out of the driver's seat.

"Yeah. Ryder figured I could handle it. It was great." Ian looked excited and very pleased with himself.

Ryder came up and put an arm around Ian's shoulders giving him a squeeze. "Ian's a natural driver. He was awesome out there. I'm quite proud of him. He did great for his first lesson."

Tana seemed to relax after hearing Ryder's words of praise for her son. "Well, then I'm proud of you too Ian. Good for you."

Tana stood on tiptoe and gave Ian a quick kiss on the cheek. He was still shorter than Ryder by quite a few inches but, compared to Tana, it didn't matter. They were both tall.

Ian grinned from ear to ear. He thought his mother was going to be angry at Ryder for taking him out on the main roads so soon. But Ryder had stood up for Ian. Something his own father had yet to do.

Tana continued stretching while the two guys went into the house. Ryder took the dogs in with him, so they could get a drink of water while Tana finished up. When he unclipped the running leash from Tana's waist, he gave her a quick kiss and a wink to let her know he hadn't forgotten about his promise to her. Tana went inside not long after Ryder, planning on a quick shower to freshen up after her run.

Having done enough studying, Nikki had cleaned up her books and was in the living room with Ian and Ryder. She was listening to them tell her about Ian's first lesson. Tana was deeply touched with how Ryder was so good to both of her kids. He may not have wanted children of his own, but he was good with them. Stopping on her way to go shower, she leaned against the entryway just watching and listening to them.

Ian and Ryder were making plans to go driving each day that Ryder could and Nikki was asking if he would teach her how to drive a standard. As he agreed, he looked up and saw Tana.

"Of course, you realize that you will have to fight your mom to use the Camaro," Ryder teased as Tana walked over to him. He reached out to pull her onto his lap and kissed the side of her neck.

"Yuck. Sweat." Ryder made a face and Tana elbowed him playfully.

"It's your car Ryder," Tana said. "If Nikki wants to learn how to drive stick and you are willing to teach her, go ahead."

Nikki thanked both her mom and Ryder then set up a time for herself the next day for her first lesson. After both Nikki and Ian left to go play some video games, Ryder leaned in closer to Tana.

"Let's go shower." he said in a low sexy voice.

"*Mmmm...* now that sounds like a great idea." Tana kissed his lips and stood up.

Crossing the room, she headed for the stairs with Ryder right behind her, pinching her bottom as she jogged up the stairs to the bedroom.

~~~

The next day, Tana went through her usual routine of a morning run followed by a workout while Ryder slept. By nine thirty, she was tossing her sweaty clothes in the hamper and stepped into the shower. Ryder was still asleep when she undressed and started the water. When she rinsed the shampoo out of her hair, she was startled by the sudden appearance of hands on her hips. Her eyes flew open in the spray of the water and Ryder's hazel gaze met her instantly. He had heard the shower start and came in to join her.

"Good morning, beautiful one." Ryder murmured leaning in for a kiss.

Tana stepped forward and put her arms around her husband's neck meeting him for that kiss.

"*Mmmm*... good morning, Love. How did you sleep?"

"Very well. But then again, I always sleep well with you."

Ryder held her close for a moment as he continued to wake up with the water beating down on them both. As they showered, Tana asked what Ryder had planned for the day.

"Well, I'm giving Ian another lesson and I also promised Nikki that I'd teach her to drive stick, so I guess after Ian's lesson I'll give Nikki a dry run on the Camaro."

Tana was pulling on her jeans and looking pensive.

"Why Baby? Did you have something you wanted to do?" Ryder came over to her and caressed her face with his knuckles.

Tana thought for a moment not wanting to monopolize his time more than he was already giving with Nikki and Ian's lessons, but she needed something to do. His earlier offer of teaching her how to play guitar was still on her mind.

"It's okay. I can wait. You're spending enough time with my kids. I don't want to take up more of your time."

Ryder took her by the arms and pulled her close to him. "Hey, you're my wife. We're a family and I make time for all of you. I don't have much in my schedule that needs attention for a while. We're not working on new material right now, so if there's something you want Tana, you need to tell me."

Kissing her lightly on the mouth, he raised his brows to her, questioning her as to what was on her mind.

Tana bit her lower lip and looked up at him. "You're doing more for my kids than their own father has ever done. Helping them with driving and being so attentive. To me that's enough. I don't expect you to do this kind of stuff for them, but I do appreciate it."

"And I want to do it for them. They're great kids, and I'm happy to have them in my life. I get to do these kinds of things with them and I missed all the baby mess. As much as I do for them, I will do for you. So what is it that you wanted?" Ryder reasoned.

Tana looked up at him adoringly. "I know. I just didn't want you to feel like you're being pulled in every direction by us. I was actually thinking of your offer of teaching me to play guitar. It would give me something else to do here other than running and working out. I don't really have much of a social network here yet. Until the final move it's unlikely that I'll have one with bouncing back and forth for the next little while."

Ryder's face broke into a huge grin. "You really want to learn?"

Tana nodded and gave him a crooked grin back. "Yeah, I do. I mean I doubt I can ever keep up to you, but it would be nice for us to have something to work on together in those times when it's quiet. Nikki is moving out at the end of the year. When you're working on new material or on tour, I can practice and still feel connected to you."

"Tana, you will always be connected to me, but I get what you mean. We can start today if you want. I'll help you pick out a guitar that you like and can handle. Or if you want, we can even go and get you one of your own." Ryder kissed her, looking excited.

He loved the idea of teaching her. It was an opportunity for him to share his skill and passion. Ryder didn't fully understand her career, but it never stopped him from discussing it with her or encouraging her.

Tana put a hand up to him and pushed him back laughing at him. "How about we find out if I can even grasp the concept before we run out and buy another guitar."

Typical rocker. Any excuse to pick up a guitar and he jumped on it instantly. It was that passion that she saw in him that made her want to try.

After they both finished getting dressed, Ryder ushered Tana out of the bedroom. When she tried to put the brakes on, he simply picked her up, tossed her over his shoulder like a fireman and carried her down the stairs into the kitchen.

Setting her down on the granite of the counter, he flipped on the teakettle for her and grabbed a cup from the cupboard.

"Breakfast. I know you worked out and ran this morning, so you need to eat. What tea would you like?" Ryder wanted to take care of her this morning. Her request for guitar lessons put him in an even better mood and he was feeling playful.

"Peppermint would be great, but I can get breakfast if you want." Tana hopped off the counter.

Ryder picked her back up and promptly sat her back down. "No. You sit. Today I'm going to make you a nice breakfast."

Ryder stepped up, kissed her then turned back to making breakfast.

Tana had never seen him cook before, so she was curious to see what he was going to make. Sitting there, she watched Ryder move around his kitchen. He was getting coffee on for himself then he took eggs, sausage, onion, garlic and green pepper out of the fridge.

He chopped up the vegetables, beat the eggs together with some salt and pepper and set the eggs aside. Getting two pans out from under the cooktop Ryder turned the burners on, set the pans over the elements and dropped the sausage into one pan then began sautéing the vegetables in the other. Leaving the sausages and vegetables to cook for a bit, he poured hot water into a cup and added the tea bag for Tana.

"Your tea, my lady." Ryder bowed as she took the cup from his hands and Tana giggled.

He was in a fantastic mood and Tana was enjoying watching him. Next Ryder got a big skillet out, sprayed it with cooking spray and turned on another burner as he tended to the sausages. When the skillet reached the temperature Ryder was after, he poured the eggs in, then added the sautéed vegetables and let it cook through.

The sausages were done, so he removed them from the stove, placing them on some paper towels in the microwave to stay warm. He grabbed some grated cheese from the fridge, sprinkled it over the omelet cooking in the pan then folded it over.

Turning the heat off, Ryder grabbed a plate from the cupboard and slid the omelet from the pan onto the plate. Removing the sausage from the microwave, he brought all the food to the counter beside Tana where she still sat, sipping her tea.

Grabbing another plate, he cut off a portion of the huge omelet, sliding it on to the second plate with two sausages then turned to Tana.

"Breakfast is served." He said holding her plate like a servant's tray.

"It smells delicious," Tana said.

Ryder took a fork full and popped it into her mouth. As she chewed, he waited to hear what she thought and set her plate down on her lap for her. Tana was nodding and when she swallowed, she couldn't keep the surprised look from her face.

"Wow. Ryder, this is really good. I had no idea you could cook." Tana was impressed.

Ryder smiled at her. He served himself a part of the omelet, some sausage and stood leaning against the counter next to Tana.

"Just because you never see me cook doesn't mean I don't know how." He said to her taking a bite of his breakfast.

"I used to help my mother all the time. I picked up on what she did. I love to cook, but you always had things ready by the time I get up, so I never bothered. Plus, I enjoy your cooking."

Nikki and Ian smelled food and came into the kitchen, so Ryder served them each a plate of food.

"Wow Mom. Good omelet," Nikki said as she cleaned her plate.

Tana looked at Ryder and laughed. He looked a little disappointed.

"Actually Nikki, I didn't cook this morning. Ryder did." Tana admitted looking lovingly at her husband.

Both Nikki and Ian looked from Tana to Ryder in shock. Neither of them had seen him cook either. They've seen him help their mother in the kitchen plenty of times and help her clean up. But they had no clue he could cook at all and figured he lived off his housekeeper's cooking when their mother wasn't around.

"You cooked?" Nikki stared at Ryder wide eyed.

Ryder nodded and smirked at them. "I can do more than just sing and play guitar you know."

"Sorry Ryder. We've never seen you cook before. It was really good. Thank you." Nikki came up to him and gave him a big hug.

Ryder hugged her back. He told both the kids they were welcome then reminded Ian about going driving. "Be ready in half an hour and we can head out."

Ian gave him thumbs up and took off to get dressed. Tana turned to Nikki and told her to make sure she was ready to go when Ryder came back with Ian. She nodded then left Ryder and her mother in the kitchen.

Tana started to clean up the dishes and load the dishwasher. When the kitchen was done, Ryder was ready to take Ian out for his lesson. He sat down and discussed with Tana about taking Ian into South Langley.

"I'd like to get him into the residential areas, so he can start getting used to being around some traffic. I'm not going to take him around the busier parts of town, but definitely some light traffic would be a good thing to expose him to now." Ryder gave Tana his game plan.

Tana was pensive. "I'm confident that Ian can handle this, but I'm more concerned for your truck. I'll be honest with you. I'd feel much more relaxed about this if he was using my truck and not yours. If something happens and your truck is damaged," Tana trailed off not sure how to finish her thought.

Ryder took a hold of her left hand and held up her ring finger. "Okay, you see this? You're my wife. Those two are now my stepchildren. If something happens to the truck, it's not a big deal. As long as no one is hurt then the vehicle is not important."

Tana had never seen him so insistent before and it took her a little by surprise.

"I would worry if you were out there giving him driving lessons in Sherwood Park in your truck, not because of what could happen to your truck, but because of what could happen to the two of you. It doesn't matter what vehicle we teach Ian in, the chance of something happening is there. What you need to understand is I don't care about the truck. I care about the three of you. If I didn't care, I never would have put these rings on your finger." Ryder was adamant and it brought tears to Tana's eyes.

"Okay. I'm sorry. I'm just used to having to worry about those kinds of expenses and I don't want you to think that we're going to use you. That's not why I put that ring on your finger either." Tana stood up from her seat at the island and put her arms around Ryder.

"Tana, I know you're not using me. Just as I know the kids aren't either. Come on. You're the one who insisted on the pre-nup when I didn't want it. Somehow, I think if you were planning on pulling the same shit or even close to what Amanda did, the discussion of a pre-nup would have gone quite differently."

Ryder held her face in his hands, meeting her eyes with his own. "Now if you're quite done being irrational, I've made promises to both Ian and Nikki that I intend on keeping."

He kissed the end of her nose and stood up. "Don't worry. Especially about a truck. Ian's an attentive learner."

Tana smiled feeling foolish and pulled on his hand to get him to come to her. Standing on tiptoe, she got as close to looking him in the eye as she could.

"I love you Ryder Evans. I should have given you more credit than thinking you would be more concerned about your truck than Ian's well-being. I'm sorry." Planting a kiss on his lips, he relaxed a fair amount.

"Apology accepted." He said as he grabbed her by the belt loops of her jeans and lifted her up. "You can make it up to me later." The look he gave her dripped sin and made her feel all hot in her lower belly.

"Jeez can't you guys give it a rest for even one day?" Ian rolled his eyes at them both as he came into the kitchen looking for Ryder.

Both Tana and Ryder looked at each other and smiled.

"Don't hold your breath kid." Ryder murmured loud enough for her to hear making Tana snicker as Ryder set her back down.

"Are you ready?" Ryder asked Ian over the top of Tana's head.

Ian nodded looking excited and Ryder gave him a rundown of where they were going to go for his lesson as they left the room.

~~

Ryder backed the truck out for Ian then they swapped seats. Ian was going to drive from home to some light residential areas in South Langley then back out to the acreage.

As Ian drove up the driveway and exited the grounds, Ryder reminded Ian to watch his speed and lane position then went over some basic parking that he was hoping to cover.

For the next hour and a half, Ian drove around South Langley taking instruction from Ryder when learning how to park along with backing up with no incidents. Ian was doing great and even managed to parallel park on his first try.

When Ryder told him to head back home, Ian signaled and turned into traffic, merging into the faster moving lanes like he had been doing it for years. Ryder was very pleased with how the lessons were going and Ian was just as happy.

Ian and Ryder arrived back at the house after being gone for almost two hours. Ian parked the truck and when they hopped out, Ryder was praising him for another great lesson. They were discussing areas where Ian felt he needed more confidence and what their next lesson should entail as they entered the house. Tana heard them come in and went to see how things went.

"How was it?" she asked Ian.

"Great." Ian said walking over to the fridge and grabbing a can of pop.

"We went into town and I did some parallel parking, three point turns and lots of parking in parking lots too." Ian filled his mom in on his lesson.

Ryder had gone to knock on Nikki's door to let her know he was back and both of them were walking back into the kitchen where Ryder swapped the truck keys for the Camaro keys. Nikki looked a bit nervous and when she met her mother's eyes, Tana called her on it.

"Nikki, are you sure about this? You look nervous." Tana went over to her and tried to comfort her.

"Yeah. A little bit, but I do want to learn to drive a standard Mom. I just don't want to grind the gears or wreck the car." Nikki reassured her mother.

Ryder came up and tossed the keys to her, which she caught easily. "Don't worry. We'll get you working the pedals and shifting without starting the car first to get you used to using both feet while shifting. It's easier than it looks." He encouraged her as they headed to the garage.

Ryder got Nikki to sit in the driver's seat where she adjusted the seat and mirrors to her liking. Tana had been the last one to drive the Camaro, so Nikki didn't have to move anything very much at all.

"Okay, to start you know the concept of shifting and the clutch, right?" Ryder asked settling himself into a squatting position outside of the driver's side door.

"Yeah. Clutch goes in and you shift." Nikki replied.

Ryder got her to practice moving her feet and pressing on the pedals while shifting through all the gears. He wanted her to get comfortable with the gears and the pattern of moving both of her feet before they hit the road.

After a few minutes, he stood up and got Nikki to hop out of the car. "I'm going to back it out and turn around, so you can drive up the driveway." He explained as he squeezed in the driver's seat.

"Jesus." He complained as he had no choice but move the seat back. It was too close and he couldn't get his knees past the steering wheel to be able to reach the pedals.

Nikki laughed then stood back as Ryder backed the Camaro out of the garage, swung it around smoothly, so the front of the car was pointed in the direction of the driveway. He turned the car off and climbed back out holding the door for Nikki.

Nikki sat back down and readjusted the seat forward again, so she could reach the pedals while Ryder got into the passenger seat.

"All right, the first thing I want to make sure you know is before you start the car always check to see if it's in gear. When I park, I always leave the car in first gear to keep it from rolling where your mom always leaves it in neutral and uses the emergency brake."

Nikki checked and as Ryder had said, he left the car in first. "What do I do if it's in gear?" she asked.

"Well, you can either start the car knowing it's in first by pressing in the clutch and brake. Or you can take it out of gear before starting the car. Then you can start the car by just using the brake. If the car's in neutral, you don't need to use the clutch to start the car. Only if it's in gear or it'll lurch and stall out."

Nikki took the car out of gear and pressed her foot on the brake to keep the car from moving. "Can I start it now?"

Ryder nodded and Nikki turned the key in the ignition.

"Now press the clutch in all the way and put the car in first gear, keeping your other foot on the brake."

Nikki followed Ryder's instructions and when she had the car in gear, he told her to release the clutch while she transferred her brake foot to the gas and press down on the gas in a smooth controlled motion. When she tried, she was a little slow with getting enough gas as the clutch engaged. The car hopped forward sharply and stalled out. Ryder was thrown forward having forgotten to buckle up his seat belt when he got in the car.

"Shit!" Ryder called out as he went forward and his right forearm slammed into the dash when he put it out to stop himself from going further.

He had been sitting half turned in his seat to see Nikki better and to give her instruction.

"Ohmigod! Ryder, I'm so sorry." Nikki was near tears after seeing him get thrown into the dash.

Ryder got himself back into his seat properly and buckled his seat belt. "It's not your fault, Nikki. I didn't put my seat belt on."

"But I did something wrong and the car… and then you…" Nikki was stammering.

Ryder looked at her, smiled then patted her hand on the shifter. "It's okay. I was expecting you to bunny-hop the car at least a few times. Most people do when learning to drive stick. I was the idiot and didn't think to put my seat belt on. Totally my fault." Ryder reassured her then encouraged her to try again.

Nikki took a deep breath trying to calm herself down before she started the car again. She shifted into first and this time, Ryder got her to back out on the clutch until she could ever so slightly feel the clutch engage then press it back in quickly while she kept her foot on the brake.

"Okay, now that you know where the friction point of the clutch is, you should be able to start off better without bunny-hopping us down the driveway. When you feel the clutch engage, just ease down a little more on the gas, keeping both feet moving in that smooth motion and we should be fine."

Nikki tried again. This time the car gave a little hop and then settled into a smooth forward motion. When her RPM's reached the shifting point, he got her to shift into second teaching her to look at the tachometer and to listen to the sound of the engine, so she knew when to shift.

"Drive right to the gates. We are going out on the road." Ryder looked at her grinning.

He talked her through the fob and told her the code just like her brother the day before. When she shifted back into first and tried to get going again, she stalled out. Ryder brushed off her apology and told her to try again. The next attempt resulted in her hopping a few times before the car settled into its forward motion.

"We will have to work on your starting. It gets easier with practice." Ryder reassured her as she turned and headed out onto the main road.

He coached her on her shifting and directed her where to go, trying to give her as many stops and starts as he could. Nikki was a good little driver. She was very aware of her vehicle and position on the road. He could see a little bit of nerves still lingering in her, but she was starting to really get the hang of shifting up and gauging her distance when approaching a stop, so she could down shift when he taught her that. Really the only problems she was having was her starting.

They drove around for over two hours with Ryder even getting her to go into reverse countless times, plus all the stops he made her do. By the time they returned to the gates to get back to the house, she was much smoother with her starts. She was still a bit jerky and slow, but neither of them was being thrown forward anymore.

Nikki carefully parked the car in the garage and engaged the emergency brake. She climbed out of the driver's seat and handed the keys back to Ryder.

"Well, it was definitely harder than I thought at first, but once you showed me the friction point trick, it got easier." Nikki said as they went into the house.

"Nikki, you're actually a really good driver. You're very aware and attentive. It's just going to take some time and practice. I can bet that you'll be able to drive stick as good as I can in no time." Ryder encouraged her and even agreed to give her a few more lessons.

"Maybe I'll even let you go out on your own after you have had more practice." Ryder offered.

Nikki threw her arms around him in a big hug. "You're the best!" She said and kissed his cheek then took off down the hall to her room.

Ryder stood there looking after her smiling.

"Sounds like the lesson was successful." Tana said from behind him.

"Yeah. A little rough at first, but I expected that." He hadn't heard her come up behind him. "When do you want to have your first lesson?"

Tana slid her arms around his waist and leaned into his chest. "How about after some lunch? I made some subs while you were gone. They just need to be toasted in the oven."

"*Mmmm*... sounds tasty." Ryder called the kids to the kitchen for Tana while she went to slide the tray into the oven.

The foursome enjoyed their lunch then Ian went to play video games while Nikki went back to her room. She had been chatting online with her boyfriend and friends pretty much every spare minute and was looking forward to heading home in a few days to be with them.

Once the dishes had been cleaned up from lunch, Ryder led Tana into the studio and showed her the guitars that she could choose from. He decided to start her on an acoustic, saying it would be easier for her to practice without having to worry about the power pack or amps and cords. She could easily take it anywhere she wanted to practice.

Tana gravitated over to the dozen acoustic guitars lined up along the office wall of the studio and picked up an Aria AF-25 in a blue shade finish.

"What about this one?" she asked not sure how to tell which one would be good for a beginner.

"That one is fine." Ryder grabbed his Gibson Acoustic J-200 Custom that he bought the day he met Tana and sat down on one of the stools in the studio. He put the strap over his head settling the guitar on his lap. Tana followed his lead and sat on the stool across from him.

"First, what you need to learn is the parts of the instrument." Ryder said as he began going over the different parts to the guitars and pointing them out. Then he produced two picks from his pocket and handed one to Tana.

Next, he checked the tuning of his guitar adjusting the tuning pegs until he was satisfied with the sound. Then he reached behind himself, picked up a tuner and clipped it on the headstock of Tana's guitar.

"I don't use a tuner, but you will need to."

He explained how the tuner worked and how to tune the guitar. Tana started picking the strings as Ryder showed her and adjusting the tuning pegs until the lights on the tuner turned from red to green, signaling it was in tune.

Next, he taught her how to properly position her 'fretting hand' and how to hold the pick. Once she had her positioning right, Ryder showed her how to pick the strings in the correct manner, but Tana's first try caused the sixth string to rattle terribly.

Cringing a little Ryder reached out and corrected her motion. "Strike the string softer than you did and try not to move your arm as much."

She tried again and the sound was much better. Nodding, Ryder told her to use the same force downwards and upwards on each string individually, so she could develop good alternate picking techniques. Telling her that it would help her to become more accustomed to her hand positioning, Ryder showed her what he meant while Tana watched, then she followed what he did.

Tana was dead silent as she watched Ryder intently. When he would correct her, she would look at him and watch what he was showing her then try it herself.

She continued practicing her alternate picking until she got through all six strings downwards and upwards flawlessly a few times. Ryder then decided to start her on the Chromatic Scale.

"Okay, now I'm going to show you all the notes on each string. These are just single notes and are pretty easy. It'll get more complicated as we go along, but you'll also get better so it shouldn't be too bad for you."

Ryder showed her how to start by using her pick to play the open sixth string. "Good, now take the first finger on your fretting hand, and place it on the first fret of the sixth string. Press down on the string and strike the string with your pick."

Tana followed Ryder's instructions as he continued. "Now take your second finger and place it on the second fret."

"Do I lift my first finger off or leave it down?" Tana asked. It was the first time she had spoken since starting her lesson.

"Yes. You can take the first finger off. Strike the string again then do the same thing with the third and then the fourth fingers. That's all the notes on the sixth string. Now we will move up to the fifth string and do the same thing."

Ryder played with her, going at her pace while he watched her hands and fingers for positioning. When they were done on the fifth and fourth strings, Ryder told her to stop on the third fret on the third string as there were only those three frets played. Then they continued onto the second and first strings to the fourth fret.

On the third fret of the first string, Tana didn't get a good clear note. It sounded wrong and Ryder reminded her to curl her fingers, so she wasn't holding down all the strings with the length of her finger. Tana readjusted her finger and tried again. That time the sound was clear and clean.

Ryder smiled at her. "Much better."

They finished the scales and then Ryder got her to try them again using her alternate picking.

He stayed right with her showing her the note and positioning as she followed him, slower but meticulous. They went through the scales using the alternate picking twice more before Ryder said that she should call it quits for the day.

"Your fingers will be sore if we go much longer. You're not used to pressing down on the strings like I am." Ryder took his guitar off leaning to one side and setting it in one of the stands.

Tana looked up at him, her eyes shining with what she had learned. "I can feel it already and even in my hand holding the pick." She shook out her hands and stretched them a bit.

"I have a tennis ball, you can use to help strengthen your hands. You just squeeze it. As many reps as you can about two or three times a day. When I don't play as much between albums, I find I have to still use it before we hit the studio or go on tour."

Tana took the guitar off and set it on one of the empty stands close to her as she had seen Ryder do. "That was fun." Tana said as she stood up and stretched.

"Should I practice every day?" she asked as Ryder ushered her out of the studio, closing the door behind him.

"It's up to you. If you want to learn and get better quickly, yes practicing every day is a good idea. But if you don't, it'll just take you longer to learn." Ryder walked slightly behind her as she walked up the hall into the main part of the house.

"I tell you what, I'm not going to lock the studio unless we have a party or we're not home. Anytime you want to go in and practice, you can. That Aria is yours to use as much as you want. I don't take that one on tour or anything. So, for as long as you want to learn and play it's there for you."

Ryder put his arms around her waist pulling her to him and leaned down to kiss her. Tana leaned into his kiss practically melting into him.

"Thank you." she said pulling back just far enough to speak then returning to the kiss.

"For what?" Ryder did the same.

"Teaching me, Nikki and Ian." She reached up and wrapped her arms around his neck. He tightened his arms around her waist and tried to lift her but hissed in pain. Tana stopped and backed up instantly.

"What's wrong?" she asked.

"Nothing. I think I bruised my arm." Ryder shook his head and bent his elbow to look at the underside of his forearm and saw a deep black and purple bruise forming over most of his arm.

"Yeah, I did. Pretty good too." He said looking at his arm.

Tana grabbed his arm gently and looked at it. "Holy shit, Ryder. How the hell did you do that?"

"Oh, I was a dumbass and forgot to buckle up when I took Nikki out. She stalled on her first try and I slammed my arm into the dash." Ryder brushed it off and Tana looked worried.

"Are you sure you're okay? Was it just your arm you hit?"

Ryder put his arms back around Tana's waist. Ignoring the pain in his arm, he picked her up and kissed her hard on the mouth.

"Yes, I'm sure I'm fine and no. I didn't hit anything else. Don't worry it's just a bruise."

He kissed her again. Tana hooked one of her legs over his hip and locked her arms around his neck, kissing him back.

"Okay." She whispered looking into his eyes as their foreheads pressed together.

Ryder set her back down and looked at his watch.

"I want to go out for dinner tonight. All of us." He said still holding Tana by the waist.

"Sure. And maybe a movie or something afterwards?" she added.

Ryder agreed and they went to tell the kids.

As they got ready to go out for the evening, Ryder chose a long sleeve tight black shirt to cover his arm. He didn't want Nikki to see the bruise and feel guilty for it.

Chapter 3

By early April, everyone was back in Sherwood Park. Tana had to return to work and school was back in session for the kids. Ryder stayed back in Langley for a couple of extra days to do a radio station interview and acoustic performance in Victoria then joined his family at Tana's house in less than a week.

Tana had been extremely busy getting in touch with a realtor and getting her house on the market on top of planning for Nikki's eighteenth birthday. Over the past few weeks, she and Ryder had discussed it and seeing Nikki wasn't moving to Langley with her mother and Ian, both she and Ryder figured she was going to need her own vehicle. They were going to give one to her as her birthday and graduation gift. Because she was enjoying the standard so much, Ryder had convinced Tana that they should go ahead and buy a stick shift for her.

When Ryder made it back to Sherwood Park, he knew they only had a few days to find a car for Nikki. So on Ryder's first full day back, he dropped Tana off at work and drove around to all the dealerships in Sherwood Park looking for a good used car for Nikki. There hadn't been much in the Park, so by the time noon rolled around, he ventured into the city. After trying a few dealerships on the southeast side of the city, he still wasn't finding anything that was catching his eye, so he started heading north.

Ryder was about to stop and grab some lunch when he came across another dealership and went in. There he found a 2005 Toyota Celica that he just knew Nikki would love. He started to look it over very closely and examined the body for damage. Not finding anything of concern, he went into the dealership and looked for a sales person. An older woman in her mid-fifties greeted him.

"Can I help you?" she asked.

Ryder cleared his throat and explained that he was interested in the black Celica out front. The woman introduced herself as Mary and said she could help him. She retrieved the information on the car and the keys. She and Ryder went back out, so he could pop the hood and take a close look at the engine as well as inspect the interior. Mary asked him if he was buying for himself and Ryder explained that he wasn't.

"It's for my girl—uh wife's daughter," Ryder stumbled.

"Your stepdaughter?" Mary corrected him gently.

Ryder ran his hands through his hair. "Uh… yeah. Sorry. This is new to me. We just got married. She's turning eighteen in a few days and she is going to need a good car."

"Well," Mary shuffled her paperwork on the car, "I happen to know this car was extremely well cared for and has very low mileage. It used to be my niece's car. She recently had a baby and needed something more practical for children."

They went over the specs of the car and Ryder knew it was the one for Nikki, so he asked to take it for a test drive. He wanted to take it to see Tana at work and get her thoughts on it. Mary brought him a dealer plate and handed over the keys.

Hopping in, he started the engine and it purred to life. Ryder left the parking lot keeping the radio off, so he could listen for any strange sounds and headed to Tana's work about ten minutes away. The whole drive there he listened and heard nothing out of the ordinary nor did he feel any vibrating, pulling or shimmying in the steering or pedals.

Pulling into the parking lot of Tana's work, he parked in visitor's parking and went inside to reception. The young woman behind the desk was on the phone when he walked up and she motioned to give her a moment, so Ryder leaned on the edge of the desk waiting.

"Sorry about that. How can I help you?" She asked as she hung the receiver up and finished jotting down some notes on a pad of paper.

"Can you have Tana Evans come here?" He asked not sure where to find his wife.

"Evans? We don't have anyone with the last name Evans working here. Do you mean Tana Anderson?" She was looking at the switchboard with a puzzled expression.

"It's Evans now but yeah. Tana." Ryder was taken aback a bit with what the receptionist said.

She picked up the receiver, pressed the button for Tana's extension and waited. After a few moments, she hung up. "Sorry, she's not at her desk. Did you want to leave a message for her?"

Ryder rubbed his forehead in frustration. This girl didn't really seem to give a damn about helping him and was treating him like him being there was an inconvenience to her.

"Can't you just page her or something?"

The receptionist rolled her eyes and picked up the receiver again. A beep went off overhead and she spoke into the receiver. *"Tana Anderson to front reception please."*

Her voice resonated throughout the building and when she hung up, she finally looked up at Ryder and was about to ask him if he would like to take a seat in the chairs off to his left when she realized who was standing there.

"Holy shit." Her hand flew to her mouth.

She began stammering and tripping over her words as she apologized to Ryder. He was already not impressed but as always, he was polite and friendly.

The receptionist was up out of her seat asking for an autograph and a picture. Some of the other employees within earshot of reception could hear the commotion and were peeking around the corner to see what was going on. Ryder could hear some whispers and a few employees came up to Ryder, wanting to shake his hand and introduce themselves.

Just then Tana came around the corner and saw two of her junior buyers, the receptionist plus one of the inside sales representatives all hovering around Ryder. Surprised to see him, she walked through everyone giving her two buyers a stern look that sent them and the sales rep scrambling back to their desks while the receptionist meekly sat back down.

"What are you doing here?" Tana asked Ryder smiling and reaching up to give him a kiss.

"I found a car for Nikki, so I brought it by for you to look at."

"Tana, is everything all right? I heard you get paged." A short rather portly, balding middle-aged man came up to reception to check what was going on.

"Oh, Warren, yes. Everything's fine." Tana turned and addressed the newcomer. "Ryder, this is Warren Tachney, my boss. Warren, my husband, Ryder Evans." The two men shook hands and Warren smiled up at Ryder.

"So, this is the man that is stealing our Tana away from us." Warren joked and Ryder laughed making small talk.

"If you don't mind Warren, I'm going to step outside for a few minutes. Ryder brought a car by for me to look at for my daughter. She's turning eighteen in a few days and we want to get her a car. I won't be long." Tana explained.

"I can't believe Nicole is eighteen already. Go ahead. Take your time and make sure it's the right choice. No rush, Tana. Darlene here can hold your calls for as long as you need."

Darlene was sitting behind the reception desk completely red faced and looking down as Warren made eye contact with her. Tana thanked her boss as she and Ryder stepped outside.

Just past the last window Ryder stopped, pulled her close to him and leaned down. "Next time I come see you at work, I'm texting you from the car. That receptionist is awful."

Tana shook her head. "She's a temp. Our regular receptionist broke her leg skiing over spring break and is laid up for the next six weeks, so we had to bring in a temp. But I agree. I believe Warren is trying to find another one."

"Well, then I guess that also answers my next question." Ryder smiled at her and kissed her full on the lips.

"And what question was that?" Tana smiled and reached up to caress his face.

Ryder sighed at her loving touch. "Why she insisted that there was no Evans and asked if I meant Anderson."

Tana looked thoughtful. "HR changed everything in the computers, my email address and ordered me new business cards, but I guess they forgot to change the name on the switchboard. I'll have that fixed as soon as I go inside."

Ryder smiled and led her over to the Celica to show her the car. He gave her the rundown of what Mary had said and the history of the car.

Tana looked the car over as carefully as Ryder had, inside and out then checked under the hood.

"How does it handle?"

"Like a dream." Ryder assured her. "The engine purrs like a kitten. No rattles, no clunks, or grinding, no nothing."

"Price?" she asked raising her eyebrows, a true purchaser to the core.

"Reasonable."

"Okay." Tana sighed. "I will admit it's more car than I was planning on for her as far as type and style goes, but you're right. She'll love it."

Ryder was grinning from ear to ear. "All right. I'll deal with the paperwork, and we can handle the semantics later. I'll also send it out to be one hundred percent detailed inside and out."

"You are too good you know that?" She reached out and took his hand. Pulling him to her she wrapped herself in his arm.

"I'm not the asshole the tabloids like to make me out to be." Ryder draped his arm around her shoulders, and they started to walk back to the building.

"I know." Tana replied softly, "But you know for being as famous as you are, you're still far nicer than most other people."

Ryder walked Tana back inside and she took him on a bit of a tour of the facility, meeting some of her other colleagues before heading back to her office. She closed the door halfway to give them just a bit of privacy and he sat down on the edge of her desk, looking around.

There were pictures of her kids all over with a few of the dogs mixed in as well. Just off to one side was a large collage of pictures pinned up and practically covering an entire corkboard. The center picture Ryder recognized as one of her parents taken before her father died. All the pictures surrounding it were of Ryder and her together.

There were ones from her first trip to Langley, both Christmases and all their time in between. Even some newspaper clippings from the Juno Awards were mixed in. She had all these pictures and he had no clue. All he could do was lean over and stare at them.

Tana came over and sat in her chair, looking at her pictures smiling shyly. "You found what keeps me company when you're away."

"I had no idea you had so many pictures of us. I've seen a few but wow." Ryder was beside himself with surprise.

"I've taken a few here and there of you, but I think the kids have taken more than I have. Most of these I have no idea who took. I saw them when I downloaded my camera, so I printed them and hung them here."

Ryder pulled her chair over closer to her desk and leaned down to kiss her. "At least I know you miss me and think of me when I'm gone."

"Of course I do, Ryder. I love you." Tana stood up and hugged him. "But I do need to get back to work and you need to get back to the dealership."

Tana walked him back, said goodbye to him as he got back into the Celica and drove off. When she returned to her office where she found all four of her buyers standing there waiting for her to approve some major purchase orders before they were released. Not much was said about Ryder other than it was nice to have met her husband and he seemed like a very nice, unpretentious person. Tana quietly agreed that he was and made the necessary comments on their orders before focusing back on her work.

While Tana was sorting through production schedules and purchasing reports, Ryder was back at the dealership filling out paperwork for the Celica. He was going to have to buy the car in his name then transfer ownership of it over to Nikki because she wasn't with him to sign the papers in her name. He also arranged to have the car polished and completely detailed for Nikki, so when she did get it in a few days it would be like getting a new car.

By the time Ryder had to pick Tana up from work, the Celica was paid for and he even stopped by a registries branch to see what they would need in order to bring the car home for Nikki. He obtained a temporary transit permit, but they would have to get Nikki in to get her plate right away. Tana was going to call her insurance provider to get Nikki set up and pay for her first year of insurance as a part of the gift as well.

When he pulled back into the parking lot at Tana's work, Ryder decided to avert going inside and just texted Tana that he was outside. She responded right away telling him she would be out in a few minutes.

As people came out and saw him in Tana's truck waiting for her, they waved and he waved back. Ryder found that everyone that Tana worked with was very nice and after the initial surprise of him being there wore off, they were very professional and treated him like a regular person.

Tana came running out and slid into the passenger seat giving him a kiss hello. "How did it go at the dealership?"

Ryder filled her in on what happened telling her that the car was being detailed and would be ready in two days. Nikki's birthday was Friday, so it worked out perfectly.

Nikki was going out with her friends Friday night and was planning to be home by noon on Saturday, so her family could celebrate her birthday with her. This would give them a chance to get the car home and park it next to Tana's truck in the garage without her knowing.

~~~

On Friday morning after Tana had gone through her regular routine, she stopped by Nikki's closed bedroom door and knocked lightly. Hearing her daughter's *'yeah'*, Tana opened the door and peeked in.

"Happy birthday." Tana grinned at her daughter and put her arms out to hug her.

"Thanks Mom." Nikki hugged her. "So, tonight I'm going out for dinner with Brad, Jess and her new boyfriend. Then we're going to the bar. I think they said the Union then we're going to crash at Jess's place. Are you still okay with it?" Nikki gave her mother the rundown.

"Who's driving?" Tana was willing to drive the kids around, so there wouldn't be any drinking and driving.

"Jess's parents offered."

Tana nodded and then put her hands up surrendering. "Sounds like it's all taken care of them. And you'll be home by noon tomorrow, so we can have cake, give you your gifts and take you out for dinner?"

Nikki nodded and hugged her mom again. "Thanks Mom. You're the best."

"What? I thought I was the best." Ryder poked his head into Nikki's room pouting.

"Ha ha ha." Nikki chirped back at him.

"Oh well. I guess I can settle for second best. Come here birthday girl."

Ryder picked Nikki up in a big bear hug squeezing her and spinning around singing *'Happy Birthday'*. Tana and Nikki both laughed at Ryder after he set her back down.

"You be safe tonight and have fun. If anything at all happens or goes wrong, call. I don't care what time it is, you call. Promise?" Tana put her hands on her daughter's shoulders and stared deep into her eyes.

Nikki returned her mother's stare. "I promise Mom. I love you."

"Okay. Good. I love you too Sweetheart and we will see you tomorrow. Have fun and be safe." Tana left Nikki's room pulling the door closed behind her.

Ryder drove Tana to work again, so he could do the final preparations for Nikki's birthday. The cake needed to be picked up and he wanted to pick up a few things she would need for her car as well as order her winter tires with a spare set of rims.

~~

Tana's day flew by. She was so busy right from the time she got in all the way through to the end of her day that when reception called and told her that her husband was here for her, she was shocked to see it was ten minutes to five. She hadn't even stopped for lunch.

Gathering up her untouched lunch and her purse, Tana quickly shut down her computer and headed to the front. Ryder was there talking and laughing with Warren while he waited for her. As she approached, Ryder saw her over the top of Warren's head, his face breaking out into an adoring smile.

"Hi Baby. Have a good day?" He asked leaning down to kiss her as she came up to him.

"Insane. I don't think I stopped all day." Tana sighed looking tired.

Warren wished them a good weekend and exited the building. Ryder took hold of Tana's lunch kit and purse for her as he led her out to her truck.

"Well unfortunately, we can't go straight home. Nikki's car is ready and I've been busy all day. I think I have everything ready but once we're back at the house, I'll need you to check. I've never done this before. I hope I got it all covered." Ryder looked a little anxious as he drove to the dealership to pick up the Celica.

"I'm sure it's going to be great." Tana reassured him.

Pulling into the parking lot at the dealership, Ryder parked and they both went inside. Ryder found Mary and introduced her to Tana. Mary went over the papers with Ryder and he showed her his temporary transit permit from the registries.

"Well, the car is back and everything is ready." Mary handed the keys to Ryder. "I know your daughter will love the car." She said shaking his hand before turning to shake Tana's as well.

She led Ryder around to the shop where the Celica was parked in one of the repair bays. It looked amazing. It was shiny and perfectly polished. Ryder opened the door and looked over the interior. It had been shampooed, washed and polished as well. It smelled and looked like new. He sat in the seat and Tana leaned down kiss him.

"See you at home." She said as he started the car. He waved at her and closed the door.

Ryder drove out of the bay as Tana returned to her truck to head back to her house. Following behind Ryder, she opened the garage door for him when they pulled up to the house. Ryder pulled into the garage off to one side and Tana pulled in right beside him.

After closing the overhead door, Ryder pulled out a huge blue ribbon from the backseat of Tana's truck and started to string it across the top of the car.

"Where did you get that?" Tana asked chuckling as she gave Ryder a hand.

"At a party store I saw while driving around today." Ryder was grinning like a kid as they held the ribbon in place by closing it in the doors of the Celica.

"You're really excited about this, aren't you?" Tana was looking at Ryder.

He looked like he was about to burst with excitement as he nodded and they went inside.

Ian was at the table finishing his homework when Tana and Ryder came in. Ryder took him out to the garage to show him his sister's gift while Tana started on dinner. When the two guys came back, Ian was saying that Nikki was going to love it and he was a little jealous of her.

"She's going to be on her own in a few months and is going to need a car Ian." Tana explained.

"I know but still, it's a sweet car. She's lucky." Ian complained.

"Hey, you need to focus on getting your license first." Ryder said as he stepped behind Tana, helping her with dinner.

Ian conceded and set the table while Tana and Ryder finished cooking.

As they sat down to eat, they discussed the plans for the next day. They were going to surprise Nikki with the car, then take her out to get her plate and registration. Tana had the temporary insurance papers and Ryder had the form filled out to transfer the title of the car into her name. All Nikki had to do was sign it.

Ryder told Tana that he had picked out winter tires for her and ordered a second set of rims along with an emergency road kit and a few different gift cards for gas, car washes and oil changes.

After dinner, Ian asked to go over to his girlfriend's place until ten and Tana gave him the okay, leaving her and Ryder alone for the evening. Ryder suggested he give her another guitar lesson seeing she had been doing well with practicing and her scales were getting better. She was now able to play them much faster forwards and backwards.

Once they cleaned up from dinner, they spent the next hour and a half going over a few notes that Ryder was having her put together before he started to teach her to play chords. Tana was having a tougher time getting the hang of it, but she was as persistent with learning. It was a huge help that Ryder was incredibly patient with her.

When Tana had enough for the evening, Ryder continued to play. He sat down at the island in the kitchen and started to play *'Faithfully'*.

Tana had been about to go and workout, but she stopped and turned when Ryder began singing. She leaned against the hallway wall to watch him as he looked at her.

As Ryder sang, Tana couldn't help walking into the kitchen and across the room to stand in front of him. She was drawn to him like a magnet. Looking directly into his eyes she smiled, letting him finish the song.

When Ryder was done, Tana gently lifted the guitar from his hands laying it down on the island. Then she stepped between his bent knees and kissed him hard. He could feel the desire coming off her in waves.

"I take it you like that song?" Ryder laughed as he backed away just a fraction.

Tana looked at him her expression burning. "You know damned well what seeing you play and hearing you sing does to me."

Tana spoke through clenched teeth already pulling his shirt up and over his chest.

Still leaning back a little, Ryder smirked at her. "Yes. I know."

She stopped his words with a kiss and caressed his growing erection through his jeans. Ryder pulled her closer to him, taking the kiss deeper as he started to unbutton her blouse.

Tana leaned her head back and allowed Ryder to take control as he peeled her blouse from her and let it float to the floor. Her shirt was no sooner off and Ryder was unzipping her dress pants sliding them down her legs.

He stood up from the chair and guided her backwards until the table bumped against her backside. Lifting one hip, Tana scooted herself up onto the table as she undid Ryder's jeans, freeing him into her hands. She squeezed and stroked him for a moment as he eased her down to the tabletop.

"I hope you don't mind, but this is in my way." Ryder breathed as he tore her thong off in one quick swipe and plunged himself into her.

Tana cried out as he pushed himself deeper, her nails clawing at his back.

Ryder gasped feeling her sex surrounding him, encasing his erection in her heat. He thrusted in long slow strokes relishing in the sensation of her body. Looking down at her lying on the kitchen table, she looked back up at him her breathing matching his strokes. Ryder pulled on her legs bringing her backside right to the edge of the table.

Tana could feel Ryder going a little deeper now and her breath caught in her throat as he moved faster. When he rubbed her clit with the pad of his thumb, her jaw clenched and she gritted her teeth.

Tana's walls began to tighten. Impassioned cries escaped her as Ryder continued to pump into her. She was calling out to him and grabbing at the edge of the table as she came hard.

Ryder continued to push into her, his thumb relentless on her now super sensitive nub as his climax built deep in his gut. Tana let lose a guttural cry, coming again moments after her first orgasm as Ryder slammed into her with one final hard thrust.

"Jesus! Tana." He called out as he came, leaning forward on his hands and looking down at her.

She reached up and touched his face lovingly as he caught his breath. Taking a sideways glance at the microwave, Tana realized they should get dressed.

"Ian will be home in about fifteen minutes." She said in a sex heavy voice.

"Uh huh." Ryder acknowledged standing up and zipping his jeans back up.

Tana stood and picked up her clothes. She was about to turn to head to her bedroom when Ryder took a hold of her and tossed her over his shoulder, carrying her up the stairs.

Giggling, she asked Ryder what he was doing.

"Carrying you." He answered her simply.

"No kidding. Why are you carrying me?"

Ryder entered the bedroom and plopped her down on the bed. "Because I wanted to and because I know you had a long day."

Ryder walked over to her dresser and picked up her body lotion squirting some onto his hands. He sat behind her on the bed and rubbed the lotion into her shoulders, arms and her neck to help her relax.

"*Mmmm*... that feels so nice." Tana sighed.

Ryder smiled and kissed first one shoulder then the other. Hopping back to the floor, he picked up Tana's pajamas off the chair and brought them over to where she was still seated on the bed. He pulled the tank top over her head, holding it for her to push her arms through then helped her into her bottoms.

"There. All relaxed. Let's go watch a movie and wait for Ian to come home." Ryder suggested as he led her back down the stairs into the family room.

*** ~~~ ***

The next morning, Tana was up early with the girls and did her workout as usual. After tossing her sweaty clothes in the wash and getting started on laundry, she donned a short robe then went upstairs with the intent on starting breakfast before she woke Ryder.

When she got into the kitchen she saw Ryder sitting at the kitchen table in just his pajama pants with his iPhone in hand scrolling through an email. He looked up when she came into the room and held out an arm to her.

Tana walked over to him, and he pulled her into his lap. Her little robe fell open just enough that Ryder could see she was naked beneath it. Giving her a sinful look, he kissed her and slipped a hand inside the folds of fabric, cupping her breast.

"Good morning." He mumbled as he kissed her hotly.

Tana arched into him pressing her nipple to the palm of his hand returning his kiss.

"I was hoping to come and wake you." Tana gave him a little pout.

Sighing Ryder picked up his phone and opened the email again. "Unfortunately, this thing woke me. I'm going to have to head back to Langley on Monday. Bruce and Tyson have some dates for performances over in Japan for us to go over. We need to figure out what stage design we want to use plus get things ready to ship."

Tana looked slightly crestfallen. "When are the dates?"

"May. I will be gone from May eighteenth to June fourth. When are Nikki and Ian's grads?"

Tana blew out a breath and grabbed her phone out of her purse on the table. "Nikki's is May sixteenth and Ian's is not until June fourteenth."

Ryder looked a bit relieved. "Well at least I won't miss their grads, but I'll have to arrange to fly out from here on the seventeenth then meet up with the guys to leave on the eighteenth."

Tana was happy that he was going to be able to attend both grads, but she was sad to have him leaving again. All she could do was be grateful it wasn't going to be for four months.

"How long will it take in Langley to get everything all straightened out?"

Now Tana was hoping he wasn't going to be away for her birthday on the tenth, but if he was, she'd have no other choice but handle it. After all, it was part of being with him.

Ryder held her tight knowing where she was going with her questions. "I have no clue. It might take us a few days or a few weeks, but I can promise you this, I'm not missing your first birthday as my wife."

He leaned down and kissed her while she still sat on his lap. Reaching back into her robe, he caressed her nipple with his thumb as his fingertips trailed around the curve of her breast. Tana murmured her enjoyment into his kiss and threaded her hands into his hair.

Ryder was about to suggest they head back upstairs when his cell began to ring. Groaning with displeasure, Ryder pulled away from Tana and looked at the caller ID.

"Bruce, you have the worst timing." He answered, putting the phone on speaker then set it down as he nipped at Tana's collarbone.

"Did I wake you?" Bruce's disconnected voice came through the speaker.

"Tyson's email woke me. But I was just about to take my wife back upstairs to our bedroom." Ryder said out loud and Tana's jaw dropped as she looked at him in mock horror.

"Uh, geez. Uh-sorry Ryder. I um… was kind of hoping we could get you to fly home this afternoon instead of Monday."

"Not a chance in hell. I have a very special birthday celebration to attend this afternoon for Nikki. She just turned eighteen and I'm not missing this. If Tyson feels Monday is fine, we can stick to his plans." Ryder argued.

They could hear Bruce shuffling papers on his end before he spoke again. "It's just I thought before we start figuring out what equipment we want to take with us, maybe—"

"No." Ryder cut him off. "Look a day and a half isn't going to change anything. I see in Tyson's email that all the dates are secure and booked. We have time. I'll see you Monday."

"Okay, okay, okay." Bruce conceded.

"Thanks Bruce. Now if you don't mind, I'm hanging up now and taking my wife back to bed." Ryder was smiling at Tana.

Ryder ended the call, turning his full attention back to Tana and what she wasn't wearing under her robe.

"Shall we go upstairs?" Ryder asked slipping his hand back inside of her robe.

She swatted his hand away playfully and looked at him with a look of mock irritation. "After you blatantly tell your publicist your intentions with me?"

"Manager." Ryder corrected and held on to her tightly as he stood up with her cradled in his arms. "And for the record I didn't tell him my intentions, I just told him where I was taking you." Ryder clarified as he took her back to their bedroom and hooked the door closed with his foot.

Tana tried to stifle a giggle and put on her best look of innocence. "But now he must think I'm such a naughty girl."

Dropping her on the bed, he pulled the robe open. "Baby, you're married to me. He knows you are."

Ryder didn't give her a chance to formulate a reply.

~

An hour later, breathless and sated, Tana sat up still straddling her husband.

"Was that what your intentions were?" Tana asked giving him a devilish little smile.

"You better believe it." Ryder reached up and pulled her down with a hand on the back of her neck to kiss her.

"Then I'm quite glad you didn't tell Bruce that."

Ryder laughed and kissed her again. "Shower time Baby. Nikki will be home soon."

"You're really looking forward to giving her the car." Tana poked him in the back repeatedly, teasing him.

"Yes I am. And why shouldn't I be? This is a huge step for her. I'm just glad I get to be a part of it."

"Awe." Tana was touched and gave Ryder a big kiss.

When they got into the shower, they both washed quickly not wanting Nikki to make it home before they were out. Toweling off her hair Tana stepped out of her bathroom into her closet to get clean jeans and select a top.

Ryder had hung up a bunch of his own clothes in her closet and she had made space for him in her dressers as well. He was currently digging through one of his drawers trying to find something to wear. Finally finding what he had been looking for Ryder finished getting dressed.

"We still need to have breakfast too." Tana said pulling her jeans on and buttoning them up.

"I'm on it." Ryder said as he finished with his own jeans and walked out of the room as he threaded his belt through the belt loops.

Tana smiled to herself as she watched him leave, wondering what he was going to cook this time and pulled her top on over her head. She quickly brushed out her hair and started to blow dry it, giving Ryder a little bit of time to figure something out for breakfast.

Down in the kitchen Ryder was digging through the pantry and fridge trying to decide what to make. Nothing really caught his eye until he thought of making BLT sandwiches. There was a package of bacon in the fridge and he found all the other ingredients he needed in the crisper.

Grabbing a frying pan, he started to cook the bacon while he cut up tomatoes and washed some lettuce leaves. Ryder toasted the bread and added mayonnaise, layering on the lettuce then tomatoes with a touch of salt and cracked pepper.

He could hear Tana's hair dryer had stopped. He turned to remove the bacon from the heat, placing it on paper towels to absorb the extra grease. After a few minutes, he added the bacon to the sandwiches and cut them in half. He had made enough for more sandwiches for when Ian came out of his room and for when Nikki came home, in case they were hungry.

"Smells great. What did you make?" Tana waltzed into the kitchen looking fresh and clean.

Ryder grabbed Tana by the waist, spun her around into his arms and dipped her low, kissing her. "You smell great." He said breathing in her scent. "Promise me you'll never change perfumes."

Tana giggled and wrapped her arms around his neck. "Hey, you don't exactly smell bad yourself. I happen to love your scent too."

Ryder stood Tana up just as Ian walked into the kitchen and saw the food.

"Oh hey! BLT's." He looked at his mother first and she put her hands up signaling that she had nothing to do with it.

Ian turned to Ryder. "You cooked again?"

Ryder nodded and put a sandwich together for Ian, handing it to him then passed Tana her plate. Picking up his own plate, they went to the table and sat down.

About halfway through their meal, they heard the dogs whining and bouncing all over as Nikki came home.

"Get down, girls." She called as she made her way to her room to drop her stuff.

Walking into the kitchen she said good morning to everyone and Ryder got up to make her a BLT as she sat down at the table telling them how her night was. She thanked Ryder when he handed her a plate and dug in, suddenly very hungry.

Tana and Nikki were rambling back and forth about her party and if she had a good time. Nikki said she had, but she hadn't gotten severely drunk.

"You know Mom, I know there are going to be times when I do get absolutely hammered but because you always let me have a drink or two, I really didn't feel like I had to go all out last night. I'd rather do that at home or at Jess's place where if I pass out no one has to carry my drunken ass home."

Tana was proud of her daughter and Ryder was impressed. It was a very mature outlook for someone that had just turned eighteen.

"Are you ready for your gifts?" Tana asked Nikki then looked up at Ryder. He was trying his best not to grin.

"Sure." Nikki got up and put her plate in the dishwasher then sat back down at the table.

Ian grabbed Tana's camera and turned it on. Tana nodded her head to Ryder and he pulled the Celica's key out of his pocket, setting it on the table in front of Nikki.

"Happy birthday Nikki." Tana and Ryder said in unison.

Nikki frowned and picked up the key, looking it over. When realization kicked in, her jaw dropped and her eyes got big in her face.

"Are you serious?" It was barely more than a whisper.

Ryder came to stand beside her and pulled her out of her chair. "We're dead serious." He said leading her toward the garage.

"Come see your car." Ryder said as he and Tana walked on either side of her. Ian was right behind them, videotaping the entire thing.

"Now, we need to go get your registration and your plate still but your first year of insurance is paid. You have a new set of winter tires and rims due to come in before the summer is over and Ryder also got you gift cards for gas, car washes and oil changes." Tana filled her daughter in as she stood at the garage door.

Nikki's hands were up covering her mouth and she was crying. "Oh my God you guys. Thank you so much. This is amazing. I never would have even dreamed I was getting a car."

She gave both Ryder and her mother hugs and kisses. Ryder opened the garage door then flipped on the light.

"Go take a look." He placed a hand at the small of her back gently pushing her through the door.

Nikki stepped into the garage. She saw the sleek little black sports car with the enormous blue ribbon on it and screeched.

"Holy shit! Ohmigod! No way." she shouted and started jumping up and down, laughing and crying all at once.

Spinning around she hugged her mother with such force that Tana was almost knocked over.

"Thank you." Nikki barely managed to say through her tears.

"Ryder found it for you." Tana whispered to her daughter sniffing back her own tears.

Nikki let her mother go and turned to Ryder standing next to the steps. She jumped up throwing her arms around his neck. He caught her easily and hugged her back.

"Happy birthday Nikki." He said squeezing the girl tight. "I love you kid. I'm glad you like it."

Nikki burst into fresh tears and buried her face into Ryder's shoulder. "I love you too Ryder. Not cause of the car but cause you're here and that means more to me than the car, but I love the car too."

Ryder set Nikki back down and she dried her tears. "Thank you both so much. I can't believe this is really happening. I love you all."

"Well with your brother and I moving in a few months and you moving out on your own we figured you were going to need a car so you can around easier. Especially when you go to college." Tana said wiping tears off her own face.

"It's a combination grad and birthday gift for you. Get in and see what you think." Ryder explained a little more.

Nikki opened the car door and slid behind the wheel and immediately had to move the seat forward. "Well I know Ryder drove it home."

She adjusted her mirrors to her liking then looked over the interior. It was beautiful and Nikki absolutely loved it. It was a standard too which she was really happy with. Wiggling the shifter, she found the car was left in first gear, so she pulled the emergency brake handle up and slipped the gearshift into the neutral position.

Ryder smiled and laughed. "You're just like your mom. Maybe it's a girl thing."

He put his hand out to Nikki. "Come on, let's go get you your plate and registration so you can take it for a drive."

Everyone piled into Tana's truck to get Nikki her plate and registration. The teller at the registry's office looked over all the paperwork and in no time at all Nikki was handed a plate and her registration.

"When we get home, you can put the plate on and then I guess you're off. We'd like to head out for dinner for about six. If you want to go show your friends, be home in time to get ready to go." Tana informed Nikki as they drove back home.

As soon as Tana's truck stopped, Ryder and Nikki hopped out and he gave her a hand putting her plate on the back of her car.

"Okay, you should be good to go." He said and Nikki gave him another hug.

"Can I go with you?" Ian asked his sister.

"Yeah for sure!" Nikki offered. "Thank you so much Ryder, for everything."

"You're very welcome. Drive safe and have fun." He held the car door open for her as Ian slid into the passenger seat.

Nikki started the car and carefully backed out of the garage. Once out on the street, she shifted into first and with only a little hop, she was off on her own.

Chapter 4

It was the end of the first week of May. All members of Severe State and their crew were standing in their warehouse in North Vancouver finishing picking out what was going to be shipped over to Japan. It had taken them almost two weeks to complete everything for the Japan shows because of so many changes to accommodate the short trip, but it was still going to be a great show.

Even though they had decided to use a smaller stage, they increased the lighting and added in more laser lighting, which was always a big hit in Japan. Even the pyrotechnics were upped a bit more.

There were four shows booked for them in Japan. Tokyo, Osaka, Kyoto and Okinawa. Severe State would be in Japan for just over two weeks and they were looking forward to it. It had been a very long time since they had been to Japan and everybody was excited to return.

Ryder had been away from his new family since right after Nikki's birthday. Tana's birthday was coming up fast and he was trying to get things settled with the equipment so he could fly back to Sherwood Park in time to be with her. The band had at least one more day before Ryder could return to Sherwood Park and it looked like he was going to make it back with plenty of time before Tana's birthday.

While he was home, he had been talking to the goldsmith that had designed Tana's wedding rings and engagement ring for him. Ryder got him to make her a bracelet for her birthday. It was designed with slender links and each link housed one family member's birthstone separated by a diamond link. Her parents' stones, Dawn's, Nikki, Ian and Ryder's own along with his mother's stone were all there. He was really hoping she liked it.

The crew members were all taking inventory of what was being loaded into the sea cans to be sure they had everything that was going to be needed for the shows. Chris was selecting his guitars and Matt was over picking out his basses. Ben was counting out his spare drums to make sure he had enough as he had already decided which drum kit he wanted.

Ryder had just finished up with the microphones and lighting selections. He headed over to the cases for guitars that belonged to him and started loading them with his selections. Each guitar would have to be checked out by their equipment techs before the cases were loaded into the sea can.

"So how is married life treating you?" Ben came up to Ryder having finished his counts and leaving the loading up to their capable crew.

Ryder was sliding one of his favorite guitars into his case. "Pretty great." Ryder looked at Ben with a genuine smile on his face.

"I never thought I'd ever get married again but now that I have Tana, I can't imagine my life without her."

"That's great to hear buddy." Ben clapped him on the shoulder as Ryder continued to choose his instruments.

"We're all still thrilled for you and Tana, of course. She's an amazing woman. Beautiful, capable, intelligent, strong and perfect for you." Ben complimented.

"Don't forget great kids too. Lucky bastard. You missed out on the dirty diapers and two a.m. feedings." Chris came up to join Ryder and Ben.

"Sean still keeping you up half the night?" Ryder asked. Donna and Chris had been around his place often just catching up, so he had seen the little boy quite a few times since being back in Langley.

Sean looked so much like Chris with dark hair and dark eyes and was an extremely happy baby. His only issue was sleeping through the night. He was almost six months old and was still getting his parents up three times at night.

"Oh my God, you have no idea how I'm looking forward to Japan. Two weeks of uninterrupted sleep at night." Chris joked, but he looked tired.

"Yeah right. Inside of your first day, you are going to be crazy missing him." Matt ribbed him.

"I can believe that." Ryder said as he finished his first selections and signaled his tech to start checking over the guitars.

It was the end of the day for them and Bruce came up wanting to talk to the band about their travel plans.

"The first date we're playing is May twentieth. Considering we fly out in the afternoon of the eighteenth, that puts us in Tokyo on the nineteenth. I'm thinking that's not enough time to get adjusted to the time zone change and settled for the concert. I'm going to change the flight so we leave on the sixteenth and arrive on the seventeenth. That gives you guys extra time to make sure you're all in top shape to perform."

Ryder's shoulders dropped. The other three members of Severe State were agreeing with Bruce's idea. It looked like he was going to miss Nikki's high school graduation unless he came up with a way to convince everyone to change their minds. He stalked away from the group running his hands through his hair looking pissed off.

"Hey Ryder. What's going on?" Matt called out after him seeing storm off.

Pacing in hopes to re-gain his composure, Ryder ignored him while his mind was going a hundred different directions trying to figure out what to do. As excited as he was to go and do these Japan dates, he also wanted to be there for Tana and see Nikki get her diploma.

"Fuck!" He yelled out from the other side of the warehouse.

Everyone in the building stopped what they were doing and stared at Ryder. It wasn't like him to be this upset. The last time they had seen it was when he was dealing with Amanda.

Ryder stopped, placing his hands on the edge of one of the crates and he was leaning with his head hanging down. His wide shoulders were slumped. How was he going to tell Tana he was going to miss Nikki's grad after promising them both that he was going to be there? Nikki had even said she loved Ryder because he was there for her. This was going to hurt the two women he loved more than anything.

The one person that dared deal with Ryder when he was pissed off was Ben. They had been best friends the longest and Ben knew Ryder's temper. Even though Ryder outweighed him by at least forty pounds and had a good five inches on him in height, Ben knew him. He could reach Ryder on a level that the other band members couldn't.

He walked up to him and leaned against the same crate. "Mind telling me what's got you so pissed off?"

Ryder didn't move. "Nikki's high school graduation is on the sixteenth. I already promised her and Tana that I would be there seeing we were originally supposed to fly out on the eighteenth."

"Oh shit," Ben grimaced.

"Understatement," Ryder growled.

Ben folded his arms across his chest. "Well, why don't you still fly out on the eighteenth or even leave straight from Edmonton on the seventeenth? We don't have to all travel there together."

Ryder snapped his head up and stared at Ben. "We've always been a unified front. Arrive together, leave together. It's part of our routine. It always has been."

"Dude, we all have kids. You don't think this kind of situation isn't going to come up time and time again? We've got to be flexible and work with each other or we might as well call it quits now. None of us will be happy and our wives will all either kill us or leave us." What Ben was saying made complete sense.

Sighing with relief Ryder stood up smiling a little again. "Thanks man."

He clapped Ben on the back and they both headed over to where the others were watching them intensely and waiting. Between Ben and Ryder, they explained that Ryder would fly out the morning of the seventeenth as early as possible straight from Edmonton.

"I'm not breaking my promise to Tana and Nikki for an extra two days in Tokyo. I'd rather be tired than miss her grad." Ryder said adamantly.

All the others agreed and didn't have any issues with Ryder arriving the next day, so Bruce changed his flight again and was able to get him on a ten thirty flight out of Edmonton on the seventeenth.

They wrapped up for the day and Ryder hopped into his truck to head home. He called Tana from his truck, filling her in on what had happened and she was very grateful for the other band members being so understanding. But she mentioned to Ryder that if he hadn't been able to work it out, she and Nikki would have understood.

"Ryder, its part of your career. I'm sure changes like that happen all the time. Occupational hazard remember?" Even though it would have meant missing a big milestone, Tana still would've understood.

"God woman, I love you. But I want to be there for Nikki's grad. Seeing a video wouldn't have been the same. We're pretty much done getting ready here so I should be able to fly out at the latest Sunday morning." Ryder filled her in.

"Okay. Just let me know when I need to pick you up at the airport." Tana sounded happy to know he would be coming home again.

~~~

Tana woke up the morning of May tenth as usual to Chloe and Kordie pawing at the side of the bed. Bailey was sitting on the floor wagging her tail waiting for her to get up. The girls still woke her every morning, but since Ryder had become part of her life they never jumped on the bed unless Tana called them up or Ryder wasn't there.

"Guess I don't even get to sleep in on my birthday." Tana whispered to her dogs as she glanced at the clock and swung out of bed. It was only five a.m. The sun was coming up already and they figured it was time to go.

Quickly she dressed in her running shorts and a sports bra. After pulling on a pair of socks, she leaned down and kissed her sleeping husband lightly on his exposed chest. She stood up and turned to leave when she heard Ryder speak.

"If that's what you are going running in, I may have to take it up myself." Ryder looked at her sleepily admiring her short running shorts and sports bra.

"Go back to sleep." Tana whispered as she came up and kissed him again this time on the lips.

"Happy birthday Baby." He pulled her down onto the bed rolling her over top of himself and pinned her down.

Tana giggled. "Thank you. It's five in the morning. Let me go for my run and you can get an extra couple of hours at least."

Ryder groaned and let her go. "Those dogs need to learn how to tell time."

"Tell me about it." Tana said as she left the room pulling the door half closed.

She got her shoes on and the leash situated on her hips then left on a ten-kilometer route with all three dogs trotting happily at her side.

It was a beautiful morning and Tana had a great run. After stretching and feeding the dogs, she went back upstairs to her room to shower and get ready for work. Ryder had fallen back asleep and she smiled at him as she passed the bed heading to the bathroom.

When Tana went downstairs to have breakfast, Ian was up and wished his mother a happy birthday.

"Thank you Ian." Tana said as she sat down beside him to eat.

Nikki ran out of her room and came up to Tana hugging her. "Happy birthday Mom. Love you!" and she was off back into her room to get ready for school.

Tana finished her breakfast then went to get ready for work. She closed the bathroom door to keep her hair dryer from waking Ryder and continued with her routine. When she opened the bathroom door, Ryder was standing there waiting.

"Oh!" Tana jumped. "Ryder you scared the shit out of me."

She laughed as he pulled her into a big hug and crushed his lips down on hers.

"Do you have to leave right away?" He asked as he pulled back just enough to speak.

Tana nodded. "Yes, I do."

"That's too bad." Ryder growled into her hair his hands caressing down her back and over the curves of her ass.

He lifted one hand and spanked her bottom sharply watching her eyes spark up. "I guess I will have to wait until later."

Tana was flushed and feeling warm as Ryder took her face in his hands and tilted her face up to kiss her lips. "Have a great day at work and a happy birthday, Mrs. Evans."

He smiled giving her one more kiss before brushing past her and heading into the bathroom. As he closed the door, he winked at her.

Taking a deep breath to calm herself, Tana called out a loving goodbye to Ryder then went to gather up her purse and keys.

~~

It turned out to be a busy morning for Tana. There was a production meeting that lasted longer than planned then all the managers were pulled in for an emergency meeting to discuss some inter-department issues causing stress for assembly and inventory management that needed to get ironed out.

It was five minutes to noon by the time Tana got back to her office. As she pushed her door open, she gasped in shock. There were at least a dozen bouquets of roses and calla lilies in both red and white all over her office. Each bouquet had a card on it.

Tana went from one bouquet to another collecting the cards before sitting down at her desk to open them. Each envelope she opened had a single word written on the card.

'Smile', 'Scent', 'Laugh', 'Heart', 'Independence', 'Mind', 'Body', 'Strength', 'Lips', 'Spirit', 'Courage' 'Touch'

There was only one card that had more written on it. After seeing the flowers and reading the single words on all the other cards, Tana was near tears as she read what Ryder had written.

'Happy Birthday to my beautiful wife and the love of my life. With all that I possess in my heart, I am Forever Yours, your loving husband, Ryder.'

Tana set that card aside and spread the ones with a single word written on them out on her desk looking them over a few times before a familiar voice made her look up.

"Do you know what they mean?" Ryder was leaning his long body on the doorframe to her office.

"How did you get here? I drove myself today." Tana's surprised expression stared back at him from her chair.

Ryder grinned as he sauntered into her office. "I borrowed Nikki's car. She was more than willing to lend it to me when I told her what I wanted to do."

He sat down on the corner of her desk. "Do you know what they mean?" Ryder asked her again.

Tana looked over the words again and looked up at him trying not to cry. "Things about me you love?"

Ryder nodded. "There aren't enough flowers in the world to have a bouquet for everything that I love about you, so I picked the ones that mean the most to me. The ones I think of first when we're apart."

Tears spilled over Tana's lashes and slid down her cheeks as she listened to her husband. He reached out and wiped them away with his thumb then pulled her up to his lap. Tana curled into him and tried to compose herself.

"No one's ever said or done something so incredibly romantic like this for me before. Thank you Ryder. I really don't know what to say."

Ryder kissed her forehead. "You deserve this and more. Come on. I'm taking you out for a nice lunch. I've already talked to Warren and he knows you'll be back when you get back."

Ryder stood her up as he stood. Tana grabbed a Kleenex to dry her eyes and blow her nose before they left her office. He took her around the waist as they walked toward the main doors and everyone they passed glanced up and smiled. They had seen Ryder bringing the flowers in and knew it was Tana's birthday. They could only imagine what had been said in there but could guess that it was very touching and extremely heartfelt from the look on both Ryder and Tana's faces.

~~

Later that evening, Ryder had cooked an incredible chicken parmesan with linguini dinner for everyone and afterwards there was Tana's favorite cake for dessert, carrot cake with a cream cheese icing.

Nikki and Ian gave their mother a gift card to a local runner supply store knowing it would be well used.

When Ryder pulled out his gift, he was anxious for her to see it. There was a lot of thought put into it and he was really hoping she liked it. Tana still wore the first bracelet he had given her quite frequently and this one could be worn everyday if she wanted to. It was tiny like her wrists and Ryder hoped it fit.

Tana unwrapped the box and opened the jeweler's case. When she saw the bracelet, she picked it up to examine it a little closer. It was beautiful with links in white gold shaped like the swirls of tiny treble clef's and had stones mounted to the center of each swirl. There were diamonds in between each gemstone and each gem was a different color.

Tana tilted her head to one side trying to figure out why the stones were different. Ryder watched her closely as she ran each link gently through her fingers examining each stone. There was an emerald, ruby, topaz, sapphire, garnet, amethyst, alexandrite and black diamond.

Ryder was about to tell her what it meant when she looked up at him in shock. "It's our birthstones. All of us including my parents, my sister and your mother's. But why the black diamond?"

Ryder took the bracelet from her and wrapped it around her wrist doing up the clasp. It was a perfect fit. "Because Nikki's birthday is in April and her stone would have been another diamond, so I put it as a black diamond for contrast. Do you like it?"

"Yes! It's beautiful." Tana breathed. There were tears in her eyes again as she stood up in front of Ryder to kiss him.

"Thank you so much." Tana looked at the bracelet on her wrist and smiled. "This was incredibly thoughtful. I can't believe how much you've spoiled me today."

Ryder caressed her cheek and looked deep into her eyes. "You have lived through enough hurt and struggle in your life. I just want to give you good memories and make you happy."

Tana wrapped her arms around Ryder's neck and held him tight. "You do make me happy, very much so."

She kissed him showing him how much she desired him as her tongue danced with his. Ryder returned her passion as his hands encircled her waist pulling her to his lap.

Tana broke their contact and pressed her forehead to his. "I have the best husband in the world."

Ryder smiled back at her. "Happy birthday Baby. I hope it was a good one for you."

"The best one ever." Tana admitted as she stood up.

Ryder suggested they play a game as a family, so Tana went downstairs to grab Scrabble and brought it upstairs. For the rest of the evening the four of them played numerous games, laughing and having fun together as a family.

Later, Tana and Ryder were lying in bed and Ryder was rubbing lotion into Tana's back arms and legs. She claimed he was spoiling her immensely, yet Ryder just felt he was loving her the way she deserved to be loved.

When he told her as much, she just smiled and looked away. He knew she was used to being so strong and independent. A survivor. He wanted her to come to know life without having to just survive. He wanted to be there for her and help her really live.

Ryder knew he could never ask her to quit her job and travel with him on the road full time, especially while Ian was still at home. But he was hoping that one day she would join him on the road more frequently. Even if it was just for a few weeks at a time with a week or two off, so she could still enjoy her own time.

"*Mmmm...* Mr. Evans if you keep that up, I'm going to be so relaxed that I might just fall asleep." Tana murmured from between the mattress and her forearms.

"Well now, we definitely don't want that happening. At least not yet." Ryder said trailing kisses from her hip across her lower back and up to her neck.

Tana's skin broke out in goosebumps and she squirmed beneath him as he ran the edges of his teeth up and down her spine from her neck to that spot between her shoulder blades.

"*Mmmm...*" Tana mewled.

He ran his hands down the sides of her head all the way down her body, caressing her sides. Then down her hips and legs right down to her feet.

"I want to make love to you Tana." He whispered in her ear sending a fresh wave of shivers up her spine.

"Please." Tana begged as she turned over on the bed.

Ryder lay back down beside her with his head propped up on one bent arm. He ran his hand up her body and back down just watching her reaction to his touch. Her eyes would flutter and her lips parted as she inhaled. When she met his eyes, he could see how incredibly green they were and filled with the love she had for him.

In one smooth motion, he rolled on top of her and Tana opened her thighs to make room. With one hand he brushed the strands of hair away from her face as he leaned down to kiss her. As their tongues touched and caressed, Ryder entered her gently and lovingly.

Tana gasped into his kiss as he filled her. Ryder pulled out in long leisurely strokes and flexed back into her just as slowly, intending on making their mutual pleasure last. Tana's hands trailed from his backside, up his spine to his neck and into his hair where she fisted her hands, tugging just a little.

Ryder had to exercise self-restraint when she did that, not wanting to rush. Running one of his hands down her side as the other gently caressed her face, he kept their rhythm. He could feel her tighten around him. Even with their slowed pace and gentleness, she was so responsive to him.

He flexed forward a little harder and swiveled his hips, hitting that spot inside that pushed her over the edge every time.

Tana's back arched and her hands grasped Ryder's biceps as she cried out. Ryder continued, flexing and adding in the hip rotation with his last handful of thrusts, pushing Tana's orgasm beyond her control as his own rushed through his body. He stiffened hissing through clenched teeth as he called out to his wife in unison with her cries.

Breathing hard, he kept himself raised above her on his elbows so he could lean down to kiss her. "I love you Tana Evans."

Smiling up at him she looked peaceful and sated. "And I love you Ryder Evans. With all that I am. Thank you for the best birthday I've ever had."

"You are most welcome." He shifted off her holding her close.

Caressing her arm and side to help relax her as she drifted off to sleep in his arms.

"Sleep well, Baby." He said softly and kissed the top of her head.

Chapter 5

Both Tana and Ryder made the most of their last few days before Nikki's graduation. They knew that Ryder had to fly out from Edmonton International early the day after the grad. He would be gone for two weeks so as much as Tana's work schedule allowed, they spent time together as a family and as a couple. Numerous hours were spent with the kids playing games and there were even days Ryder went outside with Ian and played street hockey with him and a few of his friends after school.

On those days when Tana came home to see her husband and her son playing three-on-three with some of Ian's friends, she felt like she had fallen into a dream world. No one acted like Ryder was a famous rock star, just Ian's cool stepdad that had a wicked wrist shot.

There was even one day that all four of them took the softball equipment to a nearby diamond to throw the ball around and to do some hitting. They spent most of the afternoon taking turns hitting, catching and pitching. Ryder found out the hard way that Nikki was a hell of a hitter and that his wife had a deadly accurate arm.

For Tana's last turn hitting, Ryder pitched to her and she made good contact, sending the ball right out to where the short stop would be. Ian dove for it, rolling and scooping the ball up then whipping it back to Ryder who was standing by second, ready to catch his wife. Tana tried to dodge him. She was quick but with his long reach, he was able to snag her around the waist, pulling her to the ground and making her squeal.

Their time together since Ryder came off tour strengthened their bond and brought them all closer together. Even though Ryder's passion and drive for his music was still just as strong, he couldn't deny feeling the pull of his new family and wanting to be with them too.

Not once did any of them try to dissuade him from his passion. It was just the opposite they encouraged him even though they missed him when he was gone just as much as he missed them.

When the morning of Nikki's graduation came, Tana was filled with nervous energy. Not only was her little girl graduating but her husband was going away again the following morning. She got up and went through her usual routine, but having taken the day off, she didn't get dressed for work.

The cap and gown ceremony was scheduled to be held at the school at two-thirty then that evening, the banquet dinner was in downtown Edmonton at The Shaw Conference Center. Nikki had an appointment to get her hair and make-up done for eleven, so Tana didn't really need to be worried about time until then.

She worked out and tinkered around the house after Ian left for classes. Tana was allowing him to take the afternoon off to attend his sister's graduation, but he had some classes he wanted to attend in the morning. He agreed to come straight home at lunch to change into his dress pants and shirt.

Ryder was awake by nine and he found Tana out in the back yard playing catch with the dogs. He stood there watching her for a few moments before he opened the door and stepped outside. As soon as he did, all three girls stopped paying attention to Tana and made a beeline for him.

Ryder reached down and patted each dog as they jostled their way to his outstretched hands. Tana walked over to him, still in her workout clothes and gave him a good morning kiss.

"How are you today?" he asked her placing a hand at the small of her back.

Tana chewed on her bottom lip and shrugged. "My baby girl is graduating today. I'm so proud of her yet I'm sad because I know she'll be on her own soon and I'm going to miss her."

It was an honest statement and one Ryder could understand. Tana was a wonderful mother that had seen her children through some very tough times. It was only natural for her to feel this way. Especially seeing how close Nikki and Tana were.

Ryder took her hand pulling her back inside and led her upstairs. "Come on. Let's shower then have breakfast."

They undressed and got in the shower where Ryder helped Tana to temporarily forget about Nikki being all grown up. Afterwards, they got dressed then had a quick breakfast of yogurt and fruit while they waited for Nikki to return from the hair salon. As the minutes ticked by Tana couldn't help but feel anxious.

Ian arrived home before Nikki and as promised, he went to change. Tana and Ryder were both ready to go. Tana was wearing black dress pants, heels and a very pretty gold satin sleeveless top. She had pinned her hair back, draping it over one shoulder. Which helped her to look even younger and sexier.

Ryder wore nice black jeans and a white linen shirt, which he left open slightly. Over that he planned on wearing his leather jacket. He had his pendant from Tana around his neck and he looked every inch the rockstar he was.

"Goddamn Ryder. If we had time, I would strip you down and have my wicked way with you right now."

Ryder arched a brow at her. "Is that a promise or a threat?"

"That's a promise. Tonight, after we get home and the kids are in bed, I am going to make sure you are well taken care of before you have to leave." Tana sauntered over to him and ran her hands up his chest feeling the bulk underneath. Standing up on her toes, she planted a deep passionate kiss on his lips then sashayed away leaving Ryder wanting more.

Moments later, Nikki arrived home and quickly changed. She appeared from her room a few minutes later in a black skirt and blue blouse. Meeting everyone else in the kitchen, she sat down to pull on her heeled sandals.

"Um… Mom, I wanted you to know I texted Dad to see if he was coming. But I still haven't heard back from him." Nikki said looking a little irritated.

Tana shook her head and glanced quickly at Ryder. "Sweetheart, I've been trying to get him to respond since we found out the date for your grad. I'm not surprised he hasn't gotten back to you."

"Me either but at least I can say that I tried too." Nikki took her father's rejection well, but Ryder knew that was mostly because Tana tried so hard to fill both parenting roles.

So far Ryder had been spared meeting Mike and even though he knew that one day he would have to face the guy, he could honestly say he wasn't looking forward to it. From the sounds of it, he was a selfish bastard that was hardly interested in his kids at all.

Everyone piled into Tana's truck and headed off to Nikki's school. As soon as they arrived, Nikki went to get her cap and gown while the other's waited in the rotunda for her to come back. It took about ten minutes for Nikki to make it back because she kept getting stopped by her friends wanting to take pictures.

When she did finally make it back, it was Tana's turn to take pictures. Nikki even asked Jess to take a few pictures of all of them together. After Jess did a double take at Ryder and shook his hand, she snapped half a dozen shots for them.

Jess asked if Ryder would let her have a picture of him with her and Nikki. Smiling warmly at Nikki's best friend, he agreed and posed with both girls.

It was time to start the ceremony so the principal was ushering all the grads to their seats in the gym with the help of the parent's association. Tana, Ryder and Ian made their way into the gym and found some empty seats close to the stage along the center aisle.

The ceremony was starting and the students were called to attention, but there was a fair amount of whispering going through the graduating class. Many of the grads had turned to look back in the direction of Ryder and Tana. It was obvious word had spread that Ryder was here for Nikki's graduation. There was a few pointing in their direction and both Tana and Ryder hoped they would all act mature enough and not interrupt the graduation ceremony.

The principal, the vice-principal and the class valedictorian, each gave speeches then the student body president gave a short speech. He made a special point thanking all the parents for not killing them when they had been growing up through the most awkward years of their lives and being there to push them when they needed it. Whether that be simply to get up in the morning or to get their homework done.

"We may not show it much and I know I certainly didn't over the last few years, but Moms and Dads, we thank you. Without your help, none of us would be here."

There was laughter and applause for the young man's comical speech. The head of the parent's association was called up next for the parents reply to the grads then the presentation of their certificates began.

The students had been seated alphabetically. When called, each group would head up and wait backstage until their name was called. Then they would walk through the archway, shake hands with the principal and the vice-principal to receive their certificates. After they received their certificates, they stopped to have their picture taken then headed back to their seat.

Nikki was in the first group and fifth up out of just over a hundred and fifty grads in total. Tana was waiting with her camera in hand, as the other student's names were called. With each name called up, the grads, parents and family members alike all clapped and cheered for the grads.

"Nicole Emily Anderson." The vice-principal said into the microphone.

A huge cheer went through over half of the graduating class as Nikki climbed the steps and walked toward the principal. Tana stood up and snapped pictures as her daughter shook hands, received her certificate, had the tassel on her cap moved from her right to the left, signaling her graduation then she posed for a picture before leaving the stage amongst all the hoots and hollers.

Ryder was having a hard time not cheering or yelling out to Nikki. It was an incredible feeling for him to watch her receive her diploma and he was doubly glad to have not missed it. The sense of love and pride he felt for Nikki at that moment couldn't have been stronger even if she had been his own daughter.

In less than an hour, they were all seated back down as the vice-principal gave the closing speech. At the end, all the grads tossed their caps up in the air and Tana stood up to snap a picture of it.

The parents filed out of the gym as the grads turned in their gowns if they were done with pictures and kept their caps. Jess's parents came up to say hi to Tana, so she introduced Ryder to them. Tana and Jess's parents had developed a great relationship over the years through the girls. There had been numerous conversations on limits and boundaries for the girls as they grew up and thankfully, they all had the same parenting style.

Ryder saw Nikki and Jess headed for them with a huge group of grads following behind. None of them had turned in their gowns yet, and there were cameras everywhere. Knowing what was about to happen, Ryder squeezed Tana's hand and gave her a heads up.

Nikki and Jess arrived and as Jess's parents congratulated the two girls, the rest of the group of grads arrived calling to Nikki.

"Can we meet your dad Nik?" One girl asked shyly.

Nikki looked at Ryder apologetically and he came up to her and hugged her.

"Don't worry about it." He whispered to her and turned with her cradled in his arm to face the other graduating students. For the next twenty minutes or so, Ryder posed with the students for pictures and signed a few autographs.

As soon as the group dispersed, Nikki begged Ryder and her mother to head to the car, promising them she would meet them there as soon as she turned her gown in. They really had to get going in order to get changed for the banquet and to make it there on time. Ryder and Tana agreed, said good-bye to the small group of parents they had been talking to and headed back to the truck before more grads came looking for pictures with Nikki's rocker stepdad.

Back at home, Tana and Nikki changed in record time. Nikki donned her peacock blue mermaid style gown, while Tana slipped into an elegant hunter green satin halter dress with black heels.

Nikki looked beautiful and when Tana saw her, it brought tears to her eyes. Taking a picture, Tana told her daughter how proud she was of her.

When the girls came into the family room where Ryder and Ian were waiting, both guys whistled at them.

"Wow! Both of you look stunning." Ryder said going to Nikki first and giving her a kiss on the cheek and then to his wife.

"Thanks Ryder." Nikki blushed a little and grabbed her matching clutch ready to go.

"Oh Mom, Brad is going to meet us there." Nikki filled her mother in on her boyfriend's expected appearance.

"He couldn't get out of class this afternoon for the ceremony, but he will be there tonight."

Nikki and Brad had been together for almost two years now. They had gone to school together until Brad had graduated last year and he was now in his first year of university. Tana liked him and was looking forward to seeing him again to find out how he was enjoying university.

Piling back into the truck, Tana drove to downtown Edmonton where the Conference Center was right in the middle of the hill leading into the river valley. At certain parts, depending on where you were standing, you had a beautiful view of the river valley.

Brad met them out on one of the terraces and introductions were made between Ryder and Brad. He was a handsome blond and played soccer for the University of Alberta, while studying in the sports health and science fields.

Heading into the banquet hall, they looked for their table and found they were seated with Jess's parents much to Tana's relief. While they all sat and talked, numerous different parents came up to their table to introduce themselves. Tana was sure she wound up meeting every parent and grad before dinner was even served. Conversations easily flowed all throughout dinner and when the dance began, the grads were all called to the dance floor with their mother or father to have the first dance in honor of their parents. Ryder was a little surprised when Nikki stood up and took his hand.

"You have been more of a father to me over the last year and a half than my own father has my entire life. I would really like it if you would dance with me Ryder." Nikki said as he stood up.

"It would be my honor." He said standing up and leading her out to the dance floor.

Taking a few pictures, Tana watched her daughter and husband glide over the dance floor. The rest of the grads with their respective parent all glanced and nodded at Ryder dancing with Nikki. He smiled and nodded back, grateful that everyone seemed to be less interested in him and more on enjoying the graduation celebration.

When they were done, Ryder led Nikki back to Brad who took his girlfriend back out onto the dance floor where they danced for quite a while. Jess and her boyfriend were out there with them and Tana could tell they were all having a great time.

By ten, Tana was ready to go. She needed to take Ryder to the airport in the morning then she had to head to work after. She told Nikki to be safe at the after-grad and if she needed anything to call. Brad promised to drive her home afterwards then Nikki hugged her mom and Ryder, thanking them for everything before her parents and brother left to go home.

Once back at home, Ian said goodnight heading straight to bed while both Tana and Ryder headed in the direction of their room. Ryder gently closed the door behind Tana and looked her over.

"You look so lovely Tana." He had been taking pictures all day and night with his phone, saying he needed his own collage on his phone to look at while he was away again.

Tana smiled and turned to put her shoes away. When she flipped the light on in her closet, Ryder's packed bag was there staring at her, a reminder that he had to go away again. Tana stuffed the sad feeling down deciding that she was going to make him feel happy and not worry about being apart. She turned back to Ryder smiling her little smile.

"All right Mrs. Evans, I see that smile. What do you have up your sleeve?" Ryder narrowed his eyes at his wife with a half-cocked grin.

"I don't have any sleeves." Tana put her arms up playfully, showing him her bare arms as she swayed over to him.

Ryder took her wrists into his hands and pulled her against his front, holding her hands out away from him.

"You know what I mean." He growled at her and leaned down to drag his teeth across her neck.

Tana sighed into him, responding instantly to his advances. She tried to free her hands, so she could touch him, but he held her tight.

Ryder bent her arms down and behind her back, taking both wrists into one hand. With his free hand, he slipped it inside of the back of her dress and unclasped her bra with a flick of his fingers.

"Let me have my hands." Tana murmured.

"Why?" Ryder breathed into her hair inhaling her scent.

"So I can touch you." Tana pulled against his hold on her again and this time he released her.

Tana's hands instantly went to his waist and began to unbuckle his belt pulling it free from the loops in his jeans. She walked behind Ryder dropping the belt to the floor and reached around to un-do his jeans. Pulling them open, she shoved her hands into his boxers, grasping his rapidly hardening penis.

Ryder's head fell back as he inhaled deeply, letting it out in a deep throaty groan as Tana's hands manipulated and massaged the entire length of him. She pressed her body against him and he could feel her hot breath on his back as her hands started to lift his shirt. Ryder helped her by pulling it over his head and tossing it aside.

Tana ran her hands lightly all over his back and arms, following with her lips as her hands made their way to his chest. She placed her ear against Ryder's back listening to his heart beat before she made her way back around him to face him.

His gaze hot, he stood there looking down at her, letting her be in control while she worked her hands back into his jeans pushing them down. Ryder stepped out of them, kicking them off to the side then stood there completely naked in front of her.

Tana looked up at him as she slowly sank to her knees, her eyes locked to his. Taking Ryder's erection in her hands, Tana squeezed as she looked at her husband through her lashes. Hollowing her cheeks, she took him into her mouth, all the way to the back of her throat. When she pulled back, she worked her tongue over him and lightly nipped at him with her teeth.

Ryder hissed at her, his teeth clenched with the pleasure she gave him. "Baby, oh yeah." He called out to her as he felt his climax begin to build.

Tana continued and within minutes Ryder's hand clamped down on her shoulder and his muscles locked as he came with a restrained shout. Tana stayed down on her knees when he was done, rubbing and caressing his legs to calm and relax him. Ryder pulled her up looking into her eyes.

"We're not done yet." She said to him as she took his hands and placed them on her thighs.

He took her cue and lifted her dress up pulling it over her head taking her unclasped bra with it. She was left standing before him in her thong for a moment before Ryder dropped to his knees and took it off.

Trailing kisses from her navel down to each hip point then down one leg and back up the other, Tana was panting with anticipation for his next move. Ryder didn't disappoint her. Grabbing her around the waist, he stood up with her in his arms and set her on the edge of the bed. Leaning down to kiss her, Ryder parted her lips with his tongue, searching out hers.

Her arms flew around his neck, hands fisting in his hair as her desire overflowed. Ryder picked up on her fever. His own passion increased, matching hers as he lay Tana down on the bed. Tearing his lips from hers and breathless from their kiss, he worked his way down her neck to her abdomen, pausing for a moment at her pelvis before he settled his lips around the bud of her sex.

Ryder kissed and laved at her folds ramping Tana's need up even higher. As he inserted a finger into her, he suckled on her clit and her back arched instantly. He could feel her muscles quiver around his finger as she came.

Standing back up, Ryder caressed her and leaned over to nip at her breasts as she calmed slightly from her orgasm. Her breathing had just slowed when he flicked her nipple with his tongue as he lightly pinched the other one making her moan and grab at the edge of the bed.

Tana wrapped her legs around Ryder's waist and rotated her hips to him. Ryder stood up and positioned the head of his erection at her slit. He lifted her by the hips wrapping his arms underneath her bottom and lower back.

Her weight was partially in his arms and the rest on her shoulders on the bed as he slid into her depths. She gasped feeling him fill her as Ryder pulled her tight to him flexing at the same time. He watched her mouth open and her eyes flutter before making contact with his. Again, Ryder pulled her and flexed at the same time. This time Tana moaned at the feeling.

Ryder continued, enjoying the pressure this angle put on his erection as he rotated his hips. He could feel his testicles drawing up and increased the force of his thrusts, really grinding his pelvis into Tana's.

He felt her walls tightening. Ryder wanted her to come hard. On his next thrust, he moved his hips in a figure eight pattern hitting her sweet spot repeatedly causing her to cascade down over that edge into an incredibly intense orgasm. Her legs locked tight around his waist crushing her pelvis to his and her cries ramped up to shouts, finally ending with a scream which she tried to stifle.

Ryder clenched his hands at the small of her back in reaction to the force of her walls pulsing and squeezing his rock-hard penis as his orgasm burst from him with a series of thrusts and shouts.

Falling forward, he barely caught himself on his arms as he panted into Tana's chest. "You're incredible." He breathed as he fought to catch his breath.

Tana ran her hands through his hair and smiled. "*Hmmm*. So are you. God Ryder. What you do to me."

Unlocking her legs from his waist, she let him slide into bed next to her, snuggling into his chest and kissing his neck.

"I love you."

"I love you too Baby." Ryder pulled her up to kiss her mouth before letting her snuggle back down onto his chest.

As she drifted off to sleep, Ryder studied her sleeping form, etching it into his mind for himself over the next few weeks.

Chapter 6

The next morning, Tana got up and ran the dogs like any other morning. But she didn't have to rush through her morning routine because she was driving Ryder to the airport. He had to be there by eight-thirty, which gave Tana an extra forty-five minutes than she normally had. She originally tried to sleep in, but Chloe was having none of that, so Tana went for a longer run seeing she had plenty of time.

When she came back inside after stretching, she went straight to the shower. It had felt cooler out than it really was, so she had dressed in long pants and a long sleeve top with her running jacket on. Within her first kilometer, she had realized she was overdressed and by the time she got back home, she was completely soaked.

Standing in the shower and scrubbing her hair, Tana heard the shower door open. Looking over her shoulder, she smiled seeing her husband coming into join her.

"Good morning Mr. Rockstar." Tana teased as she stuck her head under the spray to rinse her hair.

Ryder mumbled a good morning back looking tired. It was going to be a long day for him, but he was hoping he could sleep on the plane. Tana finished rinsing and turned pushing Ryder into the water. Wetting his sleep-tousled hair, she shampooed it for him massaging his scalp with her fingers.

"*Mmmm*... that feels good." Ryder said as Tana turned him in order to get easier access to the back of his head.

"You need a haircut. You're starting to look like Matt with his shaggy hockey helmet hair." Tana teased.

Ryder opened one eye and arched his brow at her. "What? You don't like me with longer hair?"

Tana smirked at him and shrugged as she pushed his head back under the water to rinse his hair. Ryder wasn't prepared for it and was sputtering at her.

"I don't know how I feel about you with longer hair. I've only seen you with the style you always have."

"Maybe I'll grow it out and see what you think of it long." Ryder teased.

Tana scrunched her nose and shook her head. "No. Much longer than this and I think it would look funny on you. I like your hair the way you keep it."

Tana washed herself then turned her attention back to Ryder, washing him as well. She took her time and was extremely sensual about it. Ryder knew she was doing it deliberately. The little smile curling her lips was a dead giveaway.

Ryder let her finish before he picked her up and held her to him. After making love to her in the shower, they both remained motionless, breathing heavily with the water beating down on them.

They had been in the shower for almost an hour and the water was starting to get cold. The hot water was running out, so they quickly rinsed and got out before they were pelted with straight cold water.

Tana got dressed then went to fix something for breakfast while he finished packing and brought his bags down. Ryder loaded them in Tana's truck while she cooked him some eggs, ham, toast and coffee.

When he sat down to eat, Tana went to check on Nikki and found her soundly sleeping in her room. She must have gotten home late from her after grad party. Tana had excused her from classes like most other parents had with their graduating children seeing the grad had been held mid-week.

Tana let Ryder know Nikki was home safe and sat down to have her own breakfast. As they both ate, Tana asked about his shows in Japan. She was excited for him, and Ryder admitted he was looking forward to be going back on the road for a brief stint. As much as he loved coming home to Tana, he also couldn't deny how much he loved performing.

"I'm going to miss you." He said as he sipped his coffee. "But I'm really looking forward to this. We haven't been to Japan in about three years."

Tana got up and put her plate in the dishwasher. "You should be looking forward to this. I'll miss you too, but you have to be you. That means jetting all over the world and playing for your fans. The kids and

I will be okay. It's the first few days that are the worst. But we all adjust and just continue on until you come back home."

Tana spoke honestly, as she always did. And Ryder loved her for it. He never had to worry about feeling too guilty for leaving. She understood him in ways no other woman had even tried.

"Where's the first show?" Tana asked curious about the places he was going to see.

"Tokyo on the twentieth." Ryder finished his breakfast and thanked her, kissing her sweetly.

"Then Osaka on the twenty-fifth, Kyoto on the twenty-ninth and finally Okinawa on June third."

Tana was writing his locations and dates down on the calendar, so she knew where he was. It was something she did every time he went away. This way she could follow him and know time changes for phone calls and when he would be on stage.

It was time to go and morning traffic was heavy all the way down the highway to the international airport. Tana parked the truck and got out with Ryder helping him to grab his bags before they headed inside. Together they walked up to the desk for the private airline, got him all checked in then he turned to Tana.

"See you in two weeks. I'm going to miss you so much." He folded her into his arms and held her tight. "I love you, Tana Evans."

Tana smiled as he held her willing herself not to cry. When she looked up at him, her eyes betrayed her and filled with tears.

"Come on Baby, none of that." He smiled down at her and wiped away her tears. "I'll be home before you know it."

"I know." Tana sniffed. "I don't mean to cry. Sometimes I just can't stop it."

"I know. You're just having a moment." He teased lovingly.

Tana laughed. "Yeah, I am. I love you too."

She held him close once more then swatted his ass. "Now get out of here and wow the kimono's off of Japan."

Ryder laughed and squeezed her hand, rubbing her wedding bands with his thumb.

"My wife." He said as he slowly walked back to the customs hall, holding her hand until he had to let go.

"Bye." Tana waved after he dropped her hand and he returned her wave, kissing his fingers to her.

Tana did the same and mouthed *'I love you'* as he walked out of sight.

~~

The Friday after Ryder left, Tana finally got a chance to speak to him. He called her at nine in the evening her time, missing her voice. Tana was home all alone. Nikki was out at a friend's grad party with Brad, Jess and her boyfriend while Ian was over at his girlfriend's place until ten.

When Tana answered the long-distance call, Ryder's voice sounded as far away as he was. The connection wasn't great, but they muddled through their call regardless of the static. He was telling her he finally got caught up on sleep and over his jet lag. It had been a tough transition, but he admitted to Tana that missing Nikki's grad would have been worse than dealing with the jet lag. It was already Saturday afternoon for him and Severe State was performing again that night.

"I loved sharing the parent dance with her. I was shocked she even wanted to participate seeing her father didn't show up." Ryder admitted from his hotel room in Osaka.

"Why wouldn't she? She does love you. I'm sure she loves her father too, but not in a way that really makes much of a difference. Her feelings for Mike are more out of duty because he's her father. Believe me the kids aren't close to him."

Hearing that made Ryder remember that his own father was just as absent as Mike sounded and that was probably why he was so relieved he hadn't met Mike yet. Jack and Mike sounded like they could be cut from the same cloth.

Ryder and Tana talked for a bit longer with her asking how the first show had gone. When Ryder admitted it had been a huge success, she was incredibly happy for him. Just before they hung up, Tana wished them good luck for the rest of their shows.

"Thanks Baby. Tell the kids I love them and miss them. I love you."

Moments later, they hung up and Tana sat on the couch holding the phone to her chest smiling. She had adjusted to his absence again, but it was still good to hear his voice. The texts still came frequently, but it was hard while he was getting over jet lag and with the time zone change.

Tana finished watching the TV show she had been watching before Ryder called with little interest. Her thoughts kept wandering back to her husband and how much she loved him.

Ian came home and came into the family room to say goodnight to his mother. He saw her sitting on the couch still holding the phone to her chest and was worried.

"Hey Mom. Are you okay?" He asked sitting down on the loveseat across from her.

"Yeah, I'm fine Ian. Why?"

"Well, you're hugging the phone and you kinda look sad."

Tana laughed and released the phone. "Oh. Ryder was able to call tonight. After we hung up, I just sat here thinking."

"Miss him lots eh?" Ian smiled at his mom and Tana nodded.

"Yeah. Me too Mom. He's really a great guy. You know most of the time I completely forget who he is and what he does for a living. I see him as a regular guy until he plays, sings, or has to go away like this." Ian said as he stood up.

He gave his mother a hug goodnight. "Love you, Mom. Don't worry. He'll be home soon." He reassured her.

"Thanks Ian. You are turning into one hell of a young man."

He left her in the room, and Tana checked her phone for news from Nikki and found a text from Ryder.

'Hearing your voice tonight felt great. Music to my heart. <3 Love you so much'

Tana smiled and replied to him.

'And mine. I love you too, Mr. Evans. Have a great show tonight. <3'

There was nothing from Nikki, but Tana wasn't worried. They had gotten a ride to the party from another classmate and she warned her mother that she might stay at Jess's place if they were going to be really late.

Tana already had her weekend planned out with some shopping she needed to get done and she was going out with her girlfriends' the following night. She hadn't seen them much in the past few months and wanted to catch up with them. Putting her phone on the charger, Tana turned the lights and the TV off then went to bed.

~~

Over in Japan, Ryder was doing his sound check with the rest of the band. Everyone had gotten right back into the groove as if they had never come off tour. As they went through their checks, the lighting boards and lasers were being run through as well and the pyro was being secured. The stage was assembled and everything was almost completely ready for that night's performance.

The four guys finished up their sound check, then headed over to catering for some food before changing for the meet and greet. Ben was his usual hyper self and Matt was ribbing Chris for getting a tattoo of his son's name and birthdate on his forearm. His tattoo wasn't quite two weeks old and it was itchy as hell. Matt kept threatening to hit him in the arm like they did in school after getting vaccinations.

"So, Ryder how was the grad?" Chris asked trying to get Matt off his back by putting the focus on someone else.

Ryder was laughing at his bandmates as he filled Chris in on the grad. "It was great. Nikki was beautiful, and she even asked to dance with me for the parent dance. I really enjoyed it."

"Why would she do that? Everyone knows you dance like you play guitar. Shitty." Ben ribbed him filling a plate with some of the sushi out on the tables.

"Fuck you, Fisher." Ryder laughed. "I dance just fine."

"Notice he didn't correct me on the guitar playing." He pointed out to Matt who laughed.

Ryder flipped his middle finger up at them both.

"Well guys, you know I've been carrying him all these years covering up that he can't play." Chris joined in grateful the focus was finally off him and his tattoo.

"Assholes." Ryder laughed at them. "I'm better than you say. I've been teaching Tana and she's doing quite well."

"God the poor woman. How about once she moves to Langley, we have a real guitar player teach her if she wants to learn. I'm free most days from one to three." Chris puffed out his chest trying to act all arrogant while playing an air guitar.

Matt and Ben laughed at Ryder while he gave Chris a dirty look and shook his head. The band bantered back and forth while they ate, then at six, they went to the change rooms to get ready for the meet and greet.

~~~

Tana was sound asleep when all three of her dogs started barking like crazy and ran for the front door. She practically jumped out of bed, her heart racing from having been startled out of a deep sleep. Glancing at the clock, she saw it was two minutes after two in the morning.

Figuring Nikki had forgotten her keys and had rang the doorbell, Tana threw on her pajamas and flipped the lights on in the stairwell as she headed down to the door.

The dogs were still barking and jumping at the door, so Tana clapped her hands a few times trying to get the dogs to settle down. They backed off enough to allow her to flip the doorway lights on and open the door.

Fully expecting Nikki to come through the open door, Tana did a double take when she looked up into the eyes of an RCMP officer.

"Tana Anderson?" the officer asked.

Tana's heart was racing again as she nodded. "Actually, it's Evans now, but yes. I'm her. Is there something wrong?"

She could see the officer's name badge. His name was Dawes.

"Constable Rick Dawes. May I come in?" He asked.

Tana stepped aside and waved Constable Dawes to her front sitting room, not sure what was going on. Her sleep-muddled mind hadn't fully processed the entire situation.

"Mom? What's going on?" Ian came out of his room rubbing his eyes.

"I don't know." Tana sat down on the sofa across from the officer and looked at him. "Can you tell me what this is about Constable?"

The constable took a deep breath and removed his hat. "We don't have much time. It's about your daughter, Nicole. There's been an accident."

Tana's hands flew to her mouth and she tried to stifle a gasp. "How bad?"

It was barely audible, but the constable continued.

"Mrs. Evans, I'm afraid it's bad. Really bad. She's being airlifted to the University Hospital as we speak. We need to get you there right away."

Ian came up and held his mother as an agonizing scream escaped her. Tana clung to her son while tears coursed down her cheeks.

"Look, I can fill you in on the way to the hospital, but we really need to get you there. She needs her next of kin there, just in case."

Tana looked at the officer and her survival instinct kicked in. She stood up, still crying, and grabbed Ian. "Kennel the dogs. Now. Grab a coat and let's go."

Ian was crying as he nodded and got moving. He got the dogs down to the spare room and closed them in while Tana grabbed her coat and purse from the kitchen. She saw her phone still on the charger at the last second and grabbed it too. Ian was already waiting at the door with a hoodie in his hands as the constable ushered them out the door.

He helped them into the back seat of the patrol car and closed the door. "Hang on. I'm going to be going pretty fast. I'll have the lights on, so we shouldn't hit traffic."

The constable spun the car around, flipped the lights on and sped off heading for the freeway. As he drove, Constable Dawes filled Tana and Ian in on what witnesses said happened.

Apparently, the car Nikki, Brad and Jess had been in, had gotten T-boned by a drunk driver that ran a red light at high speed. Nikki and Brad had been in the back seat of the car and Nikki had taken the brunt of the impact.

"The truck hit the rear door on the driver's side where your daughter was seated. The accident took place out east of Ardrossan. Rescue workers have spent the last hour freeing your daughter from the car. The other passengers were easily extracted and have already been taken to the Fort Saskatchewan Hospital. Some of their injuries are serious, but not life threatening. The jaws-of-life had to be deployed to remove your daughter. I don't know about her medical condition, but STARS air ambulance isn't called in unless it's critical."

The constable was flying up the Whitemud freeway with the lights going. When he came up on traffic lights, he would flip the sirens on, slowing enough to ensure their safety before stomping the gas again and continuing to the hospital. When he was done filling them in, Tana looked at Ian with pain-ravaged eyes and saw the same hurt in her son's eyes looking back at her.

"Mom, is she—" He couldn't finish.

"No. God, please no. I can't. My little girl." Tana's body shook as fresh sobs wracked her.

Looking in her purse for some Kleenex, her hand happened on her phone and that's when she knew she had to call Ryder and Mike. They both needed to know. Just in case.

Tana called Ryder first and got his voicemail. She left a message trying to get as much information across to him as possible in the message. She told him she and Ian were on their way to the hospital, Nikki had been in a terrible accident and she would call him later with more information.

Her next call was to Mike. For once, he answered, sounding pissed off and half asleep.

"Mike, its Tana. I'm sorry to call you at this hour, but it's Nikki. She was in a horrible car accident. I'm on my way to the University Hospital now."

Mike grunted into the phone. "How bad?"

"I don't know yet. She's being airlifted by STARS." Tana sobbed trying to get through the call before they arrived at the hospital.

"Call me back when you know if she's still alive." He snapped and hung up.

Tana looked at the phone in shock her breath catching in her throat. "Okay." Was all she could muster as she put her phone back in her purse.

"Does Dad even care?" Ian asked as he wiped his eyes and nose on the sleeve of his sweater.

All Tana could do was shrug and take Ian's hand in hers as they sat back in the seat in silence while Edmonton raced past them.

The RCMP cruiser pulled up to the emergency door of the University of Alberta Hospital in less than twenty-five minutes from leaving Tana's house. Constable Dawes leapt out of the driver's seat and opened the back door letting Tana and Ian out.

Escorting them in through the doors, he spoke to the triage nurse and asked the status of Nicole Anderson.

"Are you her mother?" The nurse demanded looking at Tana and she nodded. "Good. Sign these and come with me."

Tana glanced down, saw *'Consent for Surgery'* and scrawled her name on the marked line. The nurse tossed the clipboard to another nurse and ordered her to rush it to trauma room one.

As the other nurse took off running with the surgical consent, the triage nurse lead Tana deeper into the hospital and started explaining what was going on.

"Your daughter is in critical condition. She has a fractured skull and severe swelling in her brain. Those papers are for emergency surgery to relieve the pressure on her brain. Right now, they're still trying to stabilize her for surgery. Her arm and leg are broken along with three fractured ribs and possible internal bleeding. She has numerous other cuts and bruises, which at this point are superficial. Basically, your daughter has a snowball's chance in hell of living if they don't get the swelling to stop and go down now. Her vital signs are extremely faint and if they can't get the pressure relieved soon, she won't live to see morning."

Tana felt sick. She wanted to fall down and cry right there in the middle of the hall, but she kept her feet moving. The nurse wasn't pulling any punches. There was no time to. Nikki's life was hanging on each of them focusing on their job.

"I'm taking you to her. You can see her for a few seconds as they take her to surgery, just in case she doesn't make it. I'm sorry I can't let you have more time than that, but we're trying to save her life." The nurse met Tana's eyes, and Tana nodded in understanding.

As they rounded the next corner, Tana saw a team of doctors and nurses rushing a blood-stained gurney out of one of the major trauma rooms over to the bank of elevators.

Tana was pulled even faster over to the gurney. "You have until the elevator gets here and then we have to move." The nurse told her.

Tana looked down at her daughter and sobbed. Her face was covered in blood. There was a tube down her throat with a plastic ball attached to it that one of the nurses squeezed every few seconds, breathing for her daughter. IV's were running into her good arm with multiple lines going into different bags of fluid and blood. Her arm and leg were still wrapped in makeshift casts and she had cuts everywhere.

Tana kissed her daughter's undamaged hand. "Nikki, Sweetheart, I'm here. So is Ian. We love you so much, Baby Girl. I need you to fight. Hang on and be strong, Nikki. Please."

"I love you, sis. Don't give up." Ian said quickly and squeezed her good hand.

The elevator arrived and Nikki was loaded in. "Sorry, but we have to go now. Someone will come to you when we have news." The doctor said to her.

Tana nodded. "Okay. I love you, Nikki." She called one last time as the doors slid closed. The elevator rose taking her daughter away for what could be her last living moments.

"The waiting room is over here." The triage nurse directed Tana and Ian to a small room with a TV and chairs where they both sat down to wait for news.

Tana took out her phone again and called Ryder, leaving him another message then she called Mike. This time he didn't pick up, so Tana left him the same detailed message as Ryder's, telling him that Nikki was in critical condition. She had just been taken into surgery to alleviate the pressure and swelling in her brain. She also suggested to Mike that he might want to come to the hospital as the prognosis was not looking good at the moment.

~

Severe State had just finished saying goodnight to Osaka and were heading back to their dressing room. It had been a fantastic show and all four of them were pumped.

"Who's up for some drinkin' tonight?" Ryder shouted down the hall and everyone in earshot cheered in agreement.

As they piled into the dressing room, the guys all pulled their shirts off and went to the sinks to freshen up. Ryder was washing his face when Ben brought his phone over to him.

"Hey, your phone went off."

"Probably nothing." Ryder took his phone and was about to just put it in his pocket when he thought better of it. Entering the code, he noticed he had missed a call. He opened the notification and saw that it came from Tana's cell. She had called twice, and he had two new voice mails.

'That's odd.' He thought to himself. Tana knew he was performing tonight and she never called when she knew he was going to be on stage. She knew he usually had his phone in his pocket, and it had been a fluke that he had forgotten it in the dressing room tonight after talking to her earlier.

Ryder called his voicemail and tried to listen but everyone in the room was making a lot of ruckus, so Ryder only caught bits and pieces of Tana's first message. She sounded upset and that caught his attention immediately. He managed to hear something about being on the way to the hospital and hollered for everyone to be quiet.

Listening carefully, Ryder replayed the message. Now he could clearly hear that Tana was crying as she told him Nikki had been in an accident. She was on her way to the hospital and would call again when she had more news.

"Mother fuck!" Ryder sat down hard on one of the chairs and moved onto the next message.

Everyone's attention was suddenly focused on Ryder. He looked clearly upset, but he was still on his phone, so no one asked what was going on yet.

As Ryder listened to Tana's second message, his eyes closed as if he was in immense pain and he brought his hand up to his mouth, covering it for a moment. His shoulders slumped and he swallowed hard against the lump that was already forming in his throat.

Tana told him there was no point in him rushing home, that there was nothing anyone could do but hope so he should stay in Japan and finish his shows. Her message ended saying that she would be at the hospital and for him to call when he could and that she loved him then hung up.

Ryder took the phone away from his ear, ending the call. Both of his hands flopped, hanging between his knees as his head dropped. His eyes were still closed, and he was fighting back tears.

"Ryder, what happened?" It was Matt. He had only seen Ryder look close to this devastated once before. Whatever happened this time was far worse than what Amanda had done. Right now, Ryder looked completely heartbroken.

Ryder sniffed loudly. "Nikki was in a car accident. She's in surgery. They're trying to save her life."

Everyone in the room went dead silent.

"Oh my God." Ben barely got the words out before he choked.

"Dude, you gotta go home." Matt said.

"Tana said there is nothing anyone can do but wait. Plus, she said for me to stay here and finish our shows." Ryder tried to explain her message.

"Fuck the shows man. This is your family. A child's life is on the line. Is it really that bad?" Matt asked looking pained.

Ryder nodded. "Fractured skull, three fractured ribs, broken arm and broken leg. Possible internal bleeding, but the worst is her brain is swelling. They're trying to alleviate it and get it to go down. If they can't she'll die."

All the crew quietly exited the room and left the band members alone. Everyone knew Ryder's wife and adored her. They had also met Nikki and thought her an incredibly sweet kid.

"You need to go home. Even if there's nothing to do but sit there and wait. Tana and Ian need you. That poor woman has been through enough in her life already. If she loses Nikki, she's going to need you there with her, not over here. That girl is her life. I've never seen a bond between mother and child so deep. This is probably killing both Tana and Ian." Ben tried to get through to Ryder the importance of him going back home.

"What about the last two shows?" Ryder was clearly in shock.

Having a family and his career was still all so new to him and he didn't know what to do or how to think. Severe State had never missed a show. He couldn't fathom not completing a show, let alone two, but he was also torn between staying and going home to his family. As he sat there, he wasn't even sure if he could do two more shows. Hearing about Nikki being in such bad shape completely stripped him of his desire to perform.

"Bruce and Tyson can cancel them. We can make it up to the fans when we know Nikki is going to be okay. Tyson can issue a statement that the shows are to be either cancelled or rescheduled due to a family emergency." Chris reasoned.

Matt looked at Ryder and squeezed his shoulder. "Go home to your family. Chris is right. We can make it up to the fans another day. That girl might not have a tomorrow. Regardless if she doesn't make it, you need to be there."

Ben came over and sat beside him. "Go home, Ryder. Your family needs you. Every single one of us would already be gone if it was one of our kids."

Ryder looked at all of them and nodded. He stood up while Chris called Bruce and Tyson into the room to give them the run down. Both of them told Ryder to get the hell out of there and get his ass back home.

"I'll have the plane fueled and ready to leave by the time you get to the airport. We can send your bags to Tana's later. Chris can check you out at the hotel. Just get your ass in the limo and get to the airport now." Bruce barked as he turned and started making calls.

"Thanks guys." Ryder said as everyone hugged him quickly then ushered him out the door.

He ran down the halls and out the service doors. There were fans waiting at the barriers hoping for a glimpse of the band as they left. When they saw Ryder, they began screaming for him, begging for autographs or pictures. For the first time in his career, Ryder completely ignored them and dove into the waiting limo.

The driver had already been called and knew to take him straight to the airport. Ryder tried to call Tana from the limo, but he couldn't get through. He kept losing signal, so he texted her that he was on his way home and that everyone was praying for Nikki.

When the limo pulled up to the airport, Ryder bolted out and through the doors to the terminal. He got his bearings and found the check in counter. He showed his passport and when he was asked about baggage, he quickly explained his daughter had been hit by a car and he was hurrying home. The clerk understood and ushered him through to customs.

Ryder cleared customs and was seated in the private plane in no time. The crew looked at him sympathetically and got underway. Bruce had informed them Ryder was flying home alone for a family emergency and not to waste any time. One of the flight attendants told him they would have him back in Edmonton in sixteen hours then went to her own seat to prepare for takeoff.

As soon as they had clearance from the tower, they were taxiing out to the runway and taking off. Ryder sat back and said a silent prayer for Nikki to pull through.

Chapter 7

Tana and Ian sat in the waiting room barely speaking for over six hours before anyone came to give them an update. It was nine in the morning when one of the surgical nurses came in and sat down with them. She explained that the immediate life-threatening pressure on Nikki's brain had been relieved for the moment, but the swelling was not coming down at this time.

"Mrs. Evans, your daughter is in very grave condition, but she's still with us. We're going to continue to work on her until either we bring her back or we don't."

Fresh tears coursed down Tana's cheeks as she listened to the news. It wasn't good, but at least Nikki hadn't died.

The nurse patted Tana's hand then left to go back and continue to work with the team trying to repair Nikki's broken body. Ian and Tana held each other, crying and praying for Nikki to make it.

It was few more hours before the door opened again. This time it was Jess and Brad that came through the waiting room door. Both of them were covered in cuts and bruises. Jess's arm was in a cast up to her elbow, Brad's forehead had a thick bandage on the left side and he was limping. They saw Tana and Ian and went straight to them.

"Mrs. Evans, how's Nikki?" Jess asked as she and Brad carefully eased themselves into chairs across from Ian and Tana.

"It's not good." Tana choked and told them Nikki's condition. As Tana got through another bout of tears, she looked at the two and asked them to fill her in on the details that the police didn't know.

"What happened? Where were you guys going?" Tana asked blowing her nose.

Jess was crying, and Brad was silent, but there were tears tracing down his face as he took in a ragged breath, wincing as he did and started to explain.

"We were out at that party in Ardrossan. It was at another one of our friends' place, on their acreage. Everyone was having a great time. Nothing stupid was happening. No one was even really drunk. The next thing we know, Adam, the guy Jess was with, brings out this crack pipe and starts passing around crystal meth."

"I swear, Mrs. Evans. I had no clue he did that stuff. I never would have dated him if I knew." Jess blubbered trying to reassure Tana.

Tana got up, went to the young girl and sat down next to her. She gently put an arm around her shoulders. "I know Jess. It's okay. No one is blaming you for what happened. I just need to know why you guys were out on that road."

Brad coughed and groaned in pain. "Sorry, my ribs are bruised up pretty bad."

He took another breath and went on. "Tony, our friend that drove us, wanted nothing to do with the drugs, so he called the cops then came and found us. We got out of there before the cops came and before people started getting high. That's all I remember. I remember waking up in the hospital and my parents filled in the rest."

Jess nodded. "We were all knocked out and have concussions. But mine and Brad's weren't that bad. They checked us but we insisted on being let go once the doctors saw us. They said we would to be all right enough to go home under observation, so we were released. We made our parents bring us here. We had to know how Nikki was. No one knew. They were only able to tell us where she had been taken."

"And what about Tony? Is he okay?"

Jess nodded. "He's worse off than us. Really bad concussion with a broken arm and collarbone, but he'll be okay. He's still in the hospital."

"Where are your parents?" Tana asked, thankful for the distraction for the moment.

"Waiting out front. We can't stay long, but we had to know." Brad said.

Tana nodded, understanding their concern. "Give me your numbers. I'll call when I hear anything. I promise. But both of you need to go home and get better. Neither of you should be here. You need to be at home, resting. All of you are very lucky to be alive."

They both nodded, and Tana hugged them gingerly, trying not to hurt them as she scooted them back through the door.

"Mrs. Evans? Did you want me to let your dogs out for you while you're here?" Jess asked turning back.

Tana had forgotten about them in her worry for Nikki and nodded as she handed over her house keys. "Thank you Jess, but I would prefer if you rested and see if your parents could do that for me."

Jess nodded and promised she would ask them. As they made their way slowly back to their waiting parents, Tana sat back down beside Ian and held her son while they resumed their wait for news.

~~

For Ryder, the flight home seemed to be taking longer than it did to get to Tokyo because he was so sick with worry. He couldn't call Tana or even text her to find out how Nikki was. He tried sleeping, but every time he dozed off, he woke up with a start a few minutes later. His subconscious was toying with him. He kept having dreams about not being able to get to his family. He would be running down the hall of some hospital. When he found Tana and Ian sitting by Nikki's bedside, something was preventing him from moving forward to reach them. Even when he yelled out to them, there was no sound.

Ryder looked out the window and could see the morning light streaking across the Pacific. He had no idea what time it was, but the sun was up and if he didn't feel so heart sick, he would have taken a moment to enjoy how beautiful it looked.

Right now, all Ryder could process was getting home and being there for Nikki. He got up and went to the bathroom. Splashing cold water on his face, Ryder looked at his reflection in the mirror. He looked tired and ragged. Not caring, Ryder made his way back to his seat and sat back down.

A flight attendant noticed him moving around and came by to see if he needed anything.

"Can you tell me what time it is?"

"For which time zone would you like to know?" She clarified.

"Edmonton. My destination."

She nodded and said she would go and check. A few minutes later, she came back with a coffee in hand for him.

"It's almost dinner time in Edmonton. Just before five-thirty. We should be landing in about four hours."

Ryder thanked her and took the mug. As he sipped his coffee, he continued to stare out the window willing the plane to move faster and for Nikki to still be alive.

~~

Tana was watching the clock. When it read three in the afternoon, the door opened and Mike entered the waiting room.

"Dad!" Ian exclaimed and jumped up to go hug his father.

Mike stiffened and barely touched his son in a half hug as the boy came over to him. Brushing Ian off, he faced Tana, glaring at her.

Tana had to look twice at him. Mike had changed drastically since she last saw him. It had been more than five years since they had seen each other and three years since Mike had seen either Nikki or Ian. He had gotten very grey, put on a lot of weight and now sported a full beard and moustache. Time was not being kind to him. Tana wondered exactly what he was doing with his life now, as he looked haggard and worn.

"Is she still alive?" Mike barked at her, not even saying hello to his own son.

Tana stood up and looked up at Mike. "Yes, she's still alive. They're still working on her. I haven't heard anything since before noon."

Continuing, Tana filled him in on what she knew along with what Jess and Brad had told her about why they left the party they had been at.

Mike huffed and glared at her, then moved off to the corner of the room saying nothing to her as he leaned against the wall.

He stayed that way for another half an hour before another nurse came in to speak to them. The orthopedic surgeon had just finished with Nikki's arm and leg. Both had been set and casted, but she was still in the OR. The swelling still wasn't stopping and the pressure on her brain was increasing again. Nikki was currently on life support.

"There is so much intracranial pressure in her skull right now it's affecting her brain's ability to function. The blood flow is being restricted. We put a catheter in the ventricle of her brain to help drain off the excess fluid, but the swelling is preventing that from working as quickly as we need it to. We would like permission to use diuretics to increase her urine output to help get some of that extra fluid out of her system."

Tana was agreeing and nodding her head before the nurse had finished.

"There are risks. It could decrease her blood volume and cause more damage by further reducing the blood flow to her brain, but we may be able to regulate that risk seeing she is completely sedated and intubated. Right now, machines are doing everything to keep her with us and control her breathing, so she doesn't hyperventilate. We can also pump up the IV fluids if she takes a turn for the worse or her blood pressure drops too far."

"What if we do nothing?" Mike spoke up from the corner.

The nurse looked up at him and put her hands up. "Leaving it to fate will almost certainly lead to her dying in the next twenty-four hours or if she does survive, it will be strictly because machines are keeping her alive. Essentially, she would be completely brain dead."

Tana turned to face Mike, "We have no choice. To save her, we have to try."

Mike shrugged. "Do whatever you want. It doesn't sound like she'll make it any way."

Tana stared at Mike in shock for a moment then gave her consent. The nurse thanked her, as she stood up and left to go back to Nikki.

Chapter 8

When Ryder woke up and looked out his window, he could see mountains below the airplane. He had managed to doze off again and must have gotten a few hours of rest. The last he remembered, there was still nothing but ocean around him. His heart raced knowing he would be landing soon. As he walked to the bathroom, he flagged the flight attendant down and asked her how much longer until they landed.

"In about another thirty minutes you should be safely on the ground." She told him.

Ryder went into the bathroom to wash his hands and face again, feeling extremely edgy. He was almost there, and he had no clue if Nikki was even still alive.

Taking his seat again, he watched the mountains fall away to farmland and forests thinking of Nikki. He thought of dancing with her at her grad, playing ball with her a few weeks ago and back to her birthday. How happy she had been when she got her car, hugging him and telling him that she loved him.

Tears filled his eyes and fell down his cheeks as he kept thinking of her. Standing beside her mother three months ago at their wedding, her and Tana dancing on his table and her dancing with Mia, Paige and Becky on their first trip out to Langley.

A sob escaped him as he thought of her singing Becky to sleep in Tana's arms, and the day she opened the door to Tana's house and saw him standing there for the first time. When he closed his eyes, he could see her expression clearly. Her wide eyes and jaw hanging open in shock.

Never having been one to cry, Ryder wiped his eyes and sniffed as he gave in and just let the tears flow. He took a ragged breath and let it out shakily.

"Please, God. You can't take her. I just got her." He begged as sobs shook his huge frame.

Ryder cried until the captain came over the intercom announcing they were on final approach. It was then the flight attendant came to check on Ryder, bringing him some Kleenex having heard the big man cry. She patted his shoulder as she handed him the little package then went back up front to take her seat for the landing.

The moment the plane touched down Ryder grabbed his phone and turned it on to check for news. As the plane crawled to the gate, Ryder was shaking as he waited for his phone to power up. Instantly it was vibrating with notifications. He entered the code and saw there were two texts. Both from Bruce. One a message telling him there was a car waiting for him at his usual rental place and the second one informing him that the last two shows had been temporarily cancelled. There was nothing from Tana at all, so he dialed her cell number. It went straight to voicemail.

"Shit." Ryder panicked for a moment, then he thought to call the house. There was no answer there either. Next, he tried Ian's cell and got the same results.

"Fuck!" He rasped harshly running a hand though his hair.

There was nothing he could do but head to the hospital, hoping for the best. As soon as the plane doors opened, Ryder disembarked shouting a hurried thanks over his shoulder as he ran up the gangway and across the luggage claim in Edmonton International, headed straight for customs.

When he approached the customs officer, he handed his passport over. When asked if he was returning home, he answered yes.

"Family emergency. I have no luggage with me and nothing to claim. My daughter was hit by a drunk driver. I flew home immediately."

The officer looked up at Ryder and nodded handing him back his passport.

"Good luck." He said and waved Ryder through.

Once out in the main arrivals area, Ryder went straight to the car rental where he was immediately handed keys and told where to find the car.

"Everything has been taken care of sir. You can just go. There is a GPS in the car with the hospital already programmed and ready for you.

I hope your daughter is okay." The girl at the counter said to him giving him a sad smile.

"Thank you." Ryder said genuinely and added, "So do I."

He was off running again, this time for the car, dogging people and not paying attention to anyone that recognized him. The only thing he cared about at that moment was getting to the hospital and to his family.

Ryder got to the car and practically threw himself into the driver's seat. Pulling out of the parking lot, he drove as fast as he dared to the highway then stomped on the gas as he followed the GPS's mechanical voice. He figured if he got a ticket, he didn't care. He just needed to get to the hospital.

"Fuck what I wouldn't do for a police escort right now." Ryder grumbled as he got held up by a red light.

Within forty-five minutes of landing, Ryder was pulling into the parking lot in emergency. He jumped out of the car, slammed the door shut not bothering to get a parking pass and ran as fast as he could through the doors.

Quickly scanning the waiting room, he didn't find Tana or Ian, so he went to the triage nurse.

"I'm looking for my daughter. She was brought here sometime late last night or early this morning. Nikki, I mean, Nicole Anderson."

The nurse looked up at him. She had been on shift the previous night when Nikki had been brought in. "Mr. Anderson?"

Ryder shook his head, "No, Evans. Nikki is my stepdaughter. I was over in Japan when this happened. Her mother called me. I got here as fast as I could." Ryder pleaded hoping that they would just hurry and take him to where he could see his family.

The triage nurse checked the file and nodded. "Your daughter is still in the operating room. They're trying to get the intracranial pressure and swelling to go down. I can't take you to her, but I can take you to your wife."

She guided Ryder through a series of doors and corridors then motioned to the waiting room door a few feet ahead.

"In there. We're all praying for her." The nurse added as she turned to go back to her station.

Ryder looked at the door and in two huge strides, had the knob in his hand. Throwing the door open, he burst through it like a wild man. Hearing the door bang open Tana's head snapped up from leaning on the wall behind her.

"Ryder!" She exclaimed and ran to him as he stepped further into the room, scooping her into his arms.

"What are you doing here? You're supposed to be in Japan." She sniffed and more tears flowed down her cheeks as she held her husband tight, grateful to have him there.

"I got your message and came as soon as I could. Didn't you get my text?"

Tana shook her head. "My phone's dead. It was charging when the RCMP came to the house, but it died sometime after making the last calls."

Ian came over to them and stood beside his mother, red eyed. Tana let Ryder go and immediately he pulled Ian into a big hug as he asked Tana how Nikki was.

Tana filled him in on everything from being woken up to what Nikki's injuries were, right through to the continued efforts to save her. She even told him about Jess and Brad coming to check on Nikki.

Ryder listened intently, tears filling his eyes again as he thought of Tana dealing with this alone and scared of losing her only daughter. He held her and just let her cry while he comforted her.

"You came home. Even after I said for you to stay. But what about your last two shows?" Tana looked up at him with her tear-stained face and pain ravaged eyes.

Just seeing her like this tore him apart. He held her tighter and kissed the top of her head.

"The last two shows have been cancelled. The guys and crew are taking care of getting the equipment ready to ship. I'm needed here. You shouldn't think you have to deal with this alone. Not anymore. That's part of what a husband is for. Remember? Through good times and bad. This is where I belong right now. Here with you, Ian and Nikki."

He wiped the tears from her face. "You're not alone anymore Tana. God knows you've been through enough in your life. You're not going through this alone especially if Nikki—"

He couldn't bring himself to say it. "I just wish I had been able to get here faster."

"You're here now. Thank you." She kissed him.

Ryder looked up and noticed someone standing in the corner glaring at them. Frowning, Ryder saw some resemblance in the man he couldn't place. Tana noticed where Ryder was looking and remembered Mike was still there. He had barely spoken or moved the entire time since his arrival.

"Ryder, this is Mike, Nikki and Ian's father. Mike, my husband, Ryder." Tana introduced them. Ryder crossed the small room and stuck his hand out saying it was nice to meet him. Mike just looked at it, then back up to Ryder not saying anything. His eyes were cold and full of hate.

Ryder wasn't sure if it was directed at him or at Tana, but he seemed to look at everything with that same hate filled glare. Pulling his hand back Ryder straightened himself up to his full height.

"All right then. Have it your way." He said as he turned back to Tana and Ian, checking to see if either of them needed anything. Ian asked for something to drink. Ryder nodded, checking with Tana who declined.

"Come on. There's a vending machine down the hall. Let's get some water or something." Ryder said putting his arm around Ian's shoulders.

Telling Tana he would be right back, Ryder kissed the top of her head and led Ian out the door. The door had barely closed when Mike attacked Tana.

"What the fuck is he doing here?"

"What do you mean by that? He's my husband. He has every right to be here." Tana was shocked at the sudden outburst from him.

"And I suppose the influence from his lifestyle had nothing to do with Nikki being in that accident." He spat.

Tana gaped at him. "Ryder's lifestyle? What the hell are you talking about?"

"You know exactly what I'm talking about." Mike advanced on her. "Come on. They don't call it *'Sex, Drugs and Rock n Roll'* for nothing. Drinking, partying, drugs. The driver was probably completely wasted. Not to mention Nikki was probably too drunk and stoned to be smart enough to not get in that car, no thanks to you."

"You son of a bitch!" Tana was furious. "Our daughter is lying on a table somewhere fighting for her life because she chose to get away from the drugs someone else brought to that party. Nikki wasn't doing drugs. Neither was the boy that drove them. They were the ones hit by a drunk driver! Maybe if you actually paid attention to your own kids, you'd know they are smarter than that."

"Bullshit. You expect me to believe living with a rock band and not one of you does drugs. You exposed her to this." Mike was out for blood and Tana had no idea why.

"What? No one in Ryder's band does drugs!" Tana yelled, exasperated and frustrated.

"This is all because of you and now you're dealing with the consequences of your actions."

"What the fuck is your deal Mike? I didn't do anything! She went to a graduation party. Like most kids do. Just like we did when we graduated. Or did you conveniently happen to forget you were a teen once too? Nikki was out celebrating with friends. It was shitty luck that they got hit. I wish to God it didn't happen, but it did. And in case you have forgotten, Nikki's eighteen. If I said no, she could have just gone any way."

"Maybe try putting your foot down. You're too easy on them. Stand up and be a Goddamn mother. Oh, wait. That's right. You don't know how. You never had one stick around long enough to teach you." Mike shot at her.

Tana reeled back. "That's low Mike."

He advanced on her a little more, sneering. "Maybe if your parents had lived, they could have taught you what the hell birth control was too and we wouldn't be here. I wouldn't be saddled with them or stuck dealing with you. But then again, your whore mother jumped in the sack with that psycho before your father's body even had a chance to get cold. She wasn't even smart enough to even think about leaving until it literally killed her."

Tana was in tears again. But this time, it was from Mike's vicious attack. Shaking her head, she couldn't believe he had turned into this hateful and bitter man. Throwing her parents deaths at her like this of all things. He had hurt her in the past but never like this.

"If you were a better mother, you never would have let her go. You wouldn't be sitting here begging for your daughter's life, whoring yourself out and throwing yourself all over some fucked up rock star like some teenage groupie slut. Thank God I wasn't dumb enough to marry your ass years ago. I was smart enough to ditch you before you ruined my life like you will his. Nikki is better off dead than living to see her mother as a washed-up wanna-be tossed aside as soon as guitar boy is done getting his rocks off."

"You fucking son of a bitch!" Ryder's booming voice echoed through the little room. In a flash Ryder had Mike pinned against the wall by his shoulders.

"Don't you fucken dare speak to my wife like that!" Ryder looked down at Mike, his eyes blazing with fury.

"Let. Me. Go. Unless you want a lawsuit on your hands." Mike glared back at Ryder.

Ryder didn't move. He continued to glare down at Mike until Tana came up to him and pulled on his arms.

"Let him go Ryder. This isn't the time or place." She said quietly. She knew he was just protecting her, but she had never seen him so furious.

Glancing down at Tana, Ryder let Mike go and backed up a step, putting his hands up.

"You're right." He said to Tana. "Nikki is our main concern. Not him."

Ryder turned to see Ian looking shocked and pale. Both he and Ian had heard Mike yelling at Tana all the way down the hallway and had hurried back into the room.

There was no mistaking the look of disgust on the boy's face when he looked at his father. What his father said to his mother hurt him to the core. It was becoming clear to Ian that his father had no desire to be in his or Nikki's lives and hated his mother. But that still didn't give him the right to talk to her like that. He knew nothing about their lives to make those kinds of accusations.

Tana went to Ian trying to reassure him everything was fine, that his father was just upset and concerned for Nikki. With all the commotion and yelling, no one noticed the waiting room door open let alone saw the person who walked through the doorway.

Ryder was coming back over to be with Tana and Ian when Mike lunged at him, punching him hard in the kidney.

"Dad! No! Don't!" Ian cried out as he saw Mike swing.

Ryder's lower back exploded in pain. He clenched his jaw, grimacing as he grunted through his teeth. Mike swung again with his other fist and this time connected with Ryder's half-turned face, hitting him in the jaw. More pain coursed through his jaw as Ryder spun around balling his fist and swung for Mike. His first punch landed square in Mike's cheek, knocking the man back a few steps into the wall. Ryder regained his stance and swung again, connecting with Mike's right temple.

Instantly Mike crumpled to the floor as Tana grabbed for Ryder's arm, already cocked back ready to swing again. Ian grabbed his other arm and both Tana and Ian tried to pull him back from Mike's dazed form lying on the floor.

"Stop Ryder! That's enough." Tana begged. This was all too much for her at the moment.

"Fucking son of a bitch sucker punched me!" Ryder snapped.

"I know. He started it. But enough. Please." Tana turned to look at Mike, glaring.

"You too. Enough of this shit. If the two of you want to beat the hell out of each other, then go outside where I don't have to deal with it. I've been through enough today. We all have." Tears were flowing down Tana's cheeks again.

"Goddamn it Mike, if you put half of the time that you spend hating me for some God only knows reason into caring about your kids, maybe we could all be here peacefully and not fighting. Grow the fuck up! Either be here for Nikki and be quiet, or leave." Tana was shaking.

Ryder unclenched his fists, closed his eyes for a moment to regroup himself before he took her in his arms.

"You're right. I'm sorry." He whispered to her.

"Ahem."

The sound came from the door and everyone turned to see a doctor standing there in scrubs and a bandana.

"By all means if you two want to give me more skulls to patch up, keep going. But for those of you that are interested, Nicole is finally out of immediate danger."

Tana went limp against Ryder hearing the doctor's words. He held onto her and guided her back over to the chairs.

"We're very sorry, Doctor. It's been a long and emotional wait." Ryder said looking relieved through his anger.

Tana clung to Ryder with fresh tears pooling in her eyes. Ian came over to his mother and Ryder to sit with them as the doctor walked further into the room sitting down across from them.

He looked over to where Mike was still on the floor. "Are you all right? Do you need assistance?"

Mike shook his head glowering. "No. I'm fine. Good thing he can't hit."

"Stop it Mike!" Tana yelled as she felt Ryder tense again beside her.

"I'd like to argue that." The doctor said looking at Mike's face. "You might want to have your head checked. By the looks of those bruises forming already, I'd say he can hit harder than you claim."

Mike glared at the doctor and tried to stand up. He got about halfway and wobbled, still quite dazed from the force of Ryder's punch. The doctor got up and grabbed a hold of Mike's jacket steadying him while Ryder tried to suppress a grin of satisfaction.

"I'm fine." Mike snapped and staggered almost drunkenly over to the chairs sitting down as far away from everyone else as he could get.

The doctor came back and sat down across from Tana introducing himself. "Dr. Allen Parker."

"Tana and Ryder Evans, my son Ian, and Nicole's father, Mike Harding." Tana said introducing everyone else quietly.

"Please. Dr. Parker, how is my daughter." Tana asked as Ryder took her hands.

"As I was saying, she's out of immediate danger. The swelling has finally receded enough that the catheter was able to drain off the excess fluid. Her brain is still very swollen and badly bruised, but the blood flow is back to normal. Nicole's brain does seem to be functioning normally, but we won't know the extent of any brain damage until she regains consciousness. There is no internal bleeding, her arm and leg are fully set and casted. The ribs we have to leave to heal on their own. I want to stress to you, she's not out of the woods, but she's no longer at death's door."

Dr. Parker took a breath and glanced over at Mike then returned his attention to Tana and Ryder.

"Now for the bad news, I'm afraid Nicole is in a coma. We still have her heavily sedated, but unfortunately, with all the damage she's endured, she has slipped into a coma. I can't tell you how long this will last any more than I can tell you what the extent of brain damage she may suffer, if any at all. All we can do now is let her heal and wait."

Tana's eyes never left Dr. Parker's face. "Where is she now?"

"She is being moved to ICU. She'll stay there until she either comes around or slips away, which is still a huge possibility. The next twenty-four to forty-eight hours will decide which direction she goes."

"When can we see her?" Ryder spoke sounding choked.

"I can take you to see her now provided there's no more fighting. Right now, that's the last thing your daughter needs to hear."

"Can she hear us?" Ian asked.

Dr. Parker looked at him and shrugged. "There are numerous studies that indicate people in comas do in fact hear what's going on around them. If you talk to her it might help her find her way back to you."

Everyone stood up and Dr. Parker led them to the elevators to take them up to the fourth floor. Ryder took Tana's hand in the elevator and held it tightly in his own. The ride up was silent. Again, Mike stayed as far away from everyone as possible. When the doors opened and they all filed out, Dr. Parker led them down the hall to the room where Nikki was.

There were machines beeping everywhere and a few nurses tending to Nikki, checking the machines and her vitals.

"She will be monitored constantly and her vital signs checked every half an hour for the first while. We still have her sedated and will keep her sedated for about the next twenty-four hours just in case she takes a turn for the worse and we need to go back in. It will also give her body a chance to rest. And we hope begin to repair itself." Dr. Parker informed them before he went and spoke to the nurses then walked out of the room.

Tana walked slowly over to her daughter's bedside and looked down at her. Nikki's head was wrapped in bandages and her face had been washed free of blood. The cuts and scrapes had been treated but her face was all bruised and swollen. She was still intubated and there was a machine breathing for her along with multiple tubes and wires connected to her everywhere. Tana wanted to hold her, touch her, kiss all her daughters hurts away, but she was afraid to get too close in fear of causing her more pain.

One of the nurses looked at her and smiled encouragingly. "It's okay. You can touch her. And talk to her. Let her know you're here. It will give her a reason to keep fighting. She's going to need you to help keep her strong, but she's already proven to be one hell of a fighter."

"She's just like her mother." Ryder said as he guided Tana over to the side of the bed.

Tana glanced up at him then took her daughter's hand. She leaned down and kissed it gently.

"Nikki, Sweetheart its Mom. We're all here. Ian and Ryder are with me. So is your Dad. We need you to get better, Baby Girl. We love you so much." Tana's voice cracked and she covered her mouth with her hand trying to stifle her sobs.

Ryder stepped back and waved for Mike to come over. "I think you should be the next to speak to her. It's only right."

Mike looked at Ryder, taken aback slightly by his words. Stiffly, he walked to Nikki's other side and looked down at his child, his expression unreadable. Not saying anything, Mike looked at his daughter as if he was staring at a stranger. Stepping back, he looked up at Tana, motioning for her to step away from Nikki's bedside. Stepping around Ryder, she followed Mike over to the other side of the room while Ryder watched Mike closely to make sure he didn't attack his wife again.

"I'm leaving. It was pointless for me to even come." Mike stared at Tana coldly, his expression empty and heartless.

"Mike look, whatever issue you have with me, can't you let it go? And just be here for Nikki? Ian too for Christ sake. This is stupid. They need both of us right now."

"You don't get it, do you? You never did. Why I cheated. I don't want them. I never did. I only ever wanted you. Until you had them. Once they came along, it was all different. You were different. The only reason I hung around as long as I did was I thought they would grow on me, but you know what? They didn't." Mike hissed at her.

"Keep your fucking voice down!" Tana hissed right back.

Ian walked over to his father and looked him in the eye. "If you never wanted us then why did you even bother to show up?" Ian asked with tears in his eyes.

Mike stared coldly at him and shrugged, not answering him.

Ian took a deep breath and stood tall, being more of a man than the man he was facing. Looking at his father with disgust, "Leave. Please. And do me a favor, forget we ever existed."

Mike looked at Ian. "No problem."

He turned to Tana, "Don't bother calling me if she dies."

He spoke in undertones trying not to cause a bigger scene and stalked out of the room. Tana watched him leave in shock. He truly did hate all of them. Even his own children.

"I heard what he said." One of Nikki's nurses whispered to her. "What a bastard."

Ryder came back over to Tana and put his arms around her. "Forget about him. Let's just focus on Nikki and getting her strong again."

"I don't know what I ever saw in him." Tana commented as they went back to Nikki's bedside.

The nurses left them alone for a few minutes, so they could talk to Nikki in private. It was already after ten-thirty at night. The nurses knew they should have them leave but looked the other way seeing how close to losing Nikki the family had come.

When they came back to check on Nikki's vitals again half an hour later, the nurses told them they had to go. "She needs to rest and so do all of you. She's in good hands. You can come back in the morning." She ushered them out of the room before anyone could protest but Tana slipped away and went back to her daughter.

"Nikki, we have to go. I don't want to, but the nurses want you to rest. Please hang in and fight to come back. I love you so much. Get some rest. I won't be far. I promise."

Tana leaned down and kissed Nikki's cheek being careful not to bump anything then walked back to the rest of them. The nurse she had slipped past was shaking her head but smiling at the same time.

"Slippery little thing, aren't you?" She chastised Tana and then leaned in close. "If that was my child, I would have done the same thing."

Tana smiled sadly and thanked her for helping her daughter. Ryder put his arm around her shoulders, as Tana took Ian's hand and they left the ICU. Tana stopped at the desk to ensure they had all their contact numbers. Once the file was checked and Ryder's cell number was added, Tana asked if Mike had left his contact number. The nurse checked and shook her head.

"Don't give it to them, Mom. He won't answer or care. Just leave it."

Tana smiled sadly for her son, knowing he had to be hurting from hearing his father's hateful comments. She kissed him and took his hand again as they made their way to the elevators.

Chapter 9

Tana, Ryder and Ian all went home in Ryder's rental to get some sleep. Ryder promised Tana that they would return to the hospital first thing in the morning. Ian was going to stay home with the dogs and was going to come see his sister for a few hours later in the day.

When they arrived at home, there was a note on Tana's front door. It was from Jess's parents informing Tana of their well wishes for Nikki and that the dogs had been fed as well as walked for a few hours. Also, for her to call if she needed anything at all.

"That was really nice of them." Ryder said as he read the note.

Tana nodded, as Ian opened the door with his keys to let them in. He went downstairs to let the dogs out of the spare room then climbed into his bed. He was exhausted and drained. Ryder came to see if he was all right, and Ian shrugged.

"My father is a selfish fucking asshole who hates me, plus I almost lost my sister. I think this officially counts as the worst day of my life." Ian looked up at him feeling lost.

Ryder sat on the edge of Ian's bed and leaned his elbows on his knees. "Did I ever tell you my father walked out on my mother and me when I was ten?"

Ian looked at Ryder shocked and shook his head.

"Well, he did. He just came home one day after work packed a bag and walked out. My mother tried asking him what was going on, why he was leaving. But he just told her he was done and didn't want us. Then he got in his truck and left. I've never seen or heard from him since that day."

"What did you do?" Ian asked listening to Ryder intently.

"I cried. He was my dad. I thought he loved us. He was never an overly affectionate man, but there were times when he was nice. Unfortunately, that wasn't much, but we did have some fun times. He took me fishing a few times, taught me how to ride a bike, plus a few other father and son things. But he still left. And it still hurt."

"Do you still love your dad?"

Ryder sighed and ran his hand through his hair. "I don't know. I love the memories of the good times, but it hurt so damn much watching him leave and hearing him say he didn't want us that I really don't know. It's been so long that I think I'm just indifferent in regards to him, and how I feel. But I won't lie, I do still feel that pain. The trick is to not let it control you or rule your life."

Ian thought for a moment. When he spoke again, Ryder was faced with explaining something about himself that was going to be tough for him.

"That's what you did, isn't it? Let it rule your life. That's why you never had kids of your own right?"

Ryder pressed his lips together into thin line. "Mostly yes. Ian, you're about ninety percent right on that. The other reason I never had kids was because of my career. From what I saw with my father hardly being there and then walking out, I figured if I had kids one day, they would grow up and hate me for never being around. I didn't want to disappoint any kid like I was disappointed."

Ian sat up and leaned against the headboard of his bed. "But you married mom, and she has us. I'm not disappointed if you can't be here every day. I know that you have stuff. That you have to go touring all over and that's cool."

"Ian, you may have felt differently if I was your real dad and never around to teach you those father and son things."

"But the other guys in the band have kids and everything seems fine for them." Ian frowned trying to understand Ryder's decision.

"That is true, but they have great wives, and they all work hard to make it work for them. I didn't find that until I met your mom. Even now, I still don't want kids of my own. I'm more than happy with you and your sister. I might not have been there to see you grow up as small children, but I get to see you grow into amazing adults and start families of your own one day too. I'm very happy with that. Anyway, to have a baby now? At my age? That's not for me. I like my sleep."

Ryder smiled at Ian. "Speaking of which, it's been a long day. Get some sleep. Goodnight Ian. Just try not to let your father drag you down. You are a good kid with a good and caring heart. Traits you get from your mom."

Ryder gave Ian a hug and left the room, closing the door behind him. When he turned around, he saw Tana sitting on the steps to her room just looking at him.

"Hi." He said as she sat there staring at him intently. "Um… I take it you heard me talking to Ian."

Tana nodded, a small smile playing on her lips. "You never cease to amaze me, Ryder Evans."

He walked closer to her and sat down on the step below her. "I figured telling him about my father might help him accept what his father pulled tonight. Maybe give him some hope that he'll be all right."

Tana leaned forward and planted a loving kiss on his lips. "What you did was more than that. You gave Ian someone to look up to and believe in. Someone to bond with now that he knows you share something in common with him."

Ryder smiled at her and took her hands. "I meant what I said too about being more than happy with Ian and Nikki in my life. They mean as much to me as you do."

"I know. You wouldn't have come home if you didn't care." Tana wiggled his wedding band on his finger. "And I would have never married you if you didn't care about them."

Ryder stood up pulling her up with him. "Come on. Bedtime. You need to get some sleep. Nikki might be stable, but it's going to be a long road to getting her back to being fully recovered. You're going to need your rest to help her. Me too."

They headed upstairs and got ready for bed. When Tana lay down with her head on Ryder's chest, she found she couldn't relax. Every time she tried to close her eyes, she would see Nikki lying in the hospital bed and the tears would come back.

"Shhh… Come on, Baby." Ryder held her close.

"I just want her to wake up and come home." Tana sniffed. Ryder caressed her arms and back trying to relax her.

"I know. She'll wake up. Give her time to rest and heal. She'll come back to us."

"How can you be so sure? I'm terrified that she's going to slip away from me, or she'll never wake up." Tana's voice was filled with fear and pain. Just hearing her sound that way tore Ryder apart.

"Nikki's a fighter and far too strong a person to give up. She's the only other person I know that's as stubborn as you are. She's just like you. That's how I can be so sure." Ryder turned to his side and kissed her forehead.

"Now get some sleep." He ordered as he resumed caressing her back and arms.

Slowly, he could feel Tana begin to relax and hear her breathing settle. It took a while, but she finally fell asleep in his arms. Only then did Ryder give in to jet lag and exhaustion.

Chapter 10

The next morning, Tana ran the dogs more out of habit than out of desire. Even though all she wanted to do was go to the hospital and stay with Nikki, she figured she should give the dogs their run and that it would help keep her a little less agitated. She stretched afterward as usual and was shocked when she went back inside to find Ryder in the kitchen making a light breakfast.

"Ah… good. You're back." He said as he placed a cup of tea on the island for her and handed her a bowl of fruit.

Tana sipped at the tea, thanking him and declined the fruit. "I'm not hungry." She said as Ryder looked at her sternly.

"I know for a fact you didn't eat all day yesterday, and you just went for a run. If you don't eat something, Dr. Parker is going to have another head trauma patient from you passing out on me. I don't care if you're hungry or not, eat at least some of this."

Ryder pushed the bowl back in front of Tana crossing his arms across his chest as he stared at her. Tana took the bowl and picked up the spoon, taking a bite.

As soon as the food hit her stomach, she found she was hungry. Within a few minutes, she had cleaned out the bowl.

"Better?" she asked looking up at him apologetically.

"Much. Thank you for eating." Ryder put her dish in the dishwasher then suggested they get ready to go back to the hospital.

After showering and getting dressed Tana left a note for Ian saying they would be back in the afternoon to pick him up to go see Nikki. Tana made sure the dogs were fed and let out then decided to bring a book with her. She went down to her book cabinets in the basement, grabbed a few kids' books and one that she knew Nikki liked of hers. When she headed back upstairs, Ryder was waiting for her at the garage door.

"What do you have there?" he asked looking at the books in her arms.

Tana rifled through the books listing off the titles. *"The Velveteen Rabbit, The Giving Tree, Goodnight Moon, Green Eggs and Ham* and *Watchers* by Dean Koontz."

Ryder looked at Tana questioningly. "Children's books?"

Tana ran her fingertips over the cover of one and looked down at it. "I used to read these to Nikki when she was little. These were her favorites. I kept them to give to her when she had a child of her own one day."

"I get that, but why are you bringing them to the hospital?"

Tana looked up at him with a purposeful look on her face. "To read to her. I plan on sitting with her, talking to her and reading to her until she wakes up. I'm not leaving her alone any more than I have to."

"I don't expect you to. And that's a great idea. I'll read to Nikki too. Let her hear our voices and give her a reason to fight her way back."

Tana had a look of victory on her face when Ryder spoke to her. "That's my plan."

Giving her a kiss, he opened the door to the garage for her. Tana climbed into the passenger seat of her truck letting Ryder drive back to the hospital.

When they got back to the fourth floor to the neuroscience wing, Tana and Ryder checked in at the nurse's desk to see how Nikki was doing medically.

"She's about the same. Her pulse is steady and her temperature is normal which is good. Blood pressure is a little low, but not alarmingly. Probably due to the sedation drugs. Otherwise, she's still with us and that's a good sign. Dr. Parker should be coming in around ten to check on her. He can give you a full update then."

Ryder thanked her and the twosome headed toward Nikki's room. There was another nurse in with Nikki, changing IV bags and checking on her as Tana and Ryder came in. She said good morning and told them to feel free to pull the chairs up to the bed, so they could sit closer to Nikki.

When she noticed the books in Tana's arms, she smiled. "Excellent. Read all you want to her. It helps. I've seen it."

Tana nodded at her with a small smile as Ryder brought the two chairs over and set them down side by side alongside the hospital bed.

Tana walked over to Nikki. She looked so small and frail, lying there in the bed, not moving.

Instantly, Tana teared up again then took a deep breath trying to calm herself and keep from crying. Ryder came over to hold her, kissing her cheek and whispering in her ear. "It's okay. She's going to get better from here."

Nodding Tana looked up at him. "It's just she was always so lively and full of energy. She looks so frail and so broken. It hurts."

Ryder brushed her hair off her face. "I know. It's only temporary. She'll be herself again. Give her time."

He let her go and they each sat down in a chair. Tana took Nikki's hand and kissed it. "Good morning, Sweetheart."

"Hey kid. Your mom and I are back to keep you company." Ryder said giving her un-casted arm a light squeeze and leaving his hand resting there.

For the next hour, Tana and Ryder talked to Nikki, telling her how worried they were for her and about Ryder coming home all the way from Japan to be with them. As well as a little bit of the arguments with Mike plus what Ian and Ryder had talked about.

Tana let Nikki know that Jess and Brad were okay, promising to call them later to tell them how she was doing. She even said she would let them come see her when they were a little better.

It was early morning and the nurses had been in checking on Nikki every thirty minutes. Each time they checked for responses, there was nothing. Tana's heart fell each time they lifted her hand, and it fell limply back to the bed or when they poked her feet, and there was no reaction.

"It's still early. She might just need more time. She is still quite heavily sedated, so don't be discouraged." They told her.

Ryder picked up *'The Giving Tree'* book and opened it. He looked over at Tana and started reading it out loud to Nikki.

Tana watched her husband reading a children's story to her daughter as if Nikki wasn't lying in a hospital bed fighting for her life, but a small child being told a bedtime story and was touched beyond words. There was no denying his love for Nikki.

Tana reached out her hand and placed it lovingly on Ryder's forearm as she held Nikki's hand with her other hand. Ryder glanced at Tana smiling as he continued to read the story. When he was done, they noticed Dr. Parker had come in to check on Nikki. Tana and Ryder both got up out of their seats.

Tana leaned down to kiss Nikki. "Sweetie, the doctor is here to check on you. Ryder and I are just going to the other side of the room."

Dr. Parker finished looking over the records in the binder with Nikki's name on it then went to her bedside to test her responsiveness. He uncovered her feet and raked the metal handle of a reflex hammer up the entire bottom of her foot to see if she reacted then checked her reflexes to no avail. There was no movement again, so he pulled her eyelids open and shone a small pen light in her eyes.

Frowning, he turned to look at Tana and Ryder. "I'd like to bring her out of the sedation and see if she breathes on her own. I don't want her body to become lazy or her brain to forget how to keep her body working."

Both Tana and Ryder looked at each other and nodded to the doctor. If Nikki was able to breathe on her own, it would be a good step.

Dr. Parker got the two nurses and the three of them administered drugs into Nikki's IV, waited for a few minutes, then removed the tube from Nikki's throat. Everyone stood back to see if she would breathe on her own or if they would have to intubate her again.

Ryder clutched Tana in his arms, his heart pounding in his chest while Tana had tucked her fists under her chin willing her daughter to breathe. They stood there, not moving a muscle for what seemed like an eternity.

None of the other machine's alarms went off and the room was much quieter without the ventilation machine running.

"I think she's breathing." Ryder whispered to Tana.

She strained her eyes to see if Nikki's chest was rising, but she couldn't tell under the blankets.

One of the nurse's went to Nikki and took her wrist, checking her pulse even though the heart rate monitor was still going at a steady rhythm. She placed her other hand lightly on Nikki's chest. Tana could see the hand rise and fall slightly.

She was breathing!

Tana fought not to jump up and down. She did feel Ryder's arms tighten around her. When she looked up at him, he had tears running down his face and he was smiling. Tana's eyes over flowed and she squeezed him back. It was the first step for Nikki on the road to recovery.

"Well, that's encouraging." Dr. Parker said as the nurses ran oxygen tubes around Nikki's head and clipped the nosepiece in place.

"We are going to continue to give her some oxygen, just so she doesn't exhaust herself trying to breathe. But this is a positive sign. As the sedation continues to wear off and leave her system, we're hoping to see some responsiveness." He explained.

"What we're looking for is some sign of awareness, pain receptors or the ability to control the fall of her hand. Some sign that her brain functions are working. It will take time, but it's routine to check her. Later today, we'll take her for some tests to see how the swelling is. If it has come down enough and the cerebral spinal fluid flow is back to normal, we can remove the catheter."

Dr. Parker and the nurses finished up then left the room, leaving Tana and Ryder alone again with Nikki. They took their seats again and shared the news with Nikki telling her everything the doctor had said.

"I bet you already feel a hell of a lot better without that damn tube shoved down your throat. God that thing looked like it went right down to your toes!" Ryder joked.

Tana laughed at him trying to lighten the mood a little and Ryder beamed. He loved hearing that sound.

They stayed with Nikki until they came to take her for more tests. Tana told her to pass them with flying colors and that they would be back in a few hours with Ian.

This time the drive home was better than the previous night. Ryder drove again, so Tana could call Jess and Brad to give them an update. Both of them promised to come and visit as soon as their parents allowed them to. They were both going to be housebound for a week at least to recover from the crash.

Ian was ready to go when the truck pulled up, but Tana and Ryder came inside to have a bite to eat first.

"How is she?" Ian asked with a worried look.

"They took the breathing tube out and she's breathing on her own now." Tana told Ian with a small relieved look.

"It's small step in the right direction at least." Ian said grateful his sister had not gotten worse.

"Your mom brought some books to read to her, if you want to bring something for her, go for it. They say it helps."

While his parents had a sandwich, Ian went downstairs and brought up a couple of small board games and a deck of cards. "If reading helps, what about playing a game? It could be a good way to talk to her too."

Ryder and Tana looked at Ian and then at each other.

"Great idea Ian." Ryder said as they got into the truck and headed back to the hospital.

Ryder hung back for a few minutes once they got to the front entrance. "You two head up. I want to check in with the band and let them know how Nikki is. I'll be right there."

Ryder was already talking to one of the band members as Tana and Ian headed up to Nikki's room.

By the time Ryder was done giving everyone updates and made it up to Nikki's room, Ian and Tana had settled in and Tana was reading her the first few pages of *'Watchers'*. When he came into the room, Tana looked up and finished the page, putting a bookmark to save her spot and told Nikki that Ryder was back.

"Hey girl. How'd you do on those tests? Good, I hope." He said sounding cheerful.

"The rest of the band and their families all send their best to us and especially to you Nikki. So does my mother. She sends her love and prayers too." Ryder informed as he sat gently on the empty corner at the foot of Nikki's bed.

Next, they played *Yahtzee* for a bit. Tana played for both herself and Nikki, conversing with Nikki as if she was playing herself and making comments on what a good roll she had or teasing her about being lazy and not adding up her own score.

The nurses came in regularly checking on Nikki and each time, they saw the family trying their best to cope in a way that everyone hoped Nikki would respond to. It brought tears to their eyes as much as it gave them hope.

Chapter 11

Over the next week, Tana and Ryder spent all day every day with Nikki in her hospital room. Tana had taken a leave of absence from work and was planning to only go back part time so she could help Nikki with her rehabilitation when and if she woke up.

The story of Ryder Evans' stepdaughter being in the hospital ICU had broken to the media and security at the hospital was not allowing any reporters or photographers in the hospital or on the premises at all. Even the floor nurses were relentless. Absolutely no one was going to get anywhere near Nikki's room.

Ian went to school during the day, then after dinner, he would go with his parents to play games and read to Nikki until the hospital told them it was time to go. It wasn't much of a way for a young teenage boy to spend his free time, but it was what he wanted to do. Helping Nikki was all any of them could think of.

Her friends came to visit every few days and Brad stopped by every day. It was hard for them to stay and see her like that, but Jess, Brad and a few other very close friends that Tana allowed to come in, all did their best. They would talk to her and keep her in the loop of all the latest gossip at school, bringing her flowers, little trinkets or stuffed animals.

It didn't take long for Nikki's room to become filled with everyone's thoughtful gifts. It had gotten to the point her room was so over run with balloons, flowers and stuffed animals, that Tana had all but certain people's gifts sent out to other wards in the hospital. The excess flowers she had sent to geriatrics and palliative care, while the stuffed toys and trinkets she sent to the children's ward. Even after doing that, Nikki's room was still well decorated.

The catheter had been removed days ago and the last tests showed that Nikki's brain was no longer swollen with very little bruising left. She was off the oxygen completely and her arm, leg, and ribs were healing nicely. Her other cuts and bruises were healing well. Even her face started to look more like the old Nikki. She had a few scars, but they were told those would fade over time.

The nurses still checked on her regularly and they would routinely move her limbs as much as possible to keep her from stiffening too much. Tana would rub her shoulders, neck, and the un-casted arm, and leg too. She was still unresponsive, but Dr. Parker remained optimistic that she would come around.

"Sometimes these things take longer than others. She was in very grave condition when she arrived here, so don't be discouraged." He reassured them.

By the first full week in June, Tana was well settled in her routine of morning runs, seeing Ian off to school, go to the hospital, then back home for dinnertime and again back to the hospital until visiting hours were over. The one thing she was grateful for was the media had finally given up on Nikki's accident. No reporters had been around for a few days.

One evening after returning to the hospital from having dinner and picking Ian up, Tana, Ryder and Ian resumed their usual positions around Nikki's bed. Everyone was taking turns playing chess. Ryder was playing against Ian and losing terribly. They were talking and laughing while Tana rubbed Nikki's arm and shoulders.

"Check again." Ian said as he moved his rook, advancing on Ryder's king.

"Jeez. Every two moves you have me in check. Hey Nikki, can you help me out here? Your brother is kicking my ass." Ryder said as he moved his king out of Ian's rook's path.

Ian smiled and glanced at his sister. He was about to say something back to Ryder, but he stopped as he examined Nikki's face.

"Mom, she's frowning." Ian's voice sounded urgent.

Ryder's head snapped up from examining the chessboard. He damn near jumped out of his chair, knocking the chessboard on the table all over Nikki's bed. Tana stopped rubbing Nikki's arm and everyone was looking at her, examining her expression. Ian was right. Nikki had a small frown on her face.

"I'm getting the nurse." Ryder said as he strode out of the room calling down the hall for one of the nurses.

"Nikki? Honey, can you hear me?" Tana was gently touching Nikki's face and holding her hand.

Ryder and Stacey, one of the regular nurses hurried back into the room. Ian moved so Stacey could look at his sister. Both he and Ryder went to Tana's side of the bed to stand with her.

"Nikki, if you can hear me try and squeeze my hand, okay?" Tana was choking up.

Stacey was checking Nikki's lines and vitals. "Anything?" She looked at Tana, and Tana shook her head. The frown was still there. "Okay, keep talking. I'm going to check her reactions."

"Come on, Nikki, give us a squeeze if you can hear us." Ryder spoke over Tana's shoulder.

Stacey uncovered Nikki's foot and pressed a pen into the sole of her foot. She dragged it up her foot and Nikki's frown deepened.

"Look! She felt that!" Ian shouted pointing to Nikki's face.

"Come on, Nikki." Tana pleaded, "Please, anything. Let me know you can hear me."

Stacey left the room and called Dr. Parker in. He arrived a few minutes later and took over for Stacey. Everyone filled him in on seeing her frown and that when her foot was stimulated, she frowned even more.

"Is she waking up?" Tana's voice filled with hope and tears were threatening to spill down her face.

"We can hope. Sometimes individuals in a coma will have small reactions and movements but still don't wake up right away and even at times not at all." Dr. Parker leaned over Nikki and pulled her eyelid open, shining a light in first one eye then the other.

Nikki's index finger twitched in Tana's hand. "Oh my God, her finger. It just moved."

The tears spilled over running down her cheeks as she looked first to the doctor then up at Ryder. Dr. Parker pinched her fingertips and Nikki frowned again.

"Well, she is definitely reacting to pain. She might be coming around. Don't get too excited. She has been in her coma for a while now. It could take as many days for her to come fully out if it. Or she may not come out at all. All we can do is to continue what we've been doing."

Dr. Parker flipped through the binder for Nikki making some notes and checking the results of her last scans. "Her last scans show normal brain functions, so we're still leaning toward that she will come out of this."

Stacey and Dr. Parker left the room while Tana and Ryder stood there looking at one another. There was hope. Nikki was responding to stimuli.

Ian began cleaning up the knocked over game and Ryder helped him to set it up again.

"We can start a new game. You heard what the doctor said. It could take a while for her to come out, so let's keep her company while she fights her way back to us." Ian said sounding determined.

They finished their game while Tana read another chapter of *'Watchers'* out loud then it was time to go.

There had been no further responses from Nikki, but they were all hanging onto the small victory that had happened. Driving home, Ryder mentioned that he wanted to bring in a guitar the next day and play for her.

"I'm enjoying the games and reading to her, but I want to try music," he said.

"I think that's a great idea." Tana reached over the center console of her truck and took Ryder's hand.

It had been nine days since the accident and things were finally looking brighter.

Chapter 12

Tana and Ryder were back at the hospital the next morning. When the nurses saw Ryder carrying a guitar case, their eyebrows rose. Fran, a sweet elderly woman who was the head nurse came into Nikki's room and gave them an update.

"I understand Miss Nikki had a big day yesterday. Frowning and her finger moved."

"Yes, she frowned three times, twice when she was subjected to stimuli and once when my son and husband were playing chess. Her finger moved when Dr. Parker looked in her eyes." Tana said looking pleased with her daughter's small progress.

"That's good. It's those little steps that will lead to bigger ones." Fran turned to Ryder, "Now I hope you don't plan on playing some of those loud screaming, banging and crashing songs of yours that my grandchildren love to listen to."

Ryder smiled and Tana was shocked to see a little tinge of red in his cheeks. "No ma'am. Just some soft ballads."

"Good." She patted Ryder's arm as she passed him and headed out the door.

"I don't believe it." Tana giggled. "You just blushed."

Ryder pursed his lips and scrunched up his nose. "You just be quiet about that."

He playfully swatted Tana's rear and pulled the chair back over to the side of Nikki's bed.

"I had no idea you could be embarrassed." Tana sat in her chair and looked at her husband, amused.

"I had no idea she knew who I am. I wasn't embarrassed, but she just kinda caught me off guard. Normally, I never blush."

Ryder unzipped his guitar case, brought out the Gibson Acoustic J-200 Custom and began tuning it. Tana picked up the novel and as Ryder tuned his guitar, she began to read.

By noon, Tana had gone through two full chapters and told Nikki that was enough for now. "My throat is dry, Baby Girl. I'm going to go and get a drink and let Ryder take over, okay?" She leaned down and kissed Nikki's head then left the room.

Ryder swapped chairs to be closer to her and grabbed the guitar. "You know what Nikki? I'm not going to read to you today. I'm a little tired of reading, so I decided to bring this." Ryder picked out a few chords on his guitar, letting the sounds fade before he spoke again.

"So, instead of reading you a book, or newspaper article or those awful teenage gossip magazines you like, I'm going to do what I do best. I'm going to play and sing."

Ryder picked away, beginning to play out a song he loved, *'Down on the Corner'*, doing his best to play and sing as softly as he could trying not to disturb anyone else. Out at the station, the nurses could all hear him and they smiled to one another finding it incredible at how determined the family was with trying to reach their daughter. They could see how they were trying to bring a sense of normalcy to Nikki's hospital room and found it encouraging seeing how close the family was through this challenge.

Tana came out of the elevator with two bottles of water in her hand. Approaching the ICU desk, she could hear Ryder's voice coming down the hall. Instantly, she smiled as she continued back to her daughter's room.

"Mrs. Evans?" Carol, one of the ICU nurses called to her.

Tana detoured over to the ICU desk where Carol was standing.

"Your daughter is one lucky girl. The dedication all of you have to seeing her recover is incredible."

Tana smiled. "Thank you. She hasn't given up her fight. There's no way we'll ever give up on ours. We'll help her find her way back."

Carol reached out and took Tana's hand, giving it a squeeze. "Her knowing she's not alone will make all the difference."

Nodding her head and squeezing Carol's hand back Tana turned and walked back to Nikki's room where Ryder was just finishing the song. He looked up at her as he sang the last few lyrics with the final notes fading in the air. Tana handed him a bottle of water and he thanked her.

"I think she prefers the music to the reading." Ryder said taking a sip.

Tana frowned at him and looked at Nikki. Nothing had changed. Her expression was the same blank sleeping look as it had been for the past ten days.

"Why do you say that?" Tana asked puzzled.

Ryder shrugged. "Because I know I would if the roles were reversed."

Tana swatted his leg and shook her head smiling at him as Ryder began playing again. This time he played *'When I See You Smile'* and looked at his wife while he played, singing to her. Tana sat on the foot of Nikki's bed watching Ryder and smiling. She could see his love for her in his eyes and all over his face as he sang. Tana had never felt such love before she knew him. The look in her eyes as she gazed back at him and her smile spoke volumes to Ryder.

Even through this horrific ordeal, their love grew and strengthened. He stayed firmly at her side, supporting her and comforting her. Without a doubt in her heart, she knew that he would never leave. He came home from Japan to be with them even though he still had two shows left, knowing it could cause major backlash with his fans but only caring for his family when they needed him the most. Even if Tana hadn't admitted that to him, he knew.

Fran and Carol poked their heads into the room and saw Ryder singing to Tana. They could see the love and the bond between them. It made them both smile.

Carol whispered to Fran, "Lucky girl."

Fran nodded, and they watched discreetly as Ryder finished then stood up to kiss Tana lovingly.

Both nurses knocked lightly on the door. When Tana and Ryder looked up, they came in.

"Sorry to disturb, but we need to check on Miss Nikki." Fran said softly.

"Of course." Tana breathed moving off the bed while Ryder got up and moved to the chair on the other side of the room, pulling Tana down to sit on his lap.

They could still see Nikki clearly as they watched the nurses check her machines and IV's, marking down their findings in the binder and then came the response tests. Fran lifted Nikki's hand a few inches off the bed and let it go. When it fell back to the bed instantly Tana couldn't help but feel dejected. She looked down at her hands in her lap trying not to let the feelings of despair show.

Fran picked Nikki's hand up again and lifted it a little higher. This time when she let it go, Nikki's hand eased back down to the mattress. Ryder's arms tightened around Tana and she looked up at him. His eyes were wide in his face and there was a hint of a smile on his lips. He nodded toward Nikki and Tana turned her head to watch.

Fran dropped Nikki's hand a third time. It stayed raised for a few seconds before easing back down to the mattress. Tana gasped when she saw it and turned to Ryder looking anxious. Ryder met her gaze with a smile and kissed her. Squeezing her tighter, he continued watch.

They scraped the bottom of Nikki's foot and again, she frowned. Fran took Nikki's hand in hers and called to her to squeeze her hand. "Come on, Miss Nikki. Let me know you can hear me. Give us a little squeeze here, okay?"

They spent the next five minutes trying to coax Nikki to squeeze their hand, but it was to no avail. It seemed Nikki was stuck just being able to frown and somewhat control the fall of her hand.

Fran and Carol made notes in Nikki's binder then encouraged Tana and Ryder to continue to work with her.

"We'll inform Dr. Parker and finish our rounds. I'm sure he'll be pleased that she's making more progress, but he may want to order more scans to see if anything new has shown up." Fran informed them then left.

Tana and Ryder stood up and went to Nikki's bed. This time Tana stood beside her daughter and took her hand asking Nikki to squeeze her hand while Ryder sat down at the foot of her bed. He leaned forward, picked up his guitar and settled himself on the bed to play.

"Baby, I have an idea. I don't know if it'll help, but it's worth a try." Ryder started to play the song that Nikki had sung Becky to sleep with on their first trip to Langley. He had learned it when he was looking at good songs to teach Tana a little while ago. Originally he wanted to keep it as a surprise for her, but Ryder figured playing it now would be better than waiting. When he started, Tana looked up at him smiling, her eyes shining with emotion.

As Ryder sang, he would glance at Tana every so often then watch Nikki, to see if there was any reaction. Tana kept a hold of her daughter's hand and leaned down to be closer to her. Kissing her forehead, she started to sing herself, although much quieter than Ryder was. When he heard her singing, he smiled nodding to her and encouraging her. The two of them sang to Nikki, Ryder's voice clear and perfectly on key while Tana was much softer as she continued to hold her daughter's hand.

When they were about halfway done the song, Nikki's head moved slightly and she squeezed her mother's hand. Tana stopped singing instantly and looked down at her hand.

"She squeezed my hand!" She called out.

Ryder stopped playing and came up to where Tana was, setting his guitar down.

"Come on, Nikki. Fight. I know you're in there." He begged her taking both Tana's and Nikki's hands into his and squeezing them.

"Squeeze my hand again, Nikki. Like you just did. You can do it, Baby Girl." Tana was in tears again coaxing her daughter.

They watched as Nikki frowned again. Her eyes fluttered, showing the whites of her eyes briefly before closing again.

Ryder put his other hand over top of Nikki's, Tana's and his other hand and pressed them together. "Oh no you don't. Don't you dare give up now. Come on. Open those eyes. You almost had it. Keep trying."

Ryder's voice was almost at a shout trying to reach through the fog and get her to come back to them. Nikki frowned again, but her eyes didn't move.

"Come on, Nikki. Please. I need you to come back. I miss you, Sweetheart." Tana was crying as she pleaded with her daughter.

Dr. Parker came in with both nurses. Ryder quickly filled them in on Nikki's recent movements while Tana continued to coax Nikki to wake up.

Standing on the opposite side of Nikki's bed, Dr. Parker lifted one of her eyelids shining the light in her eyes again. Nikki weakly turned her head away and squeezed her eyes closed again.

"That's a definitive sign. She's coming around." Dr. Parker said moving to her feet.

"That's it girl. Come on. Keep coming, you're almost there, Nikki. Don't you quit now." Ryder coaxed her again.

"Oh God! She's squeezing my hand again." Tana cried.

"I know. I can feel it too." Ryder looked at Nikki. "Look at her other hand. Her fingers are moving."

Dr. Parker uncovered Nikki's feet and pressed the tip of the reflex hammer's handle into the bottom of her heel and raked it up the sole of her foot, hard.

"Ow."

It was barely audible, but there was no mistaking it. Nikki had spoken. She felt what Dr. Parker had done and responded. Dr. Parker looked at Nikki. She was frowning again, but her eyes remained closed.

"We heard you, Nikki!" Tana cried, sniffing. "Come on Sweetheart, open your eyes. Please. I need you to look at me."

Nikki's eyes started to flutter again like she was fighting against something holding them down. Dr. Parker pressed the metal handle into her heel for a second time and again raked it up her foot using the same amount of pressure as before.

"Don't." Nikki rasped. Her voice sounded like she had laryngitis.

"Then open your eyes, or I'll do it again." Dr. Parker ordered.

Nikki's breath got shallower and her heart rate picked up like she was working hard at something. She was really fighting to come back and no one in that room was willing to let her stop now. Nikki frowned and her eyelids opened about half way showing the whites of her eyes then closed again.

Dr. Parker pressed the handle into her heel for a third time and Nikki's eyes continued to open about half way then close.

"No."

Nikki frowned, turning her head to face her mother and Ryder as she fought to open her eyes fully and keep them open.

"Then come on Sweetheart. Open those eyes, and Dr. Parker won't have to scrape your foot anymore." Tana reasoned with her.

The fingers of her casted left hand were clenching and unclenching as much as the cast would allow and she was still squeezing Tana and Ryder's hands with her other hand.

"Come on Nikki. You're so close. All you have to do is open your eyes and you'll see us. We're right here." Ryder had tears running down his own cheeks as he watched this poor child that he loved dearly fight so hard just to open her eyes.

"I want to see those incredible green eyes of yours. Come on." He gave their hands a small shake and squeezed back a little harder.

Dr. Parker raked the bottom of her foot again. This time Nikki's eyes flew open wide. She blinked a few times before they slowly closed again.

"Stop it." Nikki said sounding slightly irritated.

"Then get those eyes open and keep them open, Nikki." Dr. Parker said.

"Trying." Nikki said frowning again as she sighed.

"Try harder, Nikki. Please. For all of us." Tana said as she brushed Nikki's hair from her forehead.

Nikki's head flopped all the way over to one side then came back to where her mother's voice was coming from. Blinking repeatedly, she slowly opened her eyes and looked at her mother. Tears flowed in rivers down Tana's face as she looked into her daughter's eyes for the first time in almost two weeks.

"Hi." Nikki said faintly as she blinked and looked up at her mother.

"Welcome back." Tana said through her tears.

Nikki slowly looked from her mother to Ryder standing there silently crying as he looked down at her.

"Ryder." She said as they made eye contact.

Ryder smiled through his own tears and gave a small laugh. "Hey kid. Glad you're back."

Nikki gave them a small nod and a weak smile. "Me too."

Tana leaned down and kissed her daughter on the forehead then wiped her eyes. "You had us all really scared for quite a while."

Nikki frowned. "What happened? I don't remember."

"Nikki, I'm Dr. Parker. I'm the chief neurosurgeon here at the hospital. You might not ever remember what happened and that's quite normal. Now that you are back with us, I need to perform some tests on you and ask you a bunch of questions to assess your condition. Do you feel up to it, or would you like to rest?"

"Do what I can." Nikki said sounding a little clearer.

She lifted her hand from Ryder and Tana's and raised it to her throat. "Hurts." She swallowed and winced.

"I'll get you some water." Fran said and left the room.

"Your throat will be sore for a few days. We had you intubated from the time you were pulled from the car up until about eight days ago." Dr. Parker explained.

Nikki looked at her mother with a panicked expression. Tana leaned down and soothed her. "It's okay. Everything will be explained to you."

Dr. Parker began to explain to Nikki what happened to her then asked her what she remembered, her full name, date of birth, address, phone number and if she could tell him what her last memory was. Nikki answered everything correctly. But when she got to her last memory, she frowned. She said she remembered seeing Brad.

"I don't know where we were or what happened, but all I remember is seeing his face."

"Your parents can fill you in on the finer details, but right now, I need to assess your motor skills and run a few simple tests. Tomorrow, we will schedule more scans and tests now that you're awake. We need to see the extent of any possible brain damage. Then you can start rehab. The sooner we can get you up and moving around the better. Which means the faster you can go home."

Dr. Parker got Nikki to follow his pen with her eyes, from side to side, up and down, then touch each of the fingers on his hand and touch her nose. He checked her reflexes on her right side in her arm and leg and asked her if she could feel him touching her toes on her broken leg. Then he had her wiggle them and her fingers of her casted arm as well as turning her head side to side.

"How do you feel?" He asked after he finished with her.

"Stiff, sore, tired. My head hurts." Nikki said.

"That's why we want to get you moving as soon as possible. Your body has taken quite a beating. Lying in bed for ten days hasn't helped much either. But we'll let you rest. You fought hard this morning. Now that you're back with us, I think we can all rest easier."

Dr. Parker took Nikki's binder with him out to the nurse's station as Fran returned with some water.

"Small sips." She ordered.

Tana nodded pouring some into a cup and put the straw to Nikki's lips.

"I think it would be good for the two of you to go ahead and fill Nikki in on the other details. Then she needs to rest." Carol said as she left the room with Fran.

Tana and Ryder both looked down at Nikki. Tana asked her if she was up to hearing about the accident and what had gone on for the last ten days. Nodding, Nikki insisted that she wanted to know.

"Okay, but then after you need to rest. Ryder and I will head home for a few hours and pick Ian up then come back at dinnertime. Believe me, I don't want to let you out of my sight now that you are awake, but you need to sleep." Tana said as she caressed Nikki's cheek.

They spent the next hour filling Nikki in on the last ten days. Nikki listened intently and when they were done, she looked exhausted.

"I think it's time to go. You're beat." Ryder said taking Nikki's hand and giving it a squeeze. "We will be back before dinner, so we can visit and talk more. But right now, you get some sleep." Ryder leaned down and planted a kiss on Nikki's forehead.

Tana leaned down and kissed Nikki too. "I love you. You'll never know how scared I was of losing you."

"I know Mom. I was scared too." Nikki said looking at her mom as tears welled up in her eyes.

"You can tell me all about it later." Tana said as she made her way to the door. "Get some sleep."

They waved as they left the room heading to the elevators then made their way out to the parkade. Ryder kept his arm around Tana's waist the whole way until they got to her truck, both smiling whole-heartedly for the first time in almost two weeks.

It was after two in the afternoon by the time they got home. Tana went to the basement to let the dogs out while Ryder made some phone calls. He gave all the band members the good news then called his mother to tell her that Nikki was awake. Tana texted Jess and Brad with messages that Nikki was awake and seemed to have no noticeable damage from her head injury.

When Tana finished on the phone, she was standing in the kitchen hugging her elbows and smiling as she stared out the back window lost in the feeling of peace within her. Ryder walked into the kitchen and saw her standing there. She looked so relaxed and happy again. The past ten days had been hard on all of them, terrified that Nikki would die at first and then scared that she may never wake up. Seeing his wife happy again healed his own heartache. Nikki's accident hit him in a way he never expected to feel. The thought of her dying crushed him and if they had lost Nikki, Ryder didn't know how he would have managed it.

Now with Nikki awake and seeming to have suffered no brain damage, they could focus on getting her recovered and strong again. Ian's grad was coming up fast and they also had the move that had to be dealt with soon.

Ryder came up behind Tana and placed his hands on her shoulders, running them down her arms then around her waist. Leaning down, he placed a long kiss on her neck as he breathed in her scent.

"*Mmmm*... I've missed this." Tana breathed as she caressed his arms.

"So have I." Ryder mumbled as he kissed her neck again. "Seeing you smile and look so much happier today makes me happy. I hate seeing you sad or upset."

Tana tilted her head to one side exposing her neck a little more for Ryder. He picked up on her silent invite, nuzzling at her. Closing her eyes and letting out a little breath, Tana felt her skin break out in goosebumps.

Ryder felt her shiver and his longing took over. Turning her to face him, he devoured her with his kiss, thrusting his hands into her hair. Pouring all the fear, pain and worry that engulfed them both over the past ten days into that one kiss, Tana and Ryder's need for closeness took over.

Ryder picked her up, carrying her to her bedroom and deposited her onto the bed, his lips never leaving hers. He lay down beside her and began to undress her feverishly. Tana, feeling the same sense of urgency tore at Ryder's clothes until she managed to get his jeans and boxers off. Hers were not far behind his, getting tossed to the floor as Ryder worked himself between her parted thighs and pressed his erection into her.

Tana cried out as Ryder entered her. He wasted no time in setting a heady pace with his thrusts. It had been almost a month since they were last intimate and considering the emotional events of late, they both craved the release. Within minutes, Ryder's hard thrusts and continued hip rotations had Tana arching her back calling out to him as she came hard, all of her pent-up emotions melting away. Ryder was moments behind her yelling and plunging into her depths with his own climax letting all of his stress go as he gripped the pillow beneath Tana's head.

He collapsed down on top of his wife, pinning her to the bed as he panted from the exertion and intensity of their encounter. Tana caressed his back under his shirt and kissed his chest through the fabric. Slowly Ryder began to calm, lifting himself up onto his elbows to look down at her.

"We both needed that." He murmured as he kissed her nose smiling at her happy and elated expression.

"Yes, we did." Tana reached her hands up to his face, cupping it in her hands and pulled him to her.

She kissed him with all the love and admiration she felt inside. "Thank you for everything through all of this. You could have given up, could have left but you stayed. You were there for me. For all of us."

Tana looked up to meet his eyes. Ryder saw the tears and the heartfelt gratitude there.

"No more tears." He said as he kissed them away. "I would've had an easier time cutting my own arm off than leaving you through this. I love Nikki and Ian as if they were my own kids. I'd do anything for them. I know this damn near destroyed you. It sent me reeling for Christ sake. Letting you deal with it alone would have made me the biggest bastard in the world. I never could've done that to any of you. All of you mean too much to me."

Tana sniffed as more tears fell and slid across her temples. "What did I ever do to deserve you?"

Kissing him she snuggled into his chest.

"You lived through hell. Too much if you ask me, but you're the one who amazes me. How you keep on standing strong and pulling through. I don't know if I could ever be that tough."

Tana sighed. "You are. Look at what you've overcome and how far you've made it in your life. You never faltered or wavered through all of this. Even when Mike attacked you."

Tana's voice got very quiet. "No one's ever done that for me. I've always had to be the one that had to stand alone. You stayed. You have no idea what that means to me."

Ryder shifted off her and onto his side. "There's nowhere else I want to be than with you through anything. Good or bad. As far as Mike goes, that fucker is lucky you and Ian were there. I doubt I would have stopped otherwise. I was seeing red by then. That shit he said about you and your parents? Hurting you just for the sake of seeing you in more pain? I was ready to kill him with my bare hands."

"I know." Tana curled herself into Ryder's body. "When you're really mad like that you look kinda scary."

Ryder pulled back from Tana so he could look into her eyes. "You know I'd never hurt you. Or the kids. I used to get into fights all the time when I was younger, but I would never hurt someone I cared about."

Tana nodded and he kissed her. "Good. Now let's get dressed. Ian should be home soon too. We need to make something to eat, so we can all go back to see Nikki."

Ryder rolled over and got up off the bed putting his hand out to help Tana up. They pulled their jeans back on, then Tana went into the bathroom to brush her hair. Meeting Ryder's eyes through the mirror, she chuckled a little.

"What?" He asked coming up behind her.

"Your hair. It's messier than usual." Tana smiled as she continued to look at him in the mirror.

"That's cause you keep shoving your hands through it. Anyway, yours is worse. You've got a *just fucked* look happening back here." Ryder teased as Tana worked the brush through the tangles.

They headed into the kitchen and started to make some sandwiches that they could take back to the hospital with them. Tana worked on a chicken salad mixture, while Ryder took care of the egg salad mixture. When Ian came home both Tana and Ryder were hard at work in the kitchen and he was surprised to see them.

"What are you guys doing home?" He asked setting his backpack down on the floor then turning to look at them with a panicked look. "Is something wrong? How's Nikki?"

Ryder and Tana both looked at each other and smiled.

"She's awake." Tana said looking elated.

Ian's face burst into a huge grin and he came over and hugged his parents. "Really? Awake? Is she normal? When can I go see her?"

Ian was rambling questions off.

Tana and Ryder just let him ramble. They could see how relieved he was that his sister had finally woken up from her coma, so they let him get it out of his system before explaining the morning's events.

"But I don't get it. Why does she need to rest? She's been sleeping for the last ten days. She should be wide awake."

Ian looked confused after Tana and Ryder finished telling him about Nikki waking up, then them coming home so she could sleep for a few hours and to pick him up.

Ryder couldn't help but laugh. "Being in a coma isn't like getting a good sleep. I don't personally know what it's like, but it wasn't easy for your sister to come out of it. She fought hard. That took a lot out of her with how weak she is from the accident."

Tana finished wrapping up the sandwiches and put them in her work lunch bag. Opening the pantry, she grabbed some bottles of juice and a few snacks and added them to the bag.

"I'm sure she'll tell us what it was like for her if she remembers, but we don't want to pester her too much. We're just going to focus on getting her strong again, so she can come home."

Tana closed the bag and called the dogs downstairs to the spare room giving each of them a big chew bone to amuse them while they were at the hospital. Ryder took the food as he and Ian went into the garage to the truck waiting for Tana to finish, so they could head back to the hospital.

When they arrived back at Nikki's room, she was dozing. The nurses had raised the head of her bed, so she could sit up more and some of the machines had been disconnected and turned off. There were fewer tubes and wires around her and that put all of them even more at ease.

Tana walked up to the bed and kissed her lightly on the forehead. "Hi, Sweetheart," she whispered softly.

Nikki smiled and slowly opened her eyes to look at her mom.

"Hi." She said weakly and turned her head to look at Ryder and Ian standing beside her mother.

"Did you have a good sleep?" Ryder asked setting the food down on one of the chairs before coming to give Nikki a kiss.

She nodded slightly and raised her good hand a little in a wave to her brother. Ian was grinning and leaned over to gently give his sister a hug being careful not to touch her injured ribs.

"God, it's good to see you awake again." He said trying not to cry.

Nikki smiled and her eyes fell closed again. She was still so tired. She wanted to stay awake, but her eyelids felt so heavy.

Fran brought her in her dinner, consisting of soup broth and a piece of bread. "All right Miss Nikki, now we don't want you overdoing it with food, so it's just going to be light for the first few days. Gotta give your body a chance to get used to food again." She set the tray down.

Nikki opened her eyes again to look at the food. She scrunched her nose up at it then looked at her mom.

"You need to eat even just a little bit." Tana encouraged.

"Yes. The sooner you get some strength back, the sooner you can come home," Ryder added.

Nikki relented, allowing her mother to spoon some of the broth into her mouth and swallowed. Making a face in disgust, Nikki asked for a small piece of bread and Tana gave her one soaked in the broth to soften it for her.

Ian and Ryder watched as Tana slowly fed Nikki getting half of the broth into her and all the bread before Nikki turned the rest down. Tana cleared the food tray off the table and gave Nikki a sip of water.

"Good work Sweetheart." Tana said kissing her daughter on the forehead.

Nikki smiled weakly and fell back against the pillows with her eyes closed. They let her rest again, keeping quiet trying not to disturb her as they ate their sandwiches.

For the rest of the evening, Nikki came in and out of her dozing state, able to communicate a little bit but still very tired. By eight in the evening, they decided to say their goodnights to her and let her sleep, promising to return in the morning.

Chapter 13

The next morning, Tana and Ryder hung back at home a little later than usual to give Nikki the chance to sleep longer. They made love again after Ian left for school then Tana called her work to inform them that Nikki had finally woken up. Warren also let her know that her replacement had been hired and gave her the choice of staying on her leave of absence until she started her new position in Vancouver that fall, or returning once she felt Nikki was well enough until she moved at the end of the month. Tana told them she would think it over and get back to them later that day. When she told Ryder, he suggested that she stay on her leave with the offer to go in and help train her replacement if they needed her to.

"Either way, I want to go in and say goodbye to everyone. Plus, I have to clean out my office." She said considering Ryder's suggestion.

They discussed it in more detail over a late breakfast and all the way to the hospital.

By the time they reached the fourth floor, Tana decided that Ryder was right. Her focus should be on getting Nikki well.

As they passed the nurse's station, Stacey poked her head up and told them that Nikki had been taken for some tests. "Dr. Parker is having a CT and MRI done as well as EEG. He wants to be sure her neural pathways are clear and all her brain functions are working properly before moving her out of ICU and assigning her to rehab."

"She should be back fairly soon then she'll need to have lunch." Carol added.

"Did she eat much for breakfast?" Tana asked, as she leaned on the counter and Ryder stood behind her.

Carol nodded. "Her entire container of yogurt and almost all of the cereal. She has a banana and some orange juice on the tray in her room in case she gets hungry."

"That's great. How is she for consciousness? Still in and out of it a lot?" Ryder asked.

"Not bad. She still tires easily. When she gets tired, her speech is affected. She has a tougher time formulating her words at that point." Carol gave them a rundown of the morning's events before Tana and Ryder went into Nikki's room to wait for her to return. The room looked strangely empty with Nikki and her bed gone.

They noticed that Ryder had left his guitar there the day before. He picked it up and played *'Sweet Surprise'*, the song he had played for Liam, while they waited for Nikki.

Tana stepped over to the window and called work to give Warren her decision. He completely understood and was grateful for Tana's offer to give her replacement help if needed then told her that she was already dearly missed.

"Everyone here is pulling for Nicole to have a speedy recovery." He said as Tana arranged to clear out her office and say her goodbyes. Her replacement, Kyle, was due to start first thing Monday morning.

"Thanks Warren. Please make sure Kyle knows if he has any issues or questions, he can call me. Just give him my cell number." Tana finished her conversation and hung up.

By half past eleven, Nikki was brought back to her room and was sound asleep in her bed. Carol brought her lunch tray in shortly after and set it down.

The porter got Nikki's bed back in its proper spot then transferred the IV bags back to the poles in her room.

"She's been in and out since she got out of the MRI two hours ago. Her CT and EEG went just fine. She dozed on and off through her other two tests and has been completely out for about an hour now." The young man that had been shuttling Nikki all over the hospital explained.

"Thank you." Ryder said. "We'll let her sleep for a while longer then she can have lunch."

He suggested heading down to the cafeteria to grab some lunch for themselves and allow Nikki to sleep. Tana nodded, agreeing with him.

Ryder took her hand and they headed back down to the main floor and over to the cafeteria. After standing in line for a few minutes, they ordered then made their way to an empty table. There were hospital staff, patients and other visitors all around them and thankfully no one really paid them much attention. Most were busy with their own illnesses or were family members of other patients.

While they ate, both of their phones kept going off with received texts from everyone wanting to know how Nikki was today. The guys were texting Ryder along with some of the crew, Bruce and Tyson. Tana's girlfriends were checking in, as were Carla, Donna and Sheryl. They would read each other their texts, who they were from and then respond, letting each person know that Nikki was doing a little better and had more tests done to see if she could come out of ICU.

It took them a little longer to finish eating because they kept stopping to respond to all the messages. Seeing they had been gone from Nikki's room for over an hour and Tana had only eaten half of her sandwich, she decided to wrap it up and take it back upstairs with her.

They made their way back up to ICU and were surprised to see Dr. Parker in with Nikki and Maxine, one of the other nurses. Nikki's test results were back already and they had returned just in time to hear the results.

"Hello Mr. and Mrs. Evans." Dr. Parker addressed them as they came back into the room. "You're just in time to hear the good news."

Tana walked over to her daughter after saying hello to the doctor and kissed Nikki. She was awake and looked far more alert than she had the previous day. There was even more color in her cheeks.

"All of Nikki's tests that she endured this morning came back normal. There's nothing we can find to suggest she will have any permanent damage from her accident. The next few months will be tough on you with recovery, but I venture considering you're young and otherwise healthy, you should be fully recovered before the summer is over."

He patted Nikki's knee, "You're a very lucky girl. For a while there, we weren't sure which way you were headed, but we're sure glad you decided to stay with us."

Dr. Parker turned to leave as Tana and Ryder beamed at Nikki. Ryder gave her two thumbs up then Dr. Parker spoke again.

"Oh, and tomorrow morning you can be moved out of ICU." He smiled at Nikki then left the room to tend to his other patients.

"Where will she be moved to?" Tana asked Maxine who was uncovering Nikki's lunch and getting ready to help her eat.

"Down one floor. That will be her last move before going home. She will start on some light rehab in a day or two after she gets a little stronger. Then once she passes rehab in about two months, she should be fine to go home."

Tana and Ryder looked at each other.

"We're supposed to be moving to BC at the end of June. Can we have her transferred out there to finish her rehab?" Tana asked.

"Mom, I'm supposed to move in with Brad and Jess." Nikki said as she looked at her lunch and picked up a piece of toast.

"I know. Moving you to Langley would only be temporary. Just until you've fully recovered. Then you can come back." Tana reasoned with her daughter and Nikki relented as she nibbled on her toast.

Maxine said she didn't see any reason why Nikki couldn't finish her rehab in Langley. They would just have to find a center for her to be admitted to.

"What about keeping her at home and having a therapist come to see her?" Ryder offered.

"That's quite expensive. You would have to rent the equipment to help her around until her casts come off plus whatever else her therapist requires." Maxine told them.

"That's fine. If she'll be more comfortable at home and we don't have to worry about her being alone in a hospital, that's what we'll do." Ryder offered then added, "We can even invite Jess and Brad to come out a few times, so you have some company."

Nikki smiled and thanked Ryder as she finished her toast and moved onto her soup. Maxine made notes of their plans in Nikki's binder and said they would give them a list of qualified therapists to get in touch with before they moved.

After the nurse left the room, Tana looked at Nikki and asked her how she was feeling.

"A little better. I'm still really tired, but at least I'm not falling back asleep every five minutes."

"Well, you look better." Ryder told her as he sat on the foot of her bed. "How's your lunch?"

Nikki made a face. "Nasty. But if I want to get better, I have to eat."

Tana handed her the other half of her sandwich. "It's ham and swiss."

Nikki thanked her mom and took the sandwich. Unwrapping it, she took a small bite.

They visited with Nikki again until she started looking tired then insisted she get some sleep.

"We'll come back again tonight." Ryder promised.

They both gave Nikki a kiss as she lay back against the pillows and closed her eyes. She was asleep very shortly after her parents left the room.

Back in the truck and on their way home, Tana suggested they should stop and get some boxes.

"With Nikki's accident, I completely forgot about getting packed up and ready to move." She admitted.

Ryder agreed and asked what she planned on doing with everything. Tana shrugged and asked if he wanted her to bring anything of hers to Langley other than Ian's stuff and her personal belongings.

Ryder shook his head. "It's up to you Baby, but maybe you should see if Jess and Brad want any of it for when they move out. Otherwise you can try to sell it with the house. We can pack up what you want to keep, what you want to give to Nikki, Jess and Brad then see what's left."

Liking his idea, Tana texted Jess and Brad with the offer then made a quick stop to get moving supplies before heading home.

Once they were back home, Tana decided to start packing in the basement. So for the rest of the afternoon, she and Ryder went through all of her books, games and other belongings that were down there. The two of them packed what she wanted to keep and put aside what she didn't want or need.

When Ian came home from school, he heard the commotion downstairs and headed down to see what was going on. When Tana explained what they were doing, he agreed to start in his room on the weekend then went upstairs to do his homework.

That evening, they all went to see Nikki in the hospital again, bringing her a few light snacks and a sandwich from home. Tana had made her a roast beef and cheese sandwich plus a second one of peanut butter and jam that she could stash away in case she got hungry later. The three of them visited until they had to leave and were very thrilled to see that each time they saw her, Nikki was looking better and better.

Chapter 14

It had been a week since Nikki had woken up from her coma and she had already started her rehab. It was brutally tough for her, but she had been forewarned that it would be. The goal was to get her back to her old self as soon as possible and her therapist, Rose, was kicking her ass. Tana and Ryder were still spending most of their time with her at the hospital learning what they would need to work on with her, encouraging her and being there for her.

Brad and Jess came by regularly to visit and she was always thrilled to see them. Both of them were in tears when they saw her awake for the first time and everyone that came to see Nikki brought food in for her every chance they got.

Nikki was looking forward to the following week's check in when the cast on her leg would come off and they would switch her to a removable boot. She kept saying it would be so much better because it would make bathing much easier and she could scratch her foot when it got itchy. Her therapist said she was also going to get her starting on walking too.

As it was, Nikki was already having a hard time with the physical aspect of her rehab. She still tired easily and was very weak but every day she would try to push herself a little more. She couldn't stand for very long yet, but she was happy she could stand even if it was only for a few minutes.

The day of Ian's grade nine grad, Tana and Ryder were trying to convince the hospital to allow Nikki to attend the ceremony. Rose was hesitant on letting Nikki leave, but when Ryder suggested to have a nurse attend with them, she relented on the condition that she would be the one to go so she could keep watch.

Both Tana and Ryder agreed and Nikki was overjoyed that she was going to get out of the hospital even if it was only for a few hours.

"I need to shower first. And what about clothes?"

Tana produced a small bag that had a skirt and a tank top blouse in it that she had brought from Nikki's closet just in case.

Rose and Tana helped Nikki into the shower and she sat down in the chair to wash.

"God, I can't wait until I can pee and shower on my own again." Nikki called from behind the curtain.

Ryder heard her and was laughing out in the room. Nikki showered quickly then Rose and her mother helped her get dressed and into her wheelchair while Ryder signed her out for the rest of the day.

"We should be back by nine." Rose informed her co-workers and they all nodded.

The small group rode the elevator down and took Nikki outside into the warm June sunshine. It was almost three-thirty already. The graduation ceremony was due to start at five in the drama room of Ian's school. Then there was going to be a dinner and dance starting at seven in the gym. Ian had no idea they were bringing his sister, so it was going to be a nice surprise for him.

Rose pushed Nikki in her wheelchair out to Tana's truck. She looked pale in the bright sunshine and was squinting against the sun, so Tana reached inside the truck for her sunglasses and handed them to Nikki.

"Thanks, Mom. I guess I'm not used to the sun anymore."

Rose engaged the breaks on the wheelchair and contemplated how to get Nikki up into the truck when Ryder came over to her.

"I've got this." He bent down to pick Nikki up out of the wheelchair.

When she went to lift her casted arm over his head, she misjudged and smacked him across the head with her cast.

"Ow." Ryder said as he lifted Nikki and stepped into the doorway of the truck easing her into the seat.

Tana tried to stifle a laugh but was unable to and stood there laughing for a few minutes with Rose trying her best not to join her.

Ryder settled Nikki in the truck and leaned across to do up her seatbelt for her.

"Nice to know my wife finds it funny when I get hit in the head." He grumbled to Nikki with a smile.

"I'm sorry. It's really heavy and I thought I had cleared your head." Nikki said suppressing her own grin.

Ryder told her not to worry and made sure she was comfortable before closing the door. Rose helped Ryder to collapse the wheelchair, then he stowed it in the cargo hold while everyone else climbed into their seats.

Tana tried not to make eye contact with Ryder and had her hand up at her mouth to hide the smirk that was still there. She knew if she looked at him, she would start to giggle again.

Ryder just shook his head at her as he started the truck and pulled out of the hospital parkade to head to Ian's school.

When they got to the school, Ryder carried Nikki out of the truck and back to the wheelchair, but this time, he lifted Nikki's arm over his head, so she didn't hit him again. When Tana saw him do that, she couldn't help but snicker a little. Ryder turned and gave her a look.

As Rose pushed Nikki into the school, he leaned down and whispered in her ear, "I will get you back you realize."

Tana nodded but was still unable to suppress her smile. "Sorry, but it was funny."

Stopping at the school office, Tana wanted to talk to them for a moment and ask if they could be allowed into the drama theater ahead of everyone else. The vice-principal agreed whole-heartedly and came out to see Nikki. He remembered her from when she attended that school. When he had heard about her being in an accident, he had sent his best wishes home with Ian.

As he led them to the theater, he told Nikki he was glad to see her doing so well and Nikki smiled thanking him.

Some of the graduating students were milling around in the halls. When they saw Ryder walking down the halls of their school, most of their jaws dropped. Smiling Ryder held out his devil horns to them as they passed. The vice-principal ordered them back to class and to be quiet, reminding them he was here for the ceremony not for them to pester.

"The theater isn't wheelchair accessible, so I'm not sure how we're going to get Nikki up the steps." The vice-principal said as they stopped in front of the theater door.

"Oh, that's no problem. We have him." Rose said pointing to Ryder.

Again, Ryder effortlessly picked Nikki up out of her chair and carried her up the stairs into the theater. "Where did you want to sit?" He asked Tana looking around the room.

"How about right up front, so there are less people moving around Nikki and you for that matter." Tana suggested.

They moved one of the chairs and set up the wheelchair for Nikki. Ryder gently set her back in her seat then asked how she was feeling. Nikki gave him thumbs up. Tana and Ryder sat down with her while Rose took the seat on the other side of Nikki's chair.

As the everyone settled in, other parents and siblings just starting to arrive. Slowly, the theatre was filling up and about twenty minutes later, the graduating grade nines filed into the room and sat along the side wall in the chairs set up for them.

Shortly after all the grads were seated, the theater was called to attention. Speeches were given by both the vice-principal and the principal, followed by special award presentations to the top students for grades, sportsmanship and school spirit.

Next, came the certificate presentations for all the grade nines. Just like Nikki's graduation, they were called up one at a time alphabetically. Ian was tenth in line. When he came down the aisle dressed in pants, a shirt and a tie, he walked up the steps to the stage and shook hands with the principal then stood in front of the screen for the required picture. Tana was standing taking some pictures of her own.

Ian saw his mother and as he came down the steps to take his seat again, he saw his sister sitting in her wheelchair smiling at him. She couldn't clap her hands with the rest of the audience because of the cast, so she just sat there smiling at him and gave him a small wave as he looked at her. Ian detoured over to where his family was and bent down to give his sister a hug.

"Congrats, little brother." She whispered to him as he hugged her as tight as he dared.

"Thanks. I'm glad you could make it. It means a lot to me." He whispered back then let her go to take his seat again.

The remaining grads took under an hour to get their certificates and then there was a special speech given by the parent council president. She complimented the grads for being good examples to the younger grades this year and how proud they have made their teachers and parents, ending with wishing them all the best in their high school years ahead.

After the ceremony finished, Ian made his way back down to his family. They were waiting for everyone else to exit the theater in order for Ryder to carry Nikki back out. Most of Ian's friends followed him over to Nikki saying they were glad she was okay then looked at Ryder. A few of them said hi to him then left shyly.

When the theater was finally empty, Ryder picked Nikki up and carried her back out to the hall. Ian carried the wheelchair and helped to set it back up. Ryder put Nikki back down again before heading to the gym for the dinner and dance part of the ceremony.

There were people milling around in the gym visiting and taking pictures already. Ian wandered off quite often to hang out with some of his friends and take pictures of his own. Every so often he would come back and introduce some of his friends' parents to his own and soon there was a nice group of parents for Tana and Ryder to visit with over the buffet dinner.

Most parents had read about the accident in the local paper or heard what had happened to Nikki through their children, so when they realized that the family was here, they wanted to come over to give them their best.

After the dinner, Ian was off with some friends again goofing around a little, glad that the school year was over and feeling much happier knowing his sister really was okay. Not wanting her to feel left out, he came back with half a dozen friends. They dragged some spare chairs over to where Nikki was so they could sit and visit with his sister. The group all talked and laughed right up until the dance started.

Just like at Nikki's grad, the grads were called to share a dance with their parent, so Ian and Tana shared a dance while Ryder took some pictures for her. Then Ian was off with his friends again onto the dance floor dancing and having a good time. Nikki sat in her chair watching them dance, wishing she could join them.

Tana saw the look on her face and tried to reassure her. "Soon, Sweetheart. You will be back on your feet soon."

Nikki sighed and looked at her mom. "I know, but it just seems so long."

She yawned and Rose checked her watch.

"We should be getting her back to the hospital soon. It's eight o'clock and she's had a very busy day."

Tana agreed and motioned for Ian to come over.

"We need to get your sister back to the hospital to get some rest. Do you want to say bye to her here or come with us?" Tana asked him.

"Um… can I stay? You can pick me up later. I can say bye to her now." Ian was having fun with his friends and wanted to enjoy himself a little longer.

It had been a very long few weeks and Ian needed this break so Tana agreed and Ian went to say good night to his sister. She looked very tired and he promised to come to the hospital and see her the next day.

Rose pushed Nikki out to the truck where Ryder picked her up and put her in the truck again. Tana and Rose loaded the wheelchair while Ryder got Nikki buckled in.

It was a quiet ride back to the hospital and when Ryder parked then went to take Nikki out, he found her sound asleep in her seat. Tana and Rose had already set up the wheelchair when Ryder shook his head.

"She's passed right out. I don't want to disturb her too much. I'll just carry her."

Tana nodded and Rose snorted. "Must be nice to have someone his size around."

Tana laughed, agreeing that it did come in handy.

Ryder carried Nikki across the parkade and into the hospital while Rose pushed the empty wheelchair. Tana pushed the call button for the elevator and moments later, they stepped in as the doors opened. Nikki didn't stir the entire time from when Ryder picked her up out of the truck until he gently laid her down in her hospital bed.

Rose put the side rail up and Nikki settled into her pillows looking peaceful. She even had a small smile on her still too pale face. Ryder leaned over the rail and kissed the side of her head and whispered goodnight to her as Tana came up beside him to do the same. They left her completely dressed in her blouse and skirt, not wanting to wake her and thanked Rose for letting her go.

"It really meant a lot to Ian and to us having her there tonight. Thank you." Tana gave the woman a quick hug.

"Personally, I think it did her some good to be out and around some people closer to her own age. I hope it gives her a renewed drive to get better." Rose admitted.

Tana and Ryder both agreed then said goodnight to Rose and the other nurses on duty before they left to go pick Ian up.

Chapter 15

By the last week of June, Tana's house had sold. Everything that was being shipped to Langley, was packed up and ready to go. Tana had tried to sell the house mostly furnished but the buyers didn't need any furniture, so between her and Ryder they decided to auction off everything that wasn't going to Nikki or being taken to Langley.

Jess, Brad and Nikki all discussed what they were going to need and everything they were taking had already been moved to a storage facility for them along with Nikki's car. Both Brad and Jess made the decision to wait until Nikki was back to move out so it wasn't such a financial crunch on them.

It had been a month since the accident and Nikki's rehab was progressing well. She was even walking around the hospital now that the cast was off. She was still in a boot, so she wasn't allowed to go alone yet, but she was very happy to at least have more freedom. And to her relief, she was finally able to shower on her own.

Ryder and Tana found a physical therapist for Nikki in Langley that was willing to come to the house to work with her every day and Ryder had even gone back to Langley for a few days to prepare her room. He and her new therapist, Dan, were hard at work getting everything needed for Nikki to complete her rehab set up before her arrival. She was making such huge strides that it was much less than they originally expected, but there was still a lot to prepare. There was a walker, handrails for the bathroom, guard rail for her bed, the exercise equipment she would need and the therapy table.

Dan was even going to fly back with Ryder the next day to speak with Rose. She had insisted on going over Nikki's case, so the transfer would go smoothly. It also served as an extra added bonus because Nikki would have someone medically qualified with her on the flight back to Langley.

The previous week Tana had gone to her work and cleaned out her office with Ryder's help. It had been an emotional time for her and for many of her colleagues. Especially when they all gave her little going away cards and gifts. When she finally got to meet Kyle in person, he seemed very nice and good at what he did. He only had to contact her a few times since starting and now was looking forward to moving into Tana's old office, so he could really get down to work.

The moving trucks were due to arrive at Tana's house in two days. Everything was packed and ready. Ryder was still back in Langley, so Tana split her time between being with Nikki at the hospital and at home with Ian seeing there wasn't much left to do. She also tried to visit her friends as much as possible so she could to say goodbye. They all promised to keep in touch and Tana said she would try to visit them as often as possible.

Ian was doing the same with his friends, exchanging emails and cell numbers along with Facebook. Plus, he was hoping to come out to see his friends whenever his mother came out to visit. It was going to be a tough transition for him at first. Tana at least had the other band members' wives, where Ian had to start from scratch.

When Ryder and Dan flew in, they took Dan straight to the hospital to meet with Nikki and Rose to go over Nikki's case. He was staying at a hotel near the hospital, so he could help Rose with Nikki's therapy until they left for BC. At that point, Rose would hand the reins completely over to him.

The next morning when the trucks arrived for the move, it was chaotic. Tana was busy directing the movers making sure they knew which boxes and what furniture to load. They were emptying out Tana's bedroom first and within an hour had moved on to Ian's. Nikki's furniture had already been moved to the storage facility along with one of the couch sets, the kitchen table set, most of the kitchen stuff plus Tana's good TV and stereo. Everything else Tana was going to have sold off by an auction company. Any money from the auction, Tana decided she was going to put it away for Nikki to help with any moving expenses once she was fully recovered and moved back to Sherwood Park.

Ryder was directing the crew from the second truck in the basement on which boxes and furniture was to be loaded to be hauled to the auction company for sale. Everything was going well. Each crew knew who to ask for clarification on anything and neither Tana nor Ryder left their crew alone for too long.

By the time noon came, the basement was completely empty along with all the bedrooms. The main living spaces were going to be less complicated for the movers because there were piles in each room specifically marked *'Langley'* and *'Auction'* on the boxes. Ryder made sure to watch as each load was taken out that it went to the right truck while Tana started to clean the basement.

She swept and vacuumed the floors, having already cleaned the bathroom the day before. After checking all the windows to make sure they were closed and locked, she headed upstairs just as the last of the *'Langley'* boxes were loaded. She told her crew to head to the garage, where she pointed to the bikes, snowboarding gear and a few other boxes to be loaded.

Ryder's crew finished up with the auction stuff on the main floor, so he directed them out back to the shed instructing them to load all the stuff from there. Tana had already given away most of everything, so there wasn't much left other than some gardening tools, lawn care items, snow shovels and her patio set.

Both moving crews were completely done and the house was empty by two in the afternoon. Ryder gave the crew taking the truck to Langley instructions on how to get to his acreage and they pulled away from the house shortly after to head back to the main depot. The truck would leave the next morning from the Edmonton terminal to the Langley location, then a day after that, it would arrive at Ryder's home. The other crew already had the address of the auction house, so they left once they knew they were done.

Ryder was flying back early afternoon the next day with Dan, the kids and the dogs while Tana was planning to drive her truck back alone. The drive would take ten to twelve hours straight and Tana was hoping to do it all in one stretch. Ryder was telling her to take her time and stop for the night to rest seeing she wouldn't be leaving the city until late in the afternoon.

"I really don't like the idea of you trying to push through driving all night and possibly falling asleep behind the wheel. Having my wife killed is not what I want. Especially seeing we just got through one close call with Nikki."

"I'll be careful. I promise." Tana said as she tried to reassure him that she could handle it.

"I still don't understand why you don't sell your truck. We can get you a new one in Langley." Ryder resisted her wanting to drive her truck back to Langley since she brought it up when they got the offer on the house.

Tana was busy wiping down counters and cabinets when Ryder brought her issue back up.

"Because I like my truck. It's a good truck. The dog barrier is already in place and I have everything the way I like it. Plus, there's nothing wrong with it." Tana hopped up on the counter and began wiping the upper cabinets down while Ryder continued wiping down the appliances. They were almost done cleaning the house.

Tana had done a massive cleaning a few days ago, so they were mainly cleaning up after the movers.

"Baby I get that, but it's a long drive. It would be much easier if you just sold it and came with us on the plane tomorrow. We can get you any truck you want back home and have it set up however you like."

Tana finished the cabinets and Ryder held his hands up to help her down. Once both of her feet were back on the floor, he pulled her into his arms.

"Tana, I know how independent you are and how you don't want me to come across as trying to tell you what to do. But is a truck really worth it?"

Tana rolled her eyes and shook her head. "Ryder, you're being foolish. Hundreds of people make that drive every day. I'll be fine."

"And what if I was to say you're my wife and as your husband, what I say goes?" Ryder looked at her trying to seem serious.

"Then you'd have a huge fight on your hands. I don't take orders." Tana said looking more serious than Ryder.

"A fight? *Hmmm*, so then we could have make-up sex." Ryder slid his hands south, cupping her bottom as he pulled her close.

Tana's expression softened as she realized he wasn't serious and was just teasing her.

"I'd rather skip the fight and just have sex." She said honestly.

Ryder nodded agreeing with her. "Then you'll sell your truck and fly back with us?"

Tana dropped her head into his chest and groaned. He was relentless. She had a feeling that he wasn't going to back down until she either gave in or she left in her truck.

Not really wanting it to come to either one, she decided to appease him just a little. "What if I tell you I'll think about it?"

Ryder looked victorious. "You don't have much time. The plane leaves tomorrow afternoon."

"I'll let you know before we go to bed. How about that? Then if I decide to fly back, we can just take the truck to a dealership and set up a trade in credit. I have the entire house as profit, so I don't care about not getting top dollar. I certainly wouldn't get much for it at the auction either."

Ryder leaned down and kissed her hard. "I'd like to take you to bed right now." He murmured in her ear.

"There are no beds!" Tana laughed at him.

Ryder shrugged and suggested they could use the floor. But when Tana glanced at her watch, she shook her head.

"Tempting as hell but Ian will be home from his last day of school any minute. Plus, the realtor is due to show up soon to collect the keys. So we had better finish cleaning."

Ryder groaned and reluctantly let her go. He adjusted himself in his jeans as his substantial erection was straining painfully against the zipper.

"Cleaning isn't exactly what I was hoping to finish." He grumbled as he picked up the broom and started to sweep the floors.

Tana giggled and got back to work washing the floors behind him.

By the time Ian came home fifteen minutes later, both Tana and Ryder were loading the cleaning supplies into the back of her truck to be dropped off in Nikki's storage unit on their way to the hotel. It wasn't long after Ian came home that the realtor arrived and Tana handed over the remaining keys after she locked up. Ryder called the dogs into the truck while Tana signed the final papers, double-checking the information on file for the last papers and the funds to be couriered to.

When everything looked to be in order, she shook hands with the realtor and climbed into her truck.

She and Ian took one last look at the house then Tana backed out of the driveway for the last time. She looked pensive for a moment and Ryder asked her if she was all right.

"Yeah. It's just we only had that house for a few years but so much has happened since I bought it. I mean I met you, we're married now and well, lots of big changes."

Ryder smiled as he looked out the window. "I know. I remember walking past here the day, I met you and seeing you stretching. Then you making me face the Spanish Inquisition when I asked you out to dinner."

Tana burst out laughing. "I guess I did grill you kinda hard. But I wasn't willing to sell out my integrity for an in-town booty call."

"That wasn't my intention at all. I was just completely fascinated and intrigued by you. Yeah, I thought you were beautiful, but I wasn't looking for a booty call."

"I know." Tana said as she pulled up to the storage facility and entered the gate code. "But at the time I didn't know that, so I had to make it clear that I wasn't just your next piece of ass."

The gate rolled open and Tana drove to Nikki's unit. Hopping out, she unlocked the padlock and rolled up the door as Ryder unloaded the cleaning supplies into the storage unit. Then they closed and locked the door to the unit and headed back out to the main gate where Tana entered the code again.

"So, then why were you so open with me about your past?" Ryder was curious and had never thought to ask her until now.

Tana shrugged and was silent for a moment before she replied. "After I grilled you and you seemed so flustered with my questions, I just felt at ease with you. Like I could trust you not to judge me. It's hard to explain. I guess I just got a good vibe off you."

Ryder smiled and took her hand, kissing it. "Drawn to each other right from the beginning."

Tana glanced at him and agreed as she drove to the hotel.

"Believe me. There's not a day that goes by that I don't thank fate for having me on that trail and Chloe for tripping you." Ryder said giving her a side long glance.

Tana stared straight ahead watching the road. "Me too."

After arriving at the hotel, she parked and all three of them unloaded their bags. Tana and Ryder were planning to go to visit Nikki for a while that evening after checking in. Ian wanted to stay behind and Tana asked him to keep watch on the dogs for them.

Nikki had spent the morning in therapy and the afternoon with her friends saying a temporary goodbye until she was fully recovered and able to move back. Even Brad had been spending as much time with her as he could outside of his work schedule now that school was done for the semester.

As Tana and Ryder walked toward Nikki's room, they could hear Brad's voice and her laughing. Tana and Ryder smiled at each other and lightly knocked on the door before walking into the room.

"Hi Mom." Nikki was sitting on her bed with her boot resting on a pillow. Brad was sitting beside her, facing her with an arm across her legs.

"Hi Sweetheart. How are you feeling today?" Tana came up to kiss the top of her head and said hi to Brad.

"Not bad. Still a little tired, but Rose and Dan said that'll be normal for a while."

Ryder came up and gave her a hug. "Ready for the big move tomorrow? No more hospital food."

"Yeah. Getting out of here is going to feel great, but I still wish I didn't have to go away." She took Brad's hand and looked at him sadly.

"It's only temporary and it's for you to get better, Honey." Brad said kissing the back of her hand.

The four some visited until the night nurse came and kicked them out even though Nikki protested. She claimed that she wasn't tired and begged for them to be able to stay a little longer.

"You get paroled tomorrow morning. We can all go for a nice big breakfast before heading to the airport." Ryder whispered to her as he leaned down to hug her goodnight.

"*Mmmm*... Sounds like a plan to me. Um... can Brad come too and maybe see us off at the airport?" Nikki asked quietly.

Ryder nodded then stepped back to let Tana say goodnight.

"Night Mom. I love you." Nikki hugged her mother tight with her one arm.

"See you in the morning. I love you too, Baby Girl." Tana crossed the room to where Ryder was waiting as Brad kissed Nikki goodnight and she told him to meet her here early in the morning.

All three left the room together and as they walked to the elevator, Brad looked a little nervous. He glanced first at Tana then Ryder and let out a long sigh.

"Um… Mrs. Evans, Mr. Evans, I really need to talk to you both."

Tana and Ryder both turned to look at Brad. He was looking at them and fidgeting with his car keys.

"I really love Nikki and almost losing her last month was the worst experience of my life. I… uh, I wanted to show you this." He pulled a small box out of his pocket and showed them a two hearted white gold and diamond ring.

"It's a promise ring. I want to marry Nikki, but I want to wait till we're both done school and have lived together for a while before actually proposing to her. But I'd like both of your permission to give this to her tomorrow. So she knows I'll be here waiting for her."

Tana smiled at Brad. He was so nervous. What he was doing was sweet and she could see how much they loved each other. When she looked up at Ryder, he was looking down at her with raised eyebrows.

"I know I should be asking her real dad Mr. Evans, but she told me what happened and she said she wants nothing to do with him anymore." Brad closed the box and put it back in his pocket.

"Brad, you're both young and I see how much you do care for Nikki. I'm glad you aren't proposing now, or I might have an issue with it." Tana said.

They made it out to the parkade and were standing by Brad's car as they spoke.

"I think what you're doing is very sweet and giving Nikki that promise ring is probably the nicest gesture you could do to reassure her that you're here for her while she is recovering. As long as the two of you agree not to get married until school is done, you have my blessing." Tana said giving Brad's arm a squeeze.

Brad turned to Ryder and swallowed hard, waiting for Ryder's decision.

Ryder shrugged. "What can I say? Hurt her and I hurt you. But I don't think that'll be an issue here. You look at Nikki the same way I look at Tana. Just make sure you guys don't rush anything. Enjoy being young before you settle into marriage and kids."

Brad grinned looking relieved. "I don't want to rush anything. Seeing her in that coma made me realize what I have with her and how I want to make this last."

They congratulated Brad, said goodnight and headed off to Tana's truck as Brad got in his car and drove away. Ryder stood at the door and looked at Tana through the truck as she took her seat. He looked very sad and concerned.

"Ryder?" Tana called to him seeing he looked upset.

Ryder searched her eyes with his. "Please, Tana. Sell your truck. I know what I have too, and I don't want to risk you getting into an accident or caught in a rock slide or something."

Tana could see how much her decision to drive her truck back to Langley by herself really bothered him. Originally, she thought he was just being over protective, but seeing they had almost lost Nikki to a car accident and how it had affected each of them, she was now understanding his concern. Nikki's accident hit Ryder in a way he had never known existed.

"Okay." She whispered. "I'll sell my truck."

The words were barely out of her mouth before Ryder was on her side of the truck pulling her out and into his arms.

"Thank you." He whispered into her hair as he buried his face in her neck, just breathing her in.

After a few moments, he released her and gave her a quick kiss before they got into the truck and left the hospital.

Back at the hotel suite, Ian was watching TV in his room when Tana and Ryder called him out into the sitting area to tell him the news about Brad and Nikki.

"Oh wow. That's awesome. Brad's a cool guy and has always been good to Nik. I'm happy for them." Ian said.

"Just don't say anything yet. He asked our permission first. He's planning on giving Nikki the ring tomorrow before we fly out." Tana informed him so there was no chance of spoiling the surprise.

They told Ian that they would be going to the dealership first thing in the morning to sell the truck, so they would be getting a car and driver for the rest of the day until they had to go to the airport. Even Ian admitted he was relieved and thought it was a better idea for Tana not to make that trip alone.

"It's not that you couldn't, Mom. But you've never driven there before and without someone with you, I was worried something might happen. What if you broke down and no one came along or stopped to help?"

Ryder looked at Tana with an all-knowing look and she told Ian not to worry because it was no longer an issue.

~~

The next morning, Tana and Ryder were up early to get her truck dealt with. They left Ian and the dogs at the hotel then headed to the nearest dealership. Speaking to someone there, they were able to agree to take Tana's truck in and issue her a transferable trade in credit toward a new purchase at the dealership in Langley. It had actually gone much easier than Tana thought. When both she and Ryder removed her license plate and personal belongings from the truck, she was sadder to see her truck go than her house.

Ryder didn't harass her about making the right choice. Over the past few days, his wife had seen damn near everything she worked so hard for over the years either sold off, packed up to go to Langley or carted off to auction. He knew she was bound to be a little emotional, so he just took the bag of belongings from her and put his arm around her shoulders as they walked to the waiting limo.

Back at the hotel, Ian was up and ready. He knew that they were going to pick Nikki up from the hospital and go for breakfast before getting on the plane to BC, so he took the dogs outside to walk them for his mother while he waited for his parents to return.

He was just heading back to the front entrance when he saw a limo pull into the parking lot. It parked off to one side and Tana and Ryder climbed out.

"Hey Bud." Ryder called out to him.

Ian walked over to them and his mother thanked him for taking the girls out for her as they headed back inside. When they got back to their suite, all three of them packed their bags then gathered up the dog's travel dishes and food. Everyone was ready and checking out in less than twenty minutes. While Ryder finished with the front desk, Tana and Ian headed out to the waiting limo and got the dogs in. When Ryder was done checking out, he slid in beside Tana. A moment later, the car got moving.

It was still early so traffic was light as the driver headed to the highway to take them to the city. When they made it to the hospital, there was still plenty of time to pick Nikki and Dan up then get some breakfast before they had to be at the airport. The driver of their car had already agreed to keep the dogs while they got Nikki and even when they would stop for breakfast.

Tana was in an exceptionally good mood as they made their way up to the third floor for the last time. Her little girl was coming home. Nikki's survival and recovery were an incredible testament to her determination and Tana was never so glad to have a stubborn child.

As they walked up the hall toward Nikki's room, they saw Dan and Rose standing outside her door. When they noticed Tana, Ryder and Ian coming, Dan waved them over mouthing *'hurry'*. Tana and Ryder jogged over as Dan put his finger to his lips. Ian was right behind them and was about to ask what was going on when Dan pointed into the room.

They could see Brad had pulled the little box out of his pocket. He was holding Nikki's hand and talking to her while she was smiling up at him. Brad opened the box and slid the pretty little ring onto Nikki's left hand and the little group waiting at the doorway could hear Brad clearly.

"Nikki, I promise. I'll be here waiting for you when you're all better and can come back to me. And once we're done school, I want to marry you. But I want to wait for us to finish school first, okay?"

Tears filled Nikki's eyes. She was beaming at Brad as she nodded and kissed him. When he took her into his arms, that's when Nikki saw everyone at her doorway and laughed.

"I guess I don't have to tell you guys." She sniffed smiling.

Brad let her go then turned around as everyone came in to give Nikki hugs and to look at her ring. It was very pretty and looked lovely on her. Tana had tears in her own eyes as she hugged her daughter then gave Brad a hug as well. Ryder shook his hand as Ian smiled and told Brad that he was really happy for them.

Dan even congratulated them both then got down to the business of checking Nikki out with Rose. Tana busied herself going around Nikki's room and packing up her belongings. Brad had already agreed to take her trinkets and stuffed animals back home to his place for the time being, so he helped pack those up into a big bag the hospital gave him. Nikki grabbed a purple bear holding a heart out of the bag.

"Not this one. I'm keeping this one with me." She said as she clamped it between her cast and her side.

Brad smiled at her as she looked back at him with a serious look. He had given her that bear when she was still in her coma.

"My bear." She said adamantly and kissed him.

Nikki's ribs had healed nicely and there was very little pain left there. The cuts and bruises had healed and the scars were fading. There were only two scars on her face that bothered her the most. One was a laceration that had been pretty bad just in front her left ear and the scar from where the catheter had been inserted on her forehead just below her hairline.

Her leg was doing extremely well and she was looking forward to getting rid of her boot in the next few weeks. Her arm was going to remain casted for a bit longer. That break had been far worse than her leg and the doctors felt more time was needed to ensure it healed properly. It still ached once in a while, but it was getting better. Her head was still the worst. She was suffering from headaches and dizziness that she had been told could take weeks, months or even years to go away. She had even been warned they might never fully go away. But as annoying as they were, Nikki felt it was a small price to pay to still be alive.

Rose and Dan came back into her room with some forms for Nikki to sign and asked if she was ready to get out of there.

"Oh my God, yes." Nikki exhaled as she hobbled to her wheelchair with Brad's help.

She sat down and Tana did a final once over in the room to make sure nothing was forgotten as the group headed out of the hospital for the last time.

Down at the waiting limo, the driver had seen them all coming. He got out and took the dogs out of the back so Nikki could get in and get settled. When the dogs saw her, they started to act crazy trying to get to her, so Ryder went over to settle them down. He brought them over to Nikki one at a time, so they could sniff her and check her out. Each of them must have sensed she had been hurt because for once none of them tried to jump all over her. They stood close enough for her to reach out to them and whimpered but did not get in her way.

It was time to go, so Rose said her goodbyes to Nikki, giving her a hug before helping her into the limo. Ian and Dan followed after her, then Tana. Ryder handed the leashes in to her one at a time and each dog bailed in as they were called then finally Ryder slid in after the last dog got settled. Leaning out the limo door, he told Brad where to meet them for breakfast while the driver loaded Nikki's bags in the trunk with all the others.

After a short drive, they stopped at a nearby family style restaurant that was on their way to the airport. It was well known for their delicious breakfasts and everyone ate until they felt like bursting. Tana was impressed how much Nikki's appetite was back up and that she was looking healthier again. Brad thanked them for the meal then proceeded to say his goodbyes to Nikki, which enticed a few more tears from her.

Watching Nikki and Brad's exchanges, Ryder nudged Tana. "Remind you of someone?"

Tana smiled and laughed. "Every time I look at her, I see so much of me."

Ryder agreed then ordered a soup and sandwich meal for the driver as a small thank you for watching the dogs for them while they were inside.

Out in the parking lot, they climbed back into the limo while Ryder gave the driver the meal with a more than generous tip and he thanked Ryder graciously. Telling him they really appreciated what he had done for them, Ryder slid back into the limo and they pulled back out onto the main road.

Once the car arrived at the airport and got everyone unloaded, getting through security was a challenge. Between Nikki's chair, the dogs and everyone's bags, it took almost an hour to clear security. Ryder ushered everyone through and eventually they all headed off to the private plane. After everyone was on the plane and the dogs were in their kennels, Tana and Ryder both flopped down into their seats.

"I'm exhausted!" He gasped as the flight attendant did her pre-flight rounds.

Dan helped get Nikki in her seat then sat close to her to monitor how the pressure and altitude changes she would experience in the flight affected her.

Tana sat beside Ryder and leaned her head on his shoulder. "It's the last time we have to do this."

She tried to comfort him, but he shook his head disagreeing with her. "Nope. We'll have to do this again when Nikki is ready to move back."

"Well, it'll be easier. We won't have the dogs with us and not as many people either."

Ryder looked at Tana. "But just as much stuff I'm sure. Nikki doesn't exactly pack light."

Nikki tossed her bear at him. "Hey, don't bitch. Most of my stuff's in storage!"

Ryder tossed the bear back at her. "And you didn't have to pack any of it either. That your mother and I took care of, so I know you have a ton of stuff!"

Ryder teased and Nikki laughed then stuck her tongue out at him. The captain came over the intercom just then telling them they had clearance to push back and everyone felt the plane jolt as it began to back up.

As the plane taxied out to the runway and took off into the air, Tana and Ryder talked between themselves trying to figure out where everything was going to go. Ryder had everything they needed in his place already, so it was only Tana's personal stuff, and Ian's stuff that had to be put away. Some things like her books, movies, and the board games they had decided to keep were going to be a challenge to find a place for.

"Well, we could always put an addition onto the house and build you a home office where all that stuff could go. This way if you're working you can have a place of your own to work from." Ryder offered.

Tana gaped at him. "Are you kidding? Why not just change one of the spare rooms into a home office? That would be much easier and cheaper."

Ryder frowned. "I'm not worried about the cost if it's going to increase the functionality of the house and give you the space that you need."

"Well, I am. Ryder I'm not in this for your money. I think changing one of the current rooms would be a better idea. Do you really need five spare rooms?"

"Correction. There will only be three until Nikki is better. Then it will be four once she moves," Ryder corrected her.

"Does it really matter? That's still a lot of spare rooms." Tana didn't want him to make too much out of this.

It seemed so simple to her just to convert one spare room to a home office for her.

"Don't forget Baby, when we throw parties, I usually have people staying over in those rooms. Plus, when other people come into town to visit, with all the spare rooms we don't have to worry at all about not having space for someone."

Tana rolled her eyes still not seeing his side of it. "Well, I can't say that I agree with you. But if you want to put an addition onto the house, don't do it just on my account. Do it for more than just an office for me."

Ryder put him arm around her shoulders. "Look Baby, I know you're concerned about this, so why don't we set one of the spare rooms up for now and talk more about an addition later."

Tana glanced at Ryder then looked out the window. "I'd feel much better if we did that. I just can't justify all the expense, mess, noise and inconvenience for one room."

Ryder pulled her as close to him as he could in the airplane seat and kissed her. "I wouldn't go through all of that for just one room. We would have to figure out what else we want for space and then see if it could be done. You know, I've always wanted a full studio. One that would be capable of recording albums. I could always look at getting that done and a proper office for you as well."

Tana took his hand in hers and smiled. "Right. You and the guys rocking out in the room next to me, just what I need to listen to while on a phone conference. I'm sure that will go over great with my staff."

Ryder shrugged. "Sound-proofing isn't that big of a deal. I had it done before."

Tana relented and said that they could figure it out but wanted to wait until Nikki was better and back on her own.

The flight was peaceful. In no time, they were banking out over the Pacific Ocean to come in for their landing into Vancouver International. The captain came over the intercom and advised them of the landing as well let them know it was a very warm twenty-eight degrees outside.

Once they taxied to the gate and the doors were opened, everyone got ready to disembark. Dan set Nikki's wheelchair up just outside of the doors. Ryder helped Nikki out while Tana and Ian got the dogs out of the kennels. After Ryder got Nikki safely to Dan, he went back to help Ian and Tana gather up everyone's bags. The efficient group headed up the gangway and out into the terminal where there was a car waiting for them in their usual spot.

While Ryder and the driver got the bags in the trunk, Dan got Nikki into the car then everyone else followed, including the dogs. After everyone was in and settled the driver pulled out of the parkade and headed in the direction of Langley.

The hour drive passed by quickly for them. Ryder was excited to be back home with no more bouncing back and forth to be with the woman he loved. He held Tana close to him and looked down at her with a little half smile.

"What are you so happy for?" She asked him softly.

Ryder glanced out the window, "Oh just thinking how nice it's going to be not to have to bounce between your place and mine anymore. My family is all here now. Home."

Chapter 16

Ryder was sitting out on his back patio watching Bailey, Chloe and Kordie romp around playing in the enclosed yard. They were extremely happy to have so much more space than Tana's old backyard to play in. There was also the whole fifteen acres they could run on as well.

Tana, Ian, and Nikki were all busy putting their stuff away. Dan had helped to get Nikki inside and showed her the aids that Ryder had installed for her in her bathroom and in the other areas that she would need until she was back to her old self again. After being confident she was going to be all right, he left her to her mother's care and went home for the rest of the day.

He would be back every day for her therapy until she was cleared by the doctors. Nikki was hoping to be home by the end of July, but Dan was telling her not to push herself too hard. He would be the one to push her as hard as was safe for her.

Tana wandered into Nikki's room and found her lying down with her arm over her eyes.

"Nikki? What's wrong?" Tana came up to her and asked looking worried.

Nikki uncovered her eyes and squinted at her mom. "I'm really tired and I have a massive headache. I think it's from the flight."

Tana nodded, "It could be. I'll get your meds and some milk. Then you can have a nap."

Nikki thanked her mother as Tana left the room headed to the kitchen to get Nikki her pain killers and some milk. When she came back, Nikki hadn't moved. She looked tired and when she sat up, she put her arm out to steady herself.

"Another dizzy spell?" Tana asked quickly setting the glass and pill down, so she could grab a hold of Nikki to help stabilize her.

"Yeah. God, I hope these go away soon. They're pissing me off." Nikki looked frustrated. When her head had cleared, she took her medication and lay back down.

Tana tucked her in and kissed her. "I know. Give it time."

She left Nikki to rest. When she got back into the kitchen, she took out a notebook from one of the drawers to write down what happened.

Ryder came in and saw her writing in a notebook asking what she was doing.

"Nikki is complaining she's really tired and has a massive headache, so I gave her one of her pain killers. When she sat up, she had another dizzy spell. I'm going to keep track of this stuff in case we need to have a reference if something else happens or she falls." Tana explained without looking up.

"Good idea." Ryder said grabbing a beer out of the fridge. He grabbed a cooler for Tana and held it out to her.

"Thanks." Tana said putting the notebook aside and taking a long drink.

Ryder took her hand and led her out back to the patio. They sat down in a couple of chairs quietly sipping their drinks, just relaxing and enjoying the view until Ryder's cell interrupted them.

He answered, putting the phone on speaker. Tana could hear Ben's voice asking if everyone was back home safe.

"Yeah, we are." Ryder said out loud.

"What about Tana? She was driving, wasn't she?"

"I'm right here Ben. Ryder convinced me to sell my truck and just get a new one."

"Oh, good. So how is Nikki doing? We're all dying to come see her, but we don't want to overwhelm her if she's not up to it."

"Um… she's having a rough day today." Tana explained to Ben and he said he understood.

"I'll tell Carla she has to wait until next week then. Give her a little more time to settle in and adjust."

"Yeah that would probably be better." Ryder said.

They chatted for a bit then Ben hung up to go tell Carla the news.

"I would love to throw a party as a welcome home for you guys, but I don't want to overdo it for Nikki." Ryder said as he finished his beer.

"Yeah, me too. That would be fun, but I think maybe in a few weeks might work. She should be out of that boot by then and getting around easier. I think the more she's up and around the better the dizzy spells will get too. Now that she's out of the hospital and free to move around more, we should see some improvement. It's just hard right now with her stuck to limited mobility."

Ryder agreed. "Oh, don't forget. Tomorrow the truck is arriving. It's going to be a very busy day."

~~~

Later that evening after dinner, Tana and Ryder went into each spare room to assess which one should be turned into an office for Tana until the addition was decided on. They moved the current furniture into one of the other rooms, turning it into a double room and were satisfied with how it looked for the time being.

When they looked, Nikki was still asleep. Tana had checked on her regularly but wasn't seeing anything out of the ordinary with her, so she just left her alone. Ian was downstairs alternating between watching TV and playing video games until he went to bed.

Tana and Ryder had moved some things around in the master bedroom after dealing with the spare rooms and didn't finish until midnight. They felt that they were fully ready for when the truck arrived the next day and were both exhausted.

Ryder flopped across the enormous bed and groaned. "Thank God, I'm a musician and not a mover. I'm not cut out for that shit." The past week of packing and moving all sorts of furniture into the storage unit for Nikki plus everything in Tana's house had already taken its toll on them both.

"I hear you. I ached all over from moving that stuff in the spare room. Now after moving more in here, I'm really sore." Tana agreed.

Ryder drug his long frame off the bed and staggered into the bathroom. Within seconds, Tana could hear the Jacuzzi being filled. She perked up a little at the thought of a nice relaxing soak and wandered into the bathroom to join her husband.

He was seated on the tub's platform, completely undressed. Ryder reached back behind himself and turned the Jacuzzi on. The jets hummed to life and the huge tub was instantly filled with bubbles. He helped Tana to undress and step into the steaming water. Then stood up and stepped in himself, settling down into the relaxing heat as he pulled Tana's back to his chest.

Ryder wrapped his arms around her and rested his head back against the edge of the tub while Tana rested hers against his chest and arms. He could smell her perfume in the steam as it wafted up and around him. There was something about it that calmed him and filled his heart. Tana's scent was addictive to him and he never wanted to be without it.

~~~

The next morning when the dogs woke Tana up at seven, she peeked in on Nikki before heading out for her morning run. She was still sleeping, which made Tana frown. Nikki had been out for almost sixteen hours and she made a mental note to speak to Dan about it.

After getting the dogs clipped into their leashes, Tana slipped out the front door. It was a beautiful summer morning with the sun shining and a soft kiss of warm breeze. Pulling the door closed behind her, she took a moment, closed her eyes and inhaled the clean fresh air.

With a big smile, she slipped her sunglasses on and clapped her hands signaling to the dogs they were starting their run. At first her strides were short to warm up, then within fifty meters, they began to lengthen, her pace picking up. Reaching the gates, she snuck out quickly and turned right heading up the road falling to that coveted runner's zone.

Her feet pounded the pavement as she lost herself in the scenery. It was absolutely beautiful in the morning sunshine and the fresh air was blissful in her lungs. With her arms pumping along at her sides and her music blaring away from her iPod, Tana felt free.

For weeks, her morning runs had lost their impact on her. Since Nikki's accident she had done them more out of duty than passion. But this morning, her first morning in her new home, her passion came through all the tears, all the waiting and all the pain.

With each kilometer, Tana could feel the stress and tension of the past month's nightmares slip away, freeing her soul and recharging her spirit. She ran in this zone until her ten-kilometer playlist reset on her iPod. She stopped briefly to stretch and reset the playlist as she turned around to head back finding the same peaceful place she had been in before.

After reaching the gates again and sneaking through as they started to open, Tana sprinted up the driveway as fast as she could all the way to the house until she touched the wall by the front door. Breathing heavily, she began to stretch as she caught her breath. Knowing she had worked her muscles hard, she stretched longer than usual.

When she was done, she stepped back inside releasing the dogs from their leashes and they immediately made a beeline for their water dish. Tana followed them into the kitchen for a drink of water for herself. She was standing at the sink chugging her water with her hair plastered to her head and her clothes sticking to her with sweat when Nikki slowly made her way into the kitchen with her cane.

"Good morning, sleepyhead. How do you feel?" Tana said as she poured herself a second glass of water and pulled her iPod off.

Nikki eased herself into one of the island chairs. "Fantastic. I slept so well, I can't believe it."

Tana smiled, relieved. "No more headache?"

Nikki shook her head. "Nah. And I swear if I didn't have this boot on, I could walk much better."

"Next week, hopefully." Tana said as she kissed the side of her daughter's head. "Maybe this will be just what you needed to recover. Fresh mountain air and a nice comfy bed to rest in. You should probably get ready for Dan. He'll be here by noon and it's after ten already."

Nikki agreed and after she slowly stood up, hoping to not bring on another dizzy spell, she hobbled her way back to her room to get dressed. Dan said he would be working her hard, so she wanted to wait until after her physiotherapy session to shower. Tana saw her back to her room then ran up the stairs to her own room. Ryder was still sleeping, so Tana quietly stripped out of her running clothes and wiped herself down with a wash cloth to get the worst of the sweat off before she went back into the main bedroom.

She stood by Ryder's side and looked down at him lying there sleeping. His chest rose and fell with his breath and he looked beautifully peaceful. His light brown hair was sleep tousled and his long muscular form was stretched out across the huge bed covered only by the sheet.

Tana carefully placed a bare knee up on the bed beside him and climbed up. She lay down beside him, slipping beneath the sheet then trailed light kisses down his chest and down to his abdomen. She felt him stir and inhale deeply through his nose as she continued to kiss her way south until she reached his groin.

Using a feather light touch, she brushed the head of Ryder's penis with her fingertips then bent to place a gentle kiss in the same place as her fingers continued down the length of his stirring erection. Ryder groaned out sleepily as he woke to his wife's mouth engulfing him and sucking him right to the back of her throat.

Instantly, he went rock hard and his hands reached down to caress her. Tana continued working her tongue around the thick veins and the ridge of his head as Ryder gasped and moaned in pleasure. Continuing to torment her husband with her tongue, Tana withdrew Ryder's erection from her mouth for a moment, murmured a sultry good morning before hollowing her cheeks and sucking him back in deep into her throat.

"*Mmmm…* yeah, Baby. So nice." Ryder rasped.

Tana's head raised and lowered with every stroke of her hot silky mouth. Ryder's hips flexed in unison to her as his climax built. His left hand fisted in her hair while his right gripped the sheet beneath him and he gasped at the force of her jaws working against his engorged flesh.

"Oh God Tana." Ryder stiffened and growled through clenched teeth, twitching as he came hard.

Tana stroked and caressed him as she kissed his shaft and head then made her way back up toward his face, kissing his incredible body all the way. When she reached his face, she smiled down at him and kissed his mouth. He ran his hands up her body caressing her as she kissed him.

"Good morning Love." Tana smiled and lay down next to Ryder.

"No, not good. Great." He responded as he rolled over to caress her.

Tana writhed beneath Ryder's hands. His touch was making her skin tingle and set fire to her own need. Her sex throbbed for attention and Ryder was taking his time reaching it. She moaned as he caressed the sides of her hips and down her thighs. Leaning down to kiss her, Ryder's eyes searched his wife's.

"I love you." He breathed as he shifted down her body and planted a kiss at the apex of her thighs.

"Yes." Tana panted, "Right there. God, how I want you Ryder."

Her legs parted and her hips lifted as Ryder settled between her thighs and lowered his mouth to her pulsing clit. Tana's head fell back against the bed as his tongue caressed her nub coaxing it to come out to play. He flicked and swirled his tongue all over the exposed tip of her clit making her writhe and cry out from the exquisite sensation.

Fire built in her belly and coursed in her veins as Ryder's tongue pressed into her opening, laving at her. He rubbed her clit with the pad of his thumb sending more heat through her veins. Tana's back bowed off the bed and she inhaled sharply as Ryder's tongue caressed from her entrance right up to her clit again, swirling around the now raging bundle of nerves drawing her orgasm out. The cords in her neck stood out as she called out to Ryder moments before her body locked up and shook.

Tana was panting heavily as she came down from her high. Ryder continued to caress her, kissing her sides and stomach in an attempt to calm her.

"*Shhh*... Baby." Ryder soothed.

He made his way back up to her head and kissed her mouth. Moving carefully, Ryder made his way to the floor and pulled Tana up.

"Come Baby. Shower time."

He led her to the bathroom where he got the shower going while Tana brushed her teeth. Then Ryder brushed his before he began to shave as Tana slipped into the shower. She washed her hair and just as she began to wash her body, Ryder joined her.

"Did you like your wake-up call?" Tana asked as she spread soap all over her lithe little body.

"No. I hated it. Every miserable second." Ryder teased as he slid his hands around her giving her a kiss.

"Oh. In that case, I guess I won't do that again." Tana teased him right back.

He growled at her, pinning her against the wall then proved to her how much he loved her wake-up call by taking her from behind and pushing himself into her depths repeatedly until they both came again.

After finishing their shower and as Tana and Ryder both got dressed, Ryder offered to take her into town to look for a new truck before the moving truck arrived with all the stuff from Sherwood Park. It wasn't expected until dinnertime, so that gave them plenty of free time before it arrived.

"I know you like your independence and want to have your own vehicle, so instead of fighting with you about it being okay to use anything in the garage, how about we get your truck. Dan will be here with Nikki. So will the housekeeper and Ian. I think we can safely sneak away for a few hours."

Tana was pulling on a pair of jean shorts that made him arch a brow as a half-smile curled his lips.

"Yeah. I'd like that." She called over her shoulder as she walked into the closet to find a top.

She was rummaging around when she finally found what she was looking for. It was a nice purple sheer top with a gothic cross in black and silver studs. She had a black bra on under it and when she emerged from the closet, Ryder's half smile was wiped from his face. It was replaced with a look that dripped sinful thoughts.

"Or maybe we can just stay up here and I can rip those clothes off you." Ryder growled as he strode toward her.

Tana dodged him giggling and headed for the door. "Oh no. I want my own vehicle. We're going."

Falling to his knees, Ryder pouted as he crawled to her. "But you look so hot."

Tana giggled harder as he crawled up to her and sat back on his knees begging. Shaking her head, she planted a bare foot in the middle of his chest and shoved him back.

"Later. I want my truck."

Ryder collapsed onto the floor dramatically as Tana opened the door to leave. Growling loudly, he bolted after her. Tana screeched as he chased her down the stairs through the main floor and into the kitchen laughing. When Tana ran to one side of the island, Ryder stood on the other side with that sinful look intensely burning into Tana's eyes.

"Come here." Ryder growled again and Tana arched a brow.

"It that an order?"

Ryder shook his head. "Not at all. I just want you here in front of me so I can kiss you."

Tana slinked around the island and Ryder snatched her up in his arms, taking her right off the floor and crushing his lips down on hers.

"I should take you right back upstairs and make you beg for mercy all day. I don't want to take you out in public and share you. I want to keep you for myself." Ryder rasped and kissed her again.

She smiled back at him and ran her nails up his neck into his hair sending shivers down his spine.

"It's amazing how nuts you drive me woman." Ryder said as he set her down.

Tana held Ryder's face in her hands. "I can't get enough of you either Ryder Evans."

"Jeez you two. Take it upstairs." Ian said as he walked into the room.

"I'm trying to, but your mom won't let me. She'd rather go shopping for a new truck."

Tana swatted Ryder's ass laughing and asked Ian if he wanted to come with them. He declined but asked if he could go quadding instead. Ryder agreed providing he wore his helmet and was careful. Happy, Ian thanked them and took off to the toy barn.

Tana went to check on Nikki while Ryder spoke to Mira, letting her know that he and Mrs. Evans were going out after Dan arrived for Nikki. If there were any issues, she could reach either of them on their cell phones.

Nikki was slowly making her way back to the kitchen with her mother and Tana quickly got her something to eat. While she filled her in on their plans to go get a new truck, the doorbell rang. Dan had arrived.

"Okay Mom. I'll be fine." Nikki assured her and Ryder went to answer the doorbell.

Dan was brought to the kitchen and Nikki looked up and said hi.

"Are you ready to work hard?" He asked Nikki, teasing her that seeing she missed out on yesterday's therapy that they were going to double up today.

Tana went over her notes from the day before with him asking if there was any cause for concern with how long Nikki had slept. Dan shook his head and assured her that it was to be expected.

"No one really rests well in a hospital. With the flight plus being her first night home it was all a big change, so her body took what it needed and rested."

Feeling more relieved Tana thanked Dan and he thanked her for keeping notes.

"You'd be surprised how much that can help doctors assess what happened or narrow down what could be wrong in an emergency situation." He said encouraging Tana to continue until Nikki's recovery was complete.

With a much lighter heart and an easy step, Tana hurried over to where Ryder was waiting at the door to the garage. Kissing him with a smile, she slipped into a pair of sandals with a renewed sparkle in her eyes.

Ryder loved having his family all home and under one roof again. No more going to the hospital every day or worrying if Nikki was going to be all right. She was home for now and recovering beautifully. His wife was back to her old self, full of spunk, energy and just the happy person she had always been. The past month hit her hard and again she pulled through, beating back tragedy. Ryder was just incredibly glad that Nikki had survived and that he had been with Tana through it all, so she didn't have to go through it alone.

Grabbing the keys to the Mustang, they headed to the garage. He loved driving his Mustang so instinctively, he went to the driver's side to get in but had a change of heart and looked over to see if Tana wanted to drive. She was about to grab the passenger door handle when he held the keys out to her.

Tana did a double take and stared at the keys open mouthed. "Are you serious?"

Ryder nodded and walked over to her side of the car.

"But you've never let me drive her before."

Ryder gave her a stern look. "Now be fair. You've never asked."

Tana was in shock. "I always figured this was your baby and if you wanted me to drive, you'd offer."

"Well, I'm offering now. But if you don't want to…" Ryder tried to pull his hand holding the keys away and Tana grabbed it shouting at him.

"No! I want to! Thank you." She stood up on tiptoe and kissed him before she pranced around to the driver's side and got in.

She adjusted all the mirrors and seat while Ryder told her of the difference in the shifting pattern.

"Now give her lots of time coming in and out of reverse. Sometimes the tranny takes a bit to switch. She's old, so give her love." He coached her as Tana started the engine.

Tana nodded and took her time backing the car out of the garage then turning her around looking like she had just died and gone to heaven. Ryder rolled his window down and as Tana did the same, she tied her hair back so it wouldn't be in her face. She slid her sunglasses on then slipped the gearshift into first pulling forward easily without issue and driving smoothly up to the gate.

Playing around with the radio, Ryder found a station that he knew Tana liked. It had lots of top forty mixed in with old school rock and some new rock. He turned up the volume as she pulled through the gate heading into town.

Ryder couldn't help but notice how happy Tana looked driving the Mustang. Sports cars definitely suited her personality, but he thought it was classic cars that really made her shine. Her smile never faltered and with the the wind blowing her ponytail around, she looked sexy as hell. He got to thinking of different cars and maybe getting her one of her own.

Tana noticed him watching her and asked him something. But he couldn't hear her over the stereo, so he reached out and turned it down, asking her to repeat herself.

"Why are you looking at me like that?" She repeated.

"Like what?" He asked not sure what she was talking about.

"You're staring at me and smiling. I can't see your eyes through your sunglasses, but I can feel your eyes on me."

Ryder chuckled. He took her hand off the shifter and squeezed it. "I was just thinking that this kind of car suits you. And you obviously love it."

Tana nodded and told him it was a beautiful car. "But it's yours. I'm just glad you're letting me drive today."

Ryder was too. His sudden change of heart had given him some great ideas to think about.

Tana pulled into the dealership and parked where there were a few empty spaces around to lower the risk of someone bumping the Mustang's doors with their own.

They walked around the lot for a few minutes looking at all of the different SUV's. After a little deliberation Tana decided she loved her Acadia so much that she wanted another one again and Ryder insisted she buy new. Tana never had a brand-new vehicle before and he knew she could more than handle the expense on her own. She had the trade in credit from her old truck plus the sale of her house along with the rest of her accounts.

While she was looking over a deep red 2012 that looked to be fully loaded, with a sunroof and leather seats, Ryder went to get a salesman.

When Ryder returned with one, he lifted his sunglasses and rolled his eyes. Tana picked up on his queue and smothered her smile, letting her professional skills come through.

The salesman was six feet, very well built with jet black hair and a moustache. He introduced himself to Tana as Chad and his demeanor just oozed sleazy. He wore a heavy gold-plated chain around his neck, a big tacky gold ring that looked retro to the early eighties pimp-daddies and a gawdy looking watch. Even his suit had that dated shiny look to it and made Tana want to either laugh or cringe. She could tell he was trying to look successful but, in all reality, it was coming across more desperate, pathetic and arrogant.

When Chad shook Tana's hand, his hand was sweaty and weak, making Tana to want to wipe her hands off afterwards. She lifted her sunglasses and met his muddy dark brown eyes with her intense green ones.

"Hello there. Your husband tells me you're interested in a new Acadia." Chad looked at her, but his eyes barely met hers past his first handshake.

Chad's eyes roved over her body, checking her out. Tana could see Ryder tense his jaw when he saw this creep eying her up and down. She squared her shoulders, now wishing she had worn slacks, heels and a blouse.

"As a matter of fact, I'm interested in this one. What can you tell me about it? What features does this one have?" Tana asked.

Chad glanced at Tana long enough to tell her that it was fully loaded with all the comforts and extras that ladies of her caliber loved. Then he turned and spoke to Ryder about the mechanical and technical features of the truck.

"Excuse me Chad. I'm the one that asked the question. Not my husband. I'd appreciate you directing your answers to me." Tana snapped.

Ryder tried to hide his smile as Chad stammered for a moment then apologized. He continued, trying to excuse his actions by saying generally women like her didn't particularly care about or understand technical specifications.

It was Ryder's turn to see his wife tense as she bit back a snide comment. Instead, she took a deep breath and forced a smile. "Regardless if that's what you're used to, when I ask a question, I expect the answer to be directed to me."

Chad explained the truck's features and specs to her then offered her a test drive. When Tana agreed that would be best, he scurried off to get the keys and a plate.

"Holy shit!" Tana whispered harshly as Chad went out of earshot. "What a jerk!"

Ryder shook his head. "I know. He was the only one around. When he saw me, he just slithered over. Do you want to leave and wait for someone else on another day or go to a different dealership?"

Tana thought for a moment and shook her head. "No, I can handle him."

Ryder grinned. "That's my girl."

Chad returned with the keys and a plate handing the keys to Tana. As he put the plate on the truck, she climbed in adjusting the seats and mirrors to her liking. Ryder climbed in beside her and Chad slid into the backseat once the plate was secured.

Tana started the truck and for the whole test drive, Chad continued to point out different add-ons and luxuries in the vehicle, trumping up the safety and comfort. He also bragged constantly about how many Acadia's he sold weekly and that he had another couple interested in this one if she didn't snatch it up. Tana was sick of listening to his ego stroking by the time they were back at the dealership. The guy was so disgusting, it was nauseating and the heavy smell lingering of his cheap cologne didn't help.

"So, shall we go and crunch some numbers?" Chad spouted arrogantly.

Tana looked over at Ryder then asked Chad to give them a moment as she handed the keys back to him. Agreeing, he took the plate off the truck and headed inside to return it.

"God that was the worst test drive ever." Tana mumbled quietly as they made their way back into the dealership.

"Yeah that guy just didn't let up. I'm amazed he's able to sell cars at all let alone keep a job."

Tana glanced over at Chad quickly and a thought came to her. "How did you introduce yourself to him?"

Ryder looked at her strangely. "What do you mean?"

"Did you tell him your name?"

"Of course I did."

Tana looked at Ryder knowingly seeing Chad's angle now. "He knows who you are."

"What's your point?" Ryder asked not getting where she was going.

"You're rich, famous and he knows you can afford to pay any price. Plus, he's probably thinking that using the angle that other people are interested in the vehicle will push me to beg you to get me whatever car I want."

Ryder grinned. "Well, isn't he in for a big disappointment when he finds out it's you that's making the deal, not me."

Tana nodded and they walked over to Chad.

"All right. We've made a decision. Let's go talk numbers." Tana said as Chad grinned, leading them across the showroom floor.

As Chad escorted them to his office, Tana walked past him and Ryder noticed him clearly checking out his wife's ass. Instinctively, his fist balled. Clearing his throat, he made it clear to Chad that he noticed him staring.

Sitting down, Chad pulled out some forms. They went over the price on the truck and Tana sat back in her seat with her arms crossed in front of her chest looking non-committal and unimpressed. Ryder could see her profession coming out and almost pitied Chad for a moment before switching his thoughts back to how much he was going to enjoy watching this.

Chad misinterpreted Tana's attitude to mean she wasn't the one paying, so he switched to dealing with Ryder, trumpeting what a great deal he was giving them considering all the extras the truck had. Ryder sat back and crossed his ankle onto his knee folding his hands in his lap.

"Don't look at me, man. It's my wife's truck and her deal." Ryder said shaking his head.

Chad looked confused then Tana leaned forward placing her forearms on the desk. "Look, Chad, I'm not some idiot, you can fool with your sales tactics. It's already July. I know the factories are gearing up with manufacturing next years' models. Now we either start to talk real numbers or not only will I walk out right now, I'll also wait until the new models roll out in the fall to buy a new truck. Somehow, I doubt it will be from here."

Chad sat back as if Tana had reached out and slapped him. She wasn't what he was expecting when he figured out who Ryder was. He figured that she had to be some airhead bimbo that was just another piece of ass Ryder was trying to impress.

Tana continued, "In less than a month, you'll be trying to clear out these last models at damn near dealer cost, so here is my only offer. Five percent over dealer invoice, which you will show me, also have your service bay install a top-quality pet barrier into the truck and throw in the all-weather floor mats."

Ryder pressed a finger to his lips to help control the smile that was threatening to spread across his face. He was already literally biting his tongue to keep from laughing.

Chad was stammering and banging away on his keyboard as he punched in some numbers. "I'll have to discuss that my manager."

"You go right ahead and ask your manager. And you know what? You're going to need to bring him in because I have a credit with GM that he will also need to approve. The balance will be paid in cash so there's no need to stall me with financing or leasing offers either." Tana sat back in her seat and looked victorious as Chad looked beaten.

She knew the tactic he was going to try and use, saying his manager couldn't go that low on the truck and come back with a higher counter offer without ever speaking to a manager.

When Chad left the room, Ryder snorted. "Jesus. You're good."

Having never actually seen her work, he fully understood why Warren was so disappointed when she left. Tana just sat there and smiled. This was her zone. Getting what was wanted or needed and not paying more than was budgeted for it.

It took about fifteen minutes before Chad returned looking defeated with the manager. Both Tana and Ryder shook hands with the manager then went over the credit and the price, as well as the extras that Tana requested. He provided the forms for Tana to sign, releasing the credit to his dealership against the purchase of the Acadia and showed her the balance, including taxes. Tana pulled out her cheque book, writing a cheque for the balance. The manager took the cheque to have it verified promising to have her truck cleaned, detailed, filled and the pet barrier of her choice installed and ready for her to pick up in a few days.

"Just bring in your plate, registration and insurance. Then you can drive away with it on Monday." He said shaking both hers and Ryder's hands then handed her the bill of sale.

He knew who Ryder was and wasn't going to have his salesman dicker around with them for the sake of boosting up his commission. He wanted to give them excellent service in hopes they would return to his dealership and not the competition for other vehicles.

Ryder and Tana shook Chad's hand out of courtesy and left with Tana's proof of payment tucked in her purse. Once they were back in the Mustang with Ryder in the driver's seat, he leaned over and kissed her.

"I'm impressed. I knew you were good at what you did, or everyone wouldn't have been so sad to see you go, but wow. You had that guy's number!"

"In my career, I've dealt with some very sexist people. I've also heard pretty much every excuse and seen every trick. I knew what his game was before he even had it all planned out." Tana said as Ryder pulled out of the lot heading home.

"Well, I really enjoyed watching you make him squirm. I didn't like watching him eye you up and down though." Ryder frowned thinking of the way Chad leered at his wife.

Tana shrugged. "I didn't either, but there's no way to control who looks where."

"I know but for creeps like him I would love to control where he breathes from. And it wouldn't be through his nose." Ryder growled.

Tana just shook her head placed a hand on his arm reassuringly as he drove home.

Chapter 17

The first few weeks of July flew by with the truck arriving from Sherwood Park followed by unloading, unpacking and Tana picking up her new truck. Ian was spending a lot of time out quadding or riding his bike and was already making a few friends. Nikki's therapy was going well and Tana's guitar lessons had even resumed.

Usually Ryder and Tana would go into the studio and practice while Nikki was doing her therapy. She was getting good, but for the first few days, Ryder made her re-learn her picking, the scales and the notes all over again seeing she hadn't been practicing since Nikki's accident. It wasn't long before Tana moved onto chords again. She was struggling with it, but slowly, she was getting the hang of it. Ryder had unlimited patience with her and he was a very attentive teacher.

Nikki had been taken into the hospital to have her leg x-rayed to see if she could take her boot off permanently and when she was given the green light, she was ecstatic. Her therapy got a little more intense seeing she now had full use of both legs. She just needed to get the muscles used to being used again then build her strength and stamina back up. Her arm still had a couple of weeks before they were willing to take that cast off.

The U of A hospital had been excellent at referring Nikki to a doctor in Langley Memorial Hospital to oversee the rest of her recovery and Dan was doing a fantastic job with her physical therapy. Every day Nikki was walking better and she was much stronger since coming to Langley. A lot of that had to do with her being home and not stuck in a hospital room anymore. At home, she was constantly moving around instead of mainly being in the hospital bed. Everyone was thrilled to see her doing so well.

Ryder and Tana had even planned a party with the band members again and their families so everyone could see Nikki. Ryder had flown Brad and Jess in for four days to visit and Nikki had been over joyed when he told her. When they arrived, Brad was near tears when he saw her walking normally to greet him at the door. Even Jess had bawled like a baby seeing her doing so well and hugged her tight.

The night of the party Carla, Donna and Sheryl all cried when they first saw Nikki, telling her how worried they had been and that they were all glad she was recovering so well. Even the guys were choked up when they first saw her again. Each of them telling her when Ryder had gotten Tana's message that he looked like his whole world had just crashed down.

Nikki introduced everyone to Brad and Jess and both of them were a little dumbfounded at meeting Severe State in its entirety. They were so used to Ryder that half the time they forgot who he was until they heard him talk about a show or heard him play and sing.

When drinks were being handed around, Tana reminded Nikki not to drink yet. Her doctors had recommended for her to abstain from alcohol until the dizzy spells and headaches were gone or much less frequent. They were getting better. But every once in a while, one would hit and Nikki would get frustrated from it.

During the course of the evening, the guys decided to play a few acoustic songs for everyone seeing Jess and Brad were there for the first time. Neither of them had seen Severe State perform live before and in this little private setting, both of them were in heaven. The little kids even sat riveted watching their fathers' performance. It was a moment all of them really enjoyed. In all, the party was a huge success and all the kids loved seeing Nikki again.

The party didn't get as rowdy as normal for Nikki's sake, but everyone still had a great time. They were all just happy to have Nikki alive and doing so well. None of the band members stayed over because Jess and Brad were using the last two spare rooms, so by midnight everyone had piled kids and themselves into cars to head home. Ryder took the opportunity and used the lack of rooms to try to reopen his earlier discussion about needing an addition on the house. Tana just shook her head at him and rolled her eyes telling him that he was crazy.

Jess and Brad had an excellent visit but admitted they couldn't wait for Nikki to come home. They had already secured an apartment for the first of August, so Nikki gave them the key to the storage unit just in case she wasn't back by then. She told them that Dan was hoping that she would be fully recovered by mid-August at the latest. When the four-day visit was over, Nikki cried when they had to go back home. It was lonely for her without her friends but even Brad admitted that her progress was amazing.

"Honey, it's only a few more weeks then you can come back. With Dan's therapy and you being out of the hospital, it's done more for you than had you stayed in Edmonton. You look like your old self again." Brad reassured her as she said her goodbyes to them at the airport.

Nikki nodded as they left to go through security, turning to wave lots. When they were out of sight, Tana put her arm around her daughter's shoulders and walked back to her truck.

Chapter 18

When Bruce called a band meeting late in the second week of July, he announced that Severe State's two cancelled shows in Japan had been re-booked. They also had performances booked in Australia for the rest of the month and were due to fly out in three days seeing the plan was to use the same stage and setups for both countries.

Bruce informed them they would be gone for three weeks and that Tyson was just completing the Australian information before sending out the email. There were only two dates left to receive signed contracts before everything was final.

In all, Severe State was going back to Kyoto and Okinawa Japan for a week, then off to Australia for two weeks to perform in Sydney, Brisbane, Canberra, Melbourne, Adelaide and Perth. It was going to be a jam-packed three weeks, but the guys were used to Tyson and Bruce hammering them with tight schedules.

When the meeting was over, Ryder found Tana in the studio practicing while Nikki was getting her physio done with for the day. The door to the studio wasn't closed, so he could hear her trying some of the chords he had been teaching her. She was really getting some of them down but others were giving her more of a challenge.

He stood there watching and listening to her for a moment. Each time she made a mistake, she would stop, look at her fingering and check her sheets then try again. Impressed with her attention to detail, Ryder figured if she ever mastered it, she could eventually be a pretty good technical guitarist. She wasn't much on being creative and tended to stick to the music, but he never faulted her for what she was able to pick up.

Chris, Ben and Matt came looking for him, wanting to go over plans for the next three weeks and found him standing outside of the studio smiling. They could hear a guitar being practiced and came up to watch Tana for a few minutes.

"She's not doing too bad considering." Ben said quietly and both Chris and Matt agreed.

Ryder smiled. "I'm quite proud of how far she's come. She didn't touch the guitar the whole time Nikki was in the hospital, so she fell behind about a month, but she's picking it back up and doing well."

Tana looked up and noticed Severe State in its entirety watching her practice and hollered at them to go away.

Ben came through the partially open door. "Hey, we're not out here making fun of you. We're impressed."

"Yeah, you're doing great. Shockingly Ryder is actually doing you justice considering he's a terrible guitarist. But if you ever want to learn some cool riffs give me a call. I'd be thrilled to teach you." Chris complimented Tana and insulted Ryder in the same breath.

Tana laughed and Ryder gave him a shot in the arm.

"Fuck off Masters." He laughed as he went to his wife and kissed her.

"We need to talk." He said looking serious.

"I know what that means." Tana said as she slid off the stool and set the guitar down in the stand.

"You're going away again, right?" She said looking up at him with a knowing look in her eyes.

Ryder nodded looking excited and briefly filled her in. "Nikki's doing well and you're all moved. So I guess it's back on the road for me."

"Okay. I can handle things around here. Just keep me in the loop and I'll do the same for you."

She stood on tiptoe and kissed him. "I'm going to miss you but go and do your thing. After the past six weeks, you need the distraction. Plus, I can tell you're looking forward to it." Tana smiled at him and he smiled back at her.

"I love how you really get me." He grinned down at her.

She left them to discuss the trip telling them that if they wanted, she would have beer and sandwiches in the kitchen for them in twenty minutes.

"Okay, I love my wife more than anything, but can I have her?" Matt said looking after Tana.

"Sheryl has never done that for us and since the twins were born, she doesn't even do that for me!" He teased.

Ryder shook his head telling him there wasn't a chance in hell he could have Tana. "She's mine dude."

Once they finished their discussion, the four of them headed to the kitchen where they did in fact find sub sandwiches and beer set out on the island.

Chapter 19

The night before Ryder left for Japan, Tana decided to get creative. She blindfolded him, gave him a hot oil massage then tied Ryder to the pillars on the four-poster bed where she proceeded to torture him with her mouth, covering every inch of his body. When he was straining against the scarves to the point his muscles looked like, they would bulge right out of his skin she had eased herself down on his throbbing erection and rode him until they both were happy and sated.

By the time they finally lay peacefully next to each other, there were a few bite marks on his shoulders, plus even more scratches on his chest from the intensity of her orgasms. It was nothing new for them, but the red marks and material burns around his wrists were new. When he showed her, she put some salve on them then covered them for the rest of the night hoping they wouldn't look quite so angry in the morning. While Tana took care of his wounds, Ryder laughed, saying Chris and Ben were going to have a field day with him when they saw the marks.

Tana apologized saying she should have backed off and not teased him so much. Ryder swatted her bare bottom making a hearty smacking sound. Turning to face him with a sultry smile, Tana held up the scarves, indicating she was up for him to take control. Ryder didn't have to be asked twice. In moments, he had Tana tied to the posts and was giving her the same treatment until she was the one begging.

When he did finally enter her, he lifted her knees and spread her legs until her ankles were practically in the same location as her bound wrists above her head. Ryder slammed into her setting a pace that had her shouting at him in minutes. As she shook with yet another powerful orgasm, he made one final deep thrust, pulling her tight to him and came.

Tana sunk into the bed, panting heavily as Ryder lowered her legs. When he untied her wrists, she had the same red marks on hers but didn't have the material burns like Ryder. Laughing at the condition of her wrists, she told Ryder now they matched.

A short while later, they fell asleep in each other's arms. The next morning, Ryder finished packing while Tana ran the dogs. After her run, they showered together then Ryder went to say goodbye to Ian and Nikki while Tana dried her hair. The kids wished him luck, telling him to have a safe trip and good time.

When it was time to go, he loaded his bags into Tana's truck and they headed to the airport. It was ten thirty and the flight was due to leave at two, but they were planning on meeting the others for coffee before Severe State left.

Arriving at the airport, they quickly found parking and headed to the coffee shop to meet up with the rest of the band before they checked in. There were a few of the band's personal security guards around their group. Donna was the only other wife to come to the airport. Carla and Sheryl had said their goodbyes at the house and had decided to stay home to avoid the headache of getting all the kids in the car.

When Tana and Ryder both sat down, everyone noticed the bandages around his wrists and the red marks on Tana's. Donna smirked and looked away, where Ben looked from one to the other with raised eyebrows. Matt looked then focused on his cup of coffee shaking his head. Chris was the only one who spoke up instantly.

"Trying to keep yourself from biting your hand again?" He asked sipping his coffee and looking at Ryder dead in the eyes.

Ryder didn't miss a beat. He met Chris's gaze and shot right back. "Damn rights. With what my wife does with her mouth?"

Calmly, he set his coffee down and kissed Tana as she fought not to laugh. Ben was so caught off guard by Ryder's comment he choked on his own coffee. As he coughed and sputtered, Ryder just looked at him with a completely straight face while everyone else was laughing and begging him not to go into details.

Everyone was still chatting and enjoying their coffees when Bruce and Tyson showed up. Immediately, they gave Tana a hug and told her how relieved they were that Nikki was going to be okay. Thanking them both, she then kissed Bruce's cheek thanking him again for helping Ryder come home so fast and postponing the last two shows. He took her hand and patted it, telling her it was the least he could have done in the situation.

When he saw the red marks on her wrist, he frowned asking Tana if she was okay, figuring she had gotten hurt running her dogs.

"Bruce man, when it comes to her and Ryder, don't ask. You won't want to know the answer." Ben said.

Bruce looked over at Ryder and saw bandages on his wrists in the same place as the red marks on Tana's. He looked momentarily confused then turned beet red as he realized what they meant.

"It's okay, Bruce. I'm fine. Nothing but a little fun." Tana said as he turned even redder letting go of her hand.

"You two are definitely different. More unconventional than I think I wanted to know." He said as he turned back to Ryder. "I hope that heals by Kyoto."

"I'll be fine. If not, I have those wrist guards I sometimes wear. Not a big deal."

"Good. I really don't feel like fielding questions about a BDSM fetish or God knows what else."

Ryder looked intrigued and looked at Tana. "Not quite, hey Baby? But now that he mentions it—"

Ryder let his words trail off as Tana smirked and laughed while the others just groaned and walked away.

Bruce ushered them all over to security where Tana and Donna said goodbye to their husbands and Chris said goodbye to Sean.

"I love you." Ryder looked down at Tana and held her chin in his hand.

"I love you too. Have fun." She looked up at him and he knew by the look in her eyes, she would miss him.

His eyes softened and he kissed her with all the love he felt for her.

"I'm going to miss you too, Baby." He whispered to her as she nuzzled his chest.

He breathed her scent in before letting her go and headed to security. Just before he went out of sight, he turned to face her once more. She kissed her fingertips waiving one last time. Ryder returned the gesture then was gone.

Chapter 20

The Kyoto performance went incredibly well. Severe State started the show off with *'These Chains'* then Ryder followed that with an apology to the fans for having to cancel the original show.

"As most of you may have read in the papers, my daughter was in a horrible accident. We cancelled the show because I had to get home to her. So as soon as we could, we wanted to come back and make it up to you." He yelled into the microphone.

The crowd cheered and Ben taunted them, laying down a few drumbeats for *'Dirty Girl'* before stopping. Chris and Matt followed suit by playing a few riffs then Ryder stepped up to the microphone.

"I don't think they want it hey boys?" He taunted the crowd.

The fans screamed and Severe State played a few more chords and beats then stopped again.

"Show me how bad you want it!" Ryder screamed into the microphone then began clapping his hands and jumping around from one end of the stage to the other, riling up the crowd.

The entire jam-packed Saitama Super Arena erupted into an ear-splitting scream, clapping and stomping along with Ryder trying to show Severe State how bad they really did want it.

"I think they do want it." Matt said over his microphone as he played a chord and stopped.

"Real bad too." Chris added from his side of the stage.

Ryder took a quick drink then stepped up to his microphone.

"Well, fuck then. Let's give it to them. Are you ready for some rock and roll?" He yelled and as the crowd erupted again, all four members ripped into *'Dirty Girl'*.

The concert went on with the same energy and hard-hitting lyrics as always. When they had completed their set list, Severe State played a couple of encores then with final bursts of fire from the pyro technics, said good night.

~

The rest of Severe State's week in Japan went by without any issues. Ryder had even gotten out with Ben to do some touristy sightseeing and shopping, which is something he rarely did. In one store, he picked out a beautiful red kimono dress for Tana, a blue one for Nikki, and for Ian, he found a black samue suit with dragons printed on the back and arms. Ben picked up a few of the smaller samue suits for his kids and a very nice kimono dress for Carla.

When Ryder called home after their Kyoto performance, he was ecstatic to hear Nikki had finally gotten her cast off her arm. At her last appointment, the x-rays showed the break had healed beautifully and she was ready to start therapy to regain the strength in that arm.

"She must be thrilled." Ryder laughed into the phone as Tana told him the good news.

"Oh, you would think she just won the lottery or something. She was actually jumping around." Tana chuckled.

"Her physio is really coming along well if she's jumping."

Tana smiled on her end. "Yeah. Dan has her on the treadmill now. She started out with just walking and everyday he increases her time and pace a little. I'm very impressed with his determination to get her strong."

"Well, didn't he set a goal of her being able to be on her own again by mid to late August? What about her headaches and dizziness? How are those?"

Ryder missed being there for the daily reports on Nikki's progress, but he was also glad to be back on stage rockin out again. He knew Tana would keep him in the loop, so he enjoyed his time on the road as he always did.

"She hasn't had a dizzy spell since she started on the treadmill, unless she lets herself get dehydrated or gets up too fast. But even I get those kinds of dizzy spells, so I think its progress. As far as the headaches go, she got a nasty one after her first session on the treadmill, but those are getting less and less too. It seems the more she pushes she'll get one, but it goes away faster, then the next one isn't as bad."

"That's great!" Ryder said then had to let her go.

It was late for him and he was tired. Tana admitted she wanted to get a few more things unpacked and put away before dinner.

"I miss you Baby. I love you. I'll call when we make it to Australia."

"Sounds good. I love you and miss you too. Travel safe."

They hung up and Tana went into her make shift office where there were still piles of boxes and furniture. It still had to be organized and put away, so she took a deep breath and got to work while over in Japan, Ryder undressed and slid into the bed in his hotel room.

~~

When the band and crew all flew out of Okinawa at the end of their week in Japan, the only saving grace was the time zone change was only an hour, but the flight was still brutally long. Fifteen hours flying across the equator into the southern hemisphere still made for a long trip and some nasty jet lag.

Severe State only took a day to rest before they were rockin out down under on stage in Brisbane. They had three shows booked each week that they were going to be there. The Australian leg of the tour was going to be a very busy schedule.

With a seventeen-hour time difference, the band members barely had time to call home. The intense performing and travel schedule added to the difficulty because there was only a day to travel from one place to the next.

Ryder sent Tana a quick text when they touched down in Brisbane then again once they were in Sydney. After the Sydney show, they took the next day to get to Canberra then finally the band had a day to relax.

When Ryder woke at one in the afternoon his time, he called home wanting to check in with Tana. It was six in the morning for her and he figured she should be either up or about to get up. The dogs still got her up early for their runs but seeing she was home all day and they had much more room outside they sometimes let her sleep in a little later. He called the house number, and it rang twice before Tana answered sounding a little sleepy.

"Did I wake you?" Ryder's voice came through the receiver.

"Yeah, but I'm glad you did. I miss you." She smiled and stretched in the morning light.

Ryder yawned and told her he had just woken up too. "It's been insane. We have today off, so I got caught up on my sleep."

He sounded well rested and still slightly rough in the voice from all the performances.

"Must be nice to sleep all day like that. I don't think I could ever do it." Tana giggled, knowing he slept in the way he did because his schedule kept him up very late. "How are the Aussie's treating you guys?"

"Great! I don't think I've ever seen so many bras thrown on stage as there were the other night in Sydney. There must have been over two dozen." Ryder commented.

Tana laughed and admitted that it was those kinds of things that made some concerts really memorable. "I remember going to one where the singer actually put it on and wore it for the rest of the show. It was awesome."

"No way in hell I'm doing that!" Ryder chuckled.

"So, what did you guys do with them?" Tana asked out of curiosity.

"Each time one landed on stage we took it over and hung it on Ben's drum kit." Ryder said and Tana laughed.

"I bet he was impressed."

Ryder shrugged. "He likes to dish it out to everyone else, so when we can, we get him back. We get to move around on stage and he has to stay put so we took advantage of that."

Tana laughed telling him she was happy they were having a good time. Next, she filled him in on Nikki's progress saying that she was now lightly jogging on the treadmill. Dan had told her that when she could hold a good run for five minutes without a dizzy spell or resulting headache, he would recommend her final tests with the doctors here.

"So, it looks like she might be given a clean bill of health as soon as the middle of August." Tana sat up in bed a little and all three dogs were pawing at the edge of the bed, wanting to get going.

Sliding out of bed she wandered to her dresser and started pulling out her running clothes. While she and Ryder talked, Tana got dressed for her run. When she was done, she headed down to the kitchen and let the dogs out back while she finished gearing up. It was another gorgeous summer morning, so Tana only had her running shorts and a sports bra on. She ran the headset for her iPod like she always did and had a few sips of water.

Ryder told her about the last four shows and that he might not be able to call because they were only in Australia for another nine days, but it was long travel times between each location.

"No worries. I know you'll keep in touch when and how you can. I love you and I trust you." She was ready to go but didn't really want to let Ryder go just yet.

"I know Baby. I love you too. And I miss you like crazy. Maybe on our next tour you can come out with me some of the time if Ian isn't in school. He could bunk with some of the crew. I know he'd probably have a blast with them."

Tana said they would have to play it by ear when that time came around. Ryder told her he should let her go. "As much as I want to stay and talk, I have to go to the bathroom and I'm starving. I'll call when I can and text you later."

They said their goodbyes then Tana let the dogs in and got them onto the running leash. Clipping it around her waist, she left and headed out for her morning run with a smile.

~~

The Canberra, Melbourne and Adelaide shows were all a huge hit. The band was back in their groove and the fans were eating them up. Concert turnout was at an all-time high in all three cities and the guys did their best to leave a lasting impression for the fans in each stadium.

Ryder managed to call Tana between Melbourne and Adelaide briefly, letting her know that all was well and that he loved her and missed her. He even took a few hours before band was scheduled to leave for Perth to do some shopping. He found some cool boomerang souvenirs and lanyards for the kids. For Tana, he bought a didgeridoo and an aboriginal tapestry for her office.

The band was flying out early evening the day after the show. There had been enough time in the original schedule for the stage that was used in Melbourne to get to Perth via truck. But one of the main truck's engines had blown, leaving part of the stage and some equipment stuck in the middle of nowhere until a new truck could get there.

Once word of the truck reached Bruce and Tyson, the crew had been given orders after the Adelaide show to rush through the teardown of the stage. Because of the delay with the second stage from Melbourne, they weren't sure if they would make it to Perth in time once the replacement truck arrived. So as soon as the show was over, the crew in Adelaide was working double time to get packed up. It was going to be a tight fit time wise for either crew to make it on time.

Bruce and Tyson were keeping close tabs on both crews. They were hoping they could somehow get the stage and all the equipment from Adelaide onto cargo planes and fly it up to Perth.

So far, the delay had cost them more than a day in travel time. At this point even if the trucks from Adelaide drove non-stop to Perth, that would give the crew less than six hours before the show started to set up, run through lighting, pyro checks and do sound check.

It was just too tight, so Bruce and Tyson were really pushing to set up cargo flights to get everything leaving at the same time as the band or shortly following. The other trucks were still rolling to Perth in hopes to do even a partial set up and save some time just in case the cargo flights couldn't be arranged. As the band headed to the airport to board their flight, the news was not encouraging.

At the airport, Bruce informed them that so far the cargo flights were not happening for two days. That gave them about twenty-four hours. It was better, but it was still cutting things close. None of the guys were worried. Bruce had never let them down before and they were confident that he would pull it off again.

As they boarded their flights to Perth, Severe State was still in great spirits from the previous night's performance. The problems with the truck were nowhere in their minds as the plane took off. When they landed in Perth and got to their hotel, Ryder texted Tana letting her know about the issues with a truck breaking down and the cargo flights. It was already late evening for him when Tana called his cell. Answering, he couldn't help but smile and feel thrilled to hear her voice.

"Baby, hi. How are you?" He said as he answered his phone.

"I'm good. So, what happened?"

He filled her in on the blown engine, and Bruce's tenacity to get all their gear and stage set up on cargo flights in order to have time to get set up for their last show.

"You know sometimes these things just happen. There's nothing any of us can do about it. Usually, we have a few more days in between shows and not such a long haul between cities, but that's just the way it played out this time around." Ryder explained as he stifled a yawn.

"Oh, I'm sorry. Were you headed to bed?" Tana asked sounding apologetic.

"No. Not yet. We just got checked in. It's just been a long day. The headaches with the truck and seeing Bruce tearing his hair out trying to get everything here to Perth was tiring enough. We trust him. We know he will get it resolved. But the flight was long too." Ryder sighed.

"I should let you go then. Let you get some sleep."

"No. Don't. I want to hear your voice. I miss you and I want to talk to you for a bit." Ryder pleaded.

"Okay. I just didn't want to keep you up. When's the show?"

"In two days. The cargo planes are supposed to be touching down sometime between nine tomorrow night and one a.m. I think. Bruce knows for sure, but the crew is going to have to work twice as hard to get set up plus run through all the checks before we go on at eight."

"Here's hoping that the plane arrives on time and that the crew is able to get the stage set up without any more delays. It would be horrible to have the show delayed because of a truck, but it sounds like Bruce has it all under control."

Ryder agreed, then asked how things were going at home. Tana filled him in on how Nikki was doing and let him know that Ian had made some more friends. He was even talking about looking forward to school starting, so he could meet more people.

July was almost over, and Nikki was getting antsy about passing her final check-ups that Dan was getting scheduled for her. So far, it looked like they would take place in the next week or two.

"Otherwise, all is good here on the home front. Just missing you and keeping busy as usual." Tana chimed.

Hearing about everyone settling in and doing so well made him a little homesick, but Ryder knew he would be home by August third, so he didn't have long before he would see them all again.

Tana and Ryder talked a little longer, then Ryder admitted that he was tired and should go before he fell asleep. Tana reassured him that understood and told him she loved him as they said goodbye. Ryder was so tired that he was sound asleep minutes after hanging up.

The cargo flights with the stage and all their equipment landed the next night at one in the morning. It took over three hours to unload the cargo planes and load everything into the waiting trucks. After the trucks were loaded, it still took over an hour to get the equipment and the stage to the stadium, then it was double time to unload and get it all set up once everything arrived at nib.

By noon when Severe State came on site to check everything out, Bruce looked about ready to have a heart attack. The entire crew was busting their asses to get it all done. The stage was completely built, but the lighting was still being run and tested while the pyro was just getting started. Sound check was in four hours and until all the lighting trusses were completed, none of the speakers, amplifiers or mixers could be tested. There were too many cranes and lifts in the way for them to properly place most of the sound equipment. Trying to set that up before all the lifts were gone could result in someone was either getting hurt or something would get broken.

By two, all the lighting was done and tested, so the lifts were moved into position to help with setting up the sound system. Every person was called to get the sound system set up and tested, so the band could do sound check. By four in the afternoon, they had pulled off a miracle. Severe State was doing their sound check and damn near every member of the crew was splayed out on the floor exhausted with relief that it had all come together. But they couldn't rest for long. They still had the show to get through. But at least now, there would be a show.

The meet and greet began at six with no issues or delays. The band was pumped and ready when the fans began to file through for their autographs and pictures. Everyone was in high spirits joking and laughing with people young and old. When parents with kids came through, they always made the kids feel special in the pictures. Band members gave them little things like guitar picks, key chains, stickers, lanyards and temporary tattoos.

When the last of the fans had gone through, they all gathered back in the dressing rooms for their ritual pre-show drink, toasting Perth and for a good show. Before they knew it, Severe State was called to take the stage. Ryder pulled his phone out of his pocket and sent Tana a quick text.

'Taking the stage. Last show down under! Love you. See you soon! <3'

Then he stuffed his phone back in his pocket as he made his way from the dressing rooms to backstage.

As the lights went down, the stadium was overrun with the sound of cheering fans. Quickly, they grabbed their instruments and got into position. Ben started the still incredibly popular drum intro to *'These Chains'* and with the flash bang of huge fire jets shooting up from all four corners of the stage, the rest of Severe State kicked in, ripping into their smash hit. The fans ate it up, screaming and cheering.

When Ryder sauntered up to the microphone and belted out the lyrics, the entire stadium was pumped with an energy level so high, it was electric and the band fed off that. It was that energy that pushed them even when fate tried to stop them as it had with the truck's blown engine.

That night Severe State put on a show in Perth that none of their fans would forget, playing all their hits. When their set list was done, they moved on, playing a couple of encores. One ballad and one hard hitting fight song. They were planning to say good night with one final song. It was an old one. Their very first hit, *'Die Tryin'* and when they started playing the first few chords, the crowd erupted.

Chris was rocking out hard during the instrumental bridge. Right on cue, Ryder stepped right to the front of the stage so he could rock out closer to the fans. Just before the bridge was done, he stepped back in the direction of his microphone and the pyro fired there for the first time that night. Immediately, Ryder was hit with a fireball from the flamethrower, completely engulfing him in flames. The crowd instantly screamed out in horror.

Instantly the music stopped. Chris and Matt threw off their instruments and ran across the stage to their friend while Ben rushed out from behind his kit to join them. In seconds, crew members were on stage with fire extinguishers in hand putting out the flames coming from Ryder's body with medics right behind them. There was a murmur running through the crowd as the medics dropped to the floor around Ryder. The house lights came up and everyone on stage was over by Ryder who was lying motionless on the stage.

Standing up, Chris went and looked down at the flamethrower mounted in the floor of the stage and clearly saw it wasn't set straight in its mount. Then he looked out at the fans right in front of where the accident happened, grabbed one of the microphones while Ben and Matt stayed with Ryder. He ran a hand over his face as he turned from Ryder lying on the stage with medics still working on him and walked to the front of the stage where Ryder had been moments before.

"Is everybody all right over here?" He asked into the microphone addressing the fans and stadium workers that had been within the area of the incident and everyone nodded.

"No one needs medical attention?" He asked making sure no one in the audience was hurt before heading back over to the medics.

Chris leaned down and spoke to one of the medics for a few seconds then stood up and placed the microphone back in its stand so he could address the crowd.

"Not to worry. Ryder's going to be fine. It looks like just his leg and arm got the worst." Chris filled them in.

A stretcher was being brought out and within minutes, everyone saw Ryder sit up grimacing in pain but very much so alive and seeming to be all right. The crowd erupted in applause and cheers as they saw him wave away the stretcher and stand up with assistance.

"He needs medical attention, so unfortunately we won't be able to finish that last encore."

"Fuck that. We're finishing the song." Ryder's voice came over the sound system.

He had made his way over to Chris's microphone with the help of the medics, Ben and Matt. His shirt and jeans were scorched and charred. One leg of his jeans had been cut open to mid-thigh and his whole lower leg and right arm were wrapped in bandages.

"Someone bring me a stool and my guitar. I'm not letting Perth down." He said and the crowd clapped and cheered in surprise.

It wasn't long before Ryder was being helped onto a stool. Medics stood by completely disagreeing with Ryder's decision to continue but seeing he wasn't showing any signs of medical distress, they were willing to allow this small delay before insisting on getting him to a hospital.

Ben smiled at him. "Man, you're sick. Good on ya for finishing."

He gave Ryder a careful high five hug and went back to his kit while stagehands came out with spare guitars for Chris and Ryder and a fresh bass for Matt.

As everyone got situated, Ryder stayed on Chris' side of the stage. Using his microphone, he spoke to Chris.

"Dude, don't step over there." He said motioning to the mis-aligned flamethrower. "It's a little fucked up."

The crowd laughed at Ryder's sense of humor even though he could have been killed with what had just happened.

"Thanks captain obvious. I hadn't noticed." Chris replied into Ryder's microphone sarcastically.

The guys all looked at each other, re-grouping. When they were ready, Ryder nodded and they started *'Die Tryin'* again from the top. This time there were no mishaps and they finished the song, saying goodnight to Perth who gave them a huge standing ovation. Matt and Chris came to help Ryder off the stage with the medic's right by his side.

Backstage, Bruce was already chewing out members of the crew trying to find out who handled set up on that side of the stage and who was responsible for double-checking that the flamethrower had been secured properly in its fixture.

"Fuck man, you have no idea how lucky you are." Matt said as he came over to see how Ryder was doing.

Ryder nodded. "I know. Thank God I stepped away when I did. Shit. I thought for sure I was a dead man."

"You damn near were." Matt gave him a hug, glad to see him all right.

"I have to call Tana. Jesus. If she hears through anyone else or through the internet, she's going to flip. I have to let her know I'm okay."

Ben looked at him and nodded. "She's going to flip any way. Look, just go and get checked out. We can call her."

"No. After what she's been through with Nikki, she's gonna worry unless she hears it from me. My voice you know." Ryder explained while pulling out his phone.

The others nodded, understanding his reasons as he called home.

~~

Tana and the kids were just sitting down to dinner when the house phone rang. Standing up from the table, she went to the counter where the cordless phone was and answered it.

"Hi Baby."

It was Ryder and he sounded off.

"Ryder? What's wrong?" Tana looked worried as she heard something in her husband's voice.

Ryder took a deep breath and she swore she could hear something that she hadn't heard before as he exhaled.

"Ryder talk to me. You're scaring me." It was barely a whisper and Tana fell into her seat not liking what she could hear in his voice. "What happened? What's going on?"

Nikki and Ian stopped eating and stared at their mother looking concerned. Tana's heart was racing.

"It's okay Baby. There was an accident with the show tonight. One of the small flame throwers at the front of the stage was misaligned."

Gasping, Tana's eyes widened in fear and her mind was racing. If he was calling, it made her wonder which of the band members got hurt.

Ryder continued. "I was standing right up front. I just stepped back when it went off and I got hit."

"Oh my God!" Tana gasped her hand going to her mouth. "How bad? Are you okay?"

"I'm fine. Well, sort of. My right calf is burned pretty bad and my arm. They want to have the doctors look at it, so they're going to take me to the hospital. I'm all right Baby. I'm not going anywhere but to the hospital then I'm coming home. I just wanted to call and tell you myself.

I figured if you heard from someone else you would worry until you heard from me."

Tears were in her eyes, but she was able to compose herself. "Thank you, and yes I would worry. I'll still worry until you come home, but I'm glad you called and told me. I love you Ryder. Please, go to the hospital and make sure you're okay. Call me once the doctors have seen you."

Ryder promised her he would and told her how much he loved her before hanging up.

Medical was insisting he get to a hospital now to prevent an infection and had called for an ambulance. Ryder was able to limp a little, but the more weight he put on his leg, the more it hurt, so he hopped his way to the waiting ambulance with Ben's help.

Ryder felt foolish he got to the ambulance. He didn't think it had been bad enough that an ambulance was needed. Cringing from the pain, he reluctantly got in.

~~

Tana sat for a minute holding the phone as she fought back the tears that threatened to escape.

"Mom? What happened?" Nikki got up from the table and came over to her mother.

Tana shook her head and placed a hand on Nikki's arm. "It's okay. I think it sounds worse than it is."

She pushed her barely touched plate away, not feeling much like eating anymore. "There was an accident with one of the flame throwers on the stage tonight. It wasn't secured right and when it went off, Ryder got burned."

Both Nikki and Ian stared at their mother in horror.

"How bad is it?" Ian asked looking worried.

Tana shrugged. "He said he's fine, but also said his leg is pretty bad. The medics want him to go to the hospital to have it checked and treated."

"Holy shit Mom. He could have been cooked. Those things shoot like twenty feet in the air."

"Ryder said it was one of the smaller ones. The ones they use closer to the fans. But even still he's lucky it was only his leg."

Tana told both Nikki and Ian about the issues with the truck engine blowing and getting everything over from Adelaide to Perth via cargo plane to be able to put on their final show in Australia.

"I bet some of the checks didn't get finished because they were trying to get everything done in time." Ian guessed.

"I don't know and neither does Ryder at the moment, but I'm sure that Bruce and the rest of the band will get to the bottom of it." She got up from the table and cleaned up from dinner.

No one really felt like eating after hearing about Ryder's injury, so Tana put the leftovers into containers then in the fridge.

"I wouldn't doubt someone's head is going to roll for this." Ian said as he loaded the dishwasher for his mother and started it.

"I don't know. I'm sure they will be somewhat understanding considering it was a rush set up. All we can do now is wait to hear back from Ryder. Then when he comes home, we can see how bad it really is."

"Think about it Mom, if a crew member gets hurt the show can still go on, but the lead singer? So much for the show." Ian said.

Tana frowned and shook her head. Ryder hadn't said if they had cancelled the rest of the show or anything. He was hopefully on his way to the hospital, so she had no choice but to wait to get the details. Instead of dwelling on it, she busied herself in the kitchen cleaning up and wiping down counters while she waited for Ryder to call her back. She was drying the frying pans when Nikki came into the kitchen with her laptop.

"Mom, the accident is already on YouTube."

"Are you serious?" Tana came over to the island where Nikki had set her laptop down.

Ian came over from wiping down the table and feeding the dogs just as Nikki started the video clip on the screen.

The three of them leaned on the island as they watched Severe State finish with one song. Ryder stepped to the very front of the stage while they were playing *'Die Tryin'*. He was just stepping back with his left foot and turning to head back to his microphone when they saw the jet of fire about ten feet long shoot directly across the stage.

Tana gasped as she saw what all the fans had seen. Ryder completely disappeared in the flames. It looked like the entire fireball had eaten him up. The other band members ran to his aide along with the crew with fire extinguishers, putting flames out on Ryder's motionless form lying on the stage.

Nikki and Tana were both covering their gaping mouths as they saw the medics rush to Ryder and begin to administer help.

All of them couldn't help but cry out in relief when Ryder was helped to a sitting position. Then when Chris was addressing the fans, apologizing for not being able to finish the song, Ryder astounded his family by standing, heading over to Chris's microphone addressing the crowd himself and Severe State finished the song after a stool was brought out for Ryder to sit on.

Tana's heart filled with pride and this time, she did cry. Not out of fear but out of love and understanding. It was that same determination, passion and drive that made him a success. She saw it in him there on the screen. Even after an incident that could have killed him, he was unwilling to back down and call it quits.

In that moment, it really drove home how much she, Nikki and Ian meant to him. Ryder had left Japan to be with them, postponing two shows so he could be with his family. Even Nikki understood and when she brought it up Tana smiled and nodded.

"The crazy fool will finish a show after almost being burned to death, yet he came home to be with us when you had your accident." Tana sniffed.

Nikki closed her laptop. "I'm not gonna lie. I feel kinda special now. We all should after seeing him finish only one song. It was an encore. It's not like the fans didn't get their concert."

Tana agreed and Ian went off to his room saying he wanted to mess around on the computer for a while. He wanted to check out the comments on the video, hoping all the Severe State haters gave credit to the band for finishing the song when they clearly had every reason not to.

Nikki was about to take her laptop back to her room when the phone rang. Tana answered it and was relieved to hear Ryder's voice again.

"Hey Baby. I'm all done at the hospital and back at the hotel." He said sounding tired.

"How bad is it?" Tana sat down at the table and Nikki joined her, wanting to know how Ryder was.

Ryder breathed out a long sigh. "Second and third degree burns on most of my right calf, with some first and second degree burns on my arm. My upper leg and my side are also first degree. Those ones they aren't worried about, but they said for me to be careful with keeping the leg and arm clean and covered for a while, so it doesn't get infected. My arm hair is burnt off and some on my head got singed too. Thank God, it happened at the end of the show. I was soaked with sweat and that saved me. Had my shirt been dry it would have completely caught fire and I'd be in much worse shape. Oh, and my flying V guitar is toast. Pisses me off cause it was my favorite one too."

Tana's shoulders slumped as she relaxed. She had seen on the video clip that he was all right, but it was nice to know he had been taken care of medically and was in the clear.

"Thank God you're all right. Does anyone know what happened?"

On his end, Ryder was shaking his head. "No. Bruce is finding out how this happened. He wants to know who fucked up and why. But Ben, Matt, Chris, and I were talking. We're going to have a huge fucking meeting when we're all back home about show times and checks on this stuff."

"That sounds like a good idea. You were lucky. It could have been much worse than it was."

"Yeah. Someone could have died. It could have been a fan that got hurt. That would have been awful. I mean we know the risks when we get up there or if we get too close. We know we can get hurt, but to have an accident like that happen and if a fan gets hurt, I don't even want to think about the repercussions." Ryder said, sounding strained.

"No kidding the publicity and the backlash could be really bad not to mention the potential lawsuit." Tana agreed with him. "When are you coming home?"

"The guys and I fly out first thing in the morning. The rest of the crew has to wait for the truck to get here from Melbourne then pack up both stages and sets of equipment. I just want to get home. We need to go over the concerns and areas we need to make changes before the next round of concerts."

"That makes sense. How long is the trip home?"

"About twenty-four hours. We have a four-hour layover in Hong Kong, but it's a really long ass flight."

"Sounds like it. I guess I'll see you in about a day and a half then?" Tana said as Ryder gave her his ETA.

After reassuring her that he was fine, Tana told him about the video clip being on YouTube already and that she had watched it with the kids. Ryder wasn't shocked to hear it was on the internet already and asked her if it had looked as bad as everyone had thought. Tana told him it had and he said he'd have to watch it for himself. A few minutes later, he let her go so he could get some sleep before the flight in the morning telling her that he couldn't wait to see her again.

"All I could think of was you as I was curled up on that stage. I tried to protect myself from the fire. It was your face that came to mind." Ryder whispered to her through the phone lines.

"I love you more than anything, Tana."

"I love you just as much Ryder. You can't imagine how relieved I am that you're not more seriously hurt. Fly home safe and take care of your burn till you get home. I'll be waiting for you at the airport. Promise."

Chapter 21

Tana was at the international flight arrivals by five p.m. on the third of August, waiting for Ryder's flight to come in. Carla, Sheryl, and Donna were there with all their children. Each of them knew about Ryder's incident and gave Tana a supportive hug. Carla even admitted that one of her biggest fears was Ben getting burned.

"His kit is always surrounded by either flames or fireworks or both. There've been times where he's mentioned it to me that it was too much, too hot or his hair was singed. He's never been burned, but it still scares me. One little mistake is all it takes."

Carla was right and Tana understood her fear whole-heartedly. All she could do was hope the meeting that Severe State wanted to call would help to ensure the band's safety.

All of them were a little more emotional and anxious to see their husbands due to Ryder's close call on stage. Situations like that always brought out everyone's worst fears. Especially when they were so far away and it had been one of the band members who had been involved.

Time ticked by slowly. When the flight arrived and was in customs for clearance, all of them were pacing. Tension and nerves were high as the doors opened and other passengers coming from customs began to come through.

Within twenty minutes, they saw Bruce and Tyson come through the door and directly behind them were all four band members looking somber and tired. Ryder was slowly hopping along on crutches, not putting much weight on his burned leg while Ben and Chris flanked him, with Matt beside Ben. They all looked up and smiled when they saw their families, each breaking away to go over to them.

Everyone was quiet as they hugged and kissed, except the kids who were excited to see their father's home. Tana's eyes filled with tears seeing her husband on crutches knowing he was hurt. She walked over to him, carefully putting her arms around him, and held him close as tears fell from her lashes. Ryder leaned down on his crutches and held her tight.

"See Baby? I'm all right. I'm home." He had seen the worry and fear in her eyes as soon as she looked up at him.

Tana nodded and sniffed as she backed away from him so he could hobble forward.

Wiping her eyes, she looked over at the others as they waved goodbye, each band member and their family heading off to their vehicles. Bruce and Tyson walked with Ryder, making their way to the doors. Tana grabbed Ryder's luggage while he manipulated the crutches as they headed to her truck. Bruce gave Tana a hand with Ryder's bags, putting them into the back for her as Ryder got himself into the passenger seat. Once he was seated, he told both Bruce and Tyson that the band wanted a complete crew management team meeting to discuss the Perth incident.

Immediately they agreed and Ryder closed the truck door. When Bruce and Tyson looked at Tana, both of them apologized to her feeling somewhat responsible for Ryder's close call.

"Tana, I'm really sorry for what happened to Ryder. We're looking into who dropped the ball." Bruce looked really upset as Tana closed the back of the truck.

"I know. We were lucky. I just hope it never happens again."

Bruce nodded promising they would get to the bottom of this and said he would see her at the house in a few days then left with Tyson to catch their own ride.

As Tana climbed in the truck, Ryder smiled at her then leaned over to give her a kiss.

"How are your burns feeling?" Tana asked as she started the truck and pulled out of the parkade.

"Hurts like a bitch to be honest." Ryder said leaning back against the seat. "Every time I try to stand on my leg, the skin feels like its splitting and it throbs. I think I'd rather break my leg next time. My arm throbs too, but it's not as bad."

"Did they give you something for the pain?" Tana asked as she headed out into Vancouver.

"Yeah, but it doesn't help much. I've got cream to put on it too and all this stuff I have to do to change the dressings regularly. It's a pain in the ass."

"But if you don't, it won't heal properly, or it could get infected. I'll help you with it." Tana glanced over at him and gave him a little smile.

"I'm sorry for putting you through more. You've been through enough lately, Baby. This just sucks." Ryder took her hand and kissed her fingers, keeping her hand in his as she drove back home to Langley.

Tana just shook her head. "Don't worry about it. You didn't do it on purpose. You got hurt. It's not like you asked for it to happen. What scares me is that it could have been so much worse."

"Believe me, it scared the shit out of me too." Ryder said to her. "This meeting is going to be very important. Seeing how much this hurts and it's mainly my leg that got the worst of it, I really don't want to know how it feels to have half of my body burned."

They drove the rest of the way home in relative silence. When Tana pulled up to the house, Ian came out right away to help with Ryder's bags. He was worried about Ryder and had been watching for them to come home.

As he eased himself out of the truck, Tana was right there to hand him his crutches. Hopping his way around the truck and into the house, Ryder set Ian's mind at ease and reassured him he was fine. Ian and Tana took the bags upstairs while Ryder went straight into the living room and flopped down on the couch. Nikki came in and he sat up with a big smile.

"Hey, look who's not limping around the house anymore. And no cast on your arm either!"

Nikki gave him a look and couldn't resist. "Hey, look who's limping around the house now. You had to go and get yourself hurt and take my place?" She teased and came over to give him a hug.

"I'm really glad you weren't more seriously hurt. When we watched the video, it looked really scary."

Ryder smiled and sat up a little more. "It was scary. I saw the video too. It looked way worse than it was, but it still shouldn't have happened."

Ryder caught up with Nikki on how her recovery was going. He was thrilled to hear she was doing so well. She had tests scheduled the following week and if they all came back in the clear, she was going to be able to move back to Sherwood Park before the middle of the month.

"Wow. Already." Ryder said as he looked at her, seeing for himself that she really was doing well.

"Yup. I haven't had a dizzy spell or headache for over a week now and I don't miss them. I can hold a steady run on the treadmill for seven minutes, plus I have full use of my arm. Nothing hurts anymore. I feel great."

Nikki looked like she was back to her old self which made Ryder very relieved. Giving her a big hug, he reiterated how happy he was to see her doing so well.

"Yes, we get one back to good health then another takes her place." Tana said as she came closer to Ryder.

"When did you last change the dressings on your leg?" She asked looking at him and knowing full well it had been a while.

"Um… the morning after the hospital so about a day." Ryder admitted.

Tana rolled her eyes and shook her head. "Where's the stuff from the hospital?"

Ryder told her he put the burn cream and extra dressings that the hospital had given to him in his bag and Tana went back upstairs to get it. When she came back down, she had a couple of different towels, the dressings, the burn cream and a face cloth.

Being as careful as he could, Ryder pulled the leg of his jeans up exposing the bandage wrapping his right calf. Tana knelt right down to the floor and stuck one of the towels under Ryder's leg then stood up and headed to the kitchen. She got a pair of scissors, a bowl with warm water in it and brought it all back out to the living room.

Carefully, she cut the gauze off Ryder's leg layer by layer until she got to the last few where she could see the gauze was sticking to the burn. Taking the small hand towel she brought down, Tana dunked it in the bowl of water and squeezed some of the water out then gently laid the almost dripping towel over Ryder's leg. He grimaced as the weight and heat set off his pain receptors and Tana apologized.

"It's okay Baby. It's gotta be cleaned and changed." He tried to reassure her.

While the water soaked into the gauze on Ryder's leg, she cut the gauze off the burn on his arm and gently blotted off the old cream, cleaning the entire area. Then she carefully started peeling the loosened gauze off Ryder's leg. He was grinding his teeth in pain. Tana kept saying sorry each time he would grumble. It didn't take too long before she had his leg fully exposed to the air.

Wetting a second softer cloth, she and dabbed at the burn, careful not to rub the raw areas. There were black bits of charred flesh on his leg where it was the worst and the rest just looked red, raw, horribly blistered and very painful. Tana didn't flinch at the sight of it where Nikki and Ian got grossed out and left the room.

Tana continued to blot at the burn and rinsing the cloth regularly until all the old cream and some of the loosened dead skin was removed. Leaving it open to the air for a few minutes to dry enough to put the cream on Tana cleaned up the bowl and wet towels then came back to Ryder.

Kneeling back down, she took the cream and ever so gently spread a thick layer over the entire burn on his arm and leg then put fresh gauze over top of both.

"There. How's that?" Tana asked as Ryder carefully pulled the leg of his jeans back down over the bandage.

"Much better. Thank you." He pulled Tana over to him and kissed her passionately.

"Are you hungry?" Tana asked as Ryder's lips left hers.

"Starving." He growled into her neck, not talking about food.

Tana giggled feeling far more relaxed than she had been earlier. Now that he was home and she had seen his burn, she knew he was going to be perfectly fine.

"I wasn't talking about that right now, but we can definitely take care of that later. Do you want dinner?" Tana asked getting up off the floor.

Ryder nodded and sat up grabbing his crutches. He got himself up to a standing position and followed Tana into the kitchen. Quickly, she went through the fridge, pulling out some leftovers and warmed them up for everyone while Ian and Nikki set the table while Ryder made his way over.

After dinner was done and the kitchen cleaned back up, Ryder crutched his way back to the living room and lay down on the couch putting his leg up. It was throbbing again and he just wanted to relax. Jet lag was starting to set in, but he wanted to stay up for a few more hours so he could start to get back onto his time zone even though he was dead tired.

Tana came in and sat down with him. They talked for a while about the trip and how the shows went. When Ryder got to the Perth incident, he asked for a pad of paper and pen to jot down different things to bring up in the meeting as they came to mind.

By ten thirty, he had figured out quite a few items he wanted to discuss. If the rest of the band was on board and they could get Bruce and Tyson to make sure all their crew was on the same page, the next round of shows and their next tour would be much more enjoyable.

Setting the notes down, Ryder said he was beyond tired. Tana told him to go to bed and get some rest. As much as he wanted to protest, he knew he had no energy, so he got up and crutched his way upstairs to their room. While she helped him to undress, he fell back onto the bed and could already feel himself slipping off to sleep.

Chapter 22

By the Sunday after Severe State came back home, everyone had gotten over their jet lag and readjusted to the time zone, so the band was all gathered in Ryder's dining room for the meeting. Bruce and Tyson were there along with the head pyro technician, head of lighting, stage and set design and all their equipment technicians. All in all, there were twelve people there plus the four members of the band.

It had been five days since the Perth incident, and no one was happier to get this meeting on the go than Ryder. Especially, seeing it had been his life that had come close to ending. No one wanted to risk that happening again.

A few days ago, he had gone over his notes with Ben, Matt, and Chris. They had added some of their ideas and concerns to Ryder's list and overall, they all felt that the meeting was going to be very beneficial.

Everyone was all seated along the sides of the table with Severe State seated at the head. Bruce and Tyson were next then all the lead crew members.

Ryder cleared his throat and started the meeting. "I'm sure you all know why we're here. There's going to be some changes in the way we do things from now on because of what happened at the Perth show. And personally, I want answers on how the fuck this even happened."

Every person at the table could see that Ryder was still upset and that he was dead serious. First on the agenda, the band addressed the timing between concerts.

"We run two crews and have two complete stage setups for a reason. So that we're not rushed in the set up and teardown of our sets and leaving less chances of injury, damage or mistakes." Chris said.

"We understand the truck blowing an engine is beyond our control. Same with other mechanical issues or the weather, but that doesn't mean that our checks get thrown out the window when we're faced with a rush." Ben added with everyone nodding in agreement.

"From here on in, if there's a long distance of more than two days for both crews to have to travel, we're adding an extra day between shows as a cushion in case these kinds of delays happen. Hopefully, that way we aren't faced with a huge panic again. I would rather lose a day than have someone lose their life." Tyson said.

He had put a lot of thought into the Perth incident and understood that making a date for a show wasn't worth someone being killed.

Everyone nodded in agreement and discussed other minor changes to scheduling and to have it less taxing on everyone by scheduling in a few breaks. This way the band could have a bit of down time, which also gave the crew time to do extra maintenance and repairs.

After all the issues had been sorted out with each crew head, Ryder sat back and looked at the head pyro technician.

"Now let's discuss Perth. Who was responsible for not securing that flame thrower and why?"

Deke looked down briefly then back up at Ryder. "Ultimately, it's my fault for not checking my guy's work. I had one of my other guys working that side of the stage. He's already been fired."

Ryder looked non-impressed as he continued to stare at Deke. "Why was it left loose in the bracket? Did he explain that?"

Deke nodded. "He said that he placed the thrower in the bracket and had just gotten the lines hooked up when he was hollered at to come help work on the sound system."

"That doesn't excuse why he didn't go back and finish his job after the sound system was done." Chris said looking pissed at the lame excuse Deke had been given.

"I know. He said he forgot. That's why I fired him. You can't just forget about a half-finished job when dealing with fire and explosions. It could kill someone." Deke said.

"No shit!" Ryder snapped. "It damn near cost me my fucking life!"

"I should've checked them all myself." Deke muttered and had the decency to look really upset.

He loved working for this band. They were the best band he had ever worked for and with what happened to Ryder he was fully expecting to be fired.

"Yeah, you should have and from now on you will. Each crew head will be handing in signed sheets for your department, affirming all required checks on all the equipment you are responsible for has been completed for each show. In addition, I don't care if a lighting board doesn't work for a show or if we're down some lasers. No one from the pyro crew is ever to be hauled away from a job they're working on until it's done, and the checks are signed off on. Then they can go help but not before. Ever." Bruce added firmly.

Deke looked up and met Bruce's eyes agreeing. "Thank you. It won't happen again."

"Your Goddamn right it won't." Ryder said.

"We did tests on all the pyro. Nothing was mis-aligned in the tests, so what happened after?" Bruce asked wanting to know how it wasn't caught in the testing phase.

Deke cleared his throat and explained that each flamethrower was bolted into the brackets to prevent being knocked loose or out of line when they were set off. "It could have been jarred out of position after the test. Even the movement on stage or the vibrations of the music could have knocked it loose. That unfortunately we'll never know."

Now that they had answers and new procedures along with more safety checks, plus Deke had the band backing him up with agreeing his guys couldn't be pulled away unless their jobs were done and signed off on, everyone felt much better. Even Ryder looked more relaxed and like his easy going self.

The meeting had gone extremely well with all of their concerns addressed. With the changes they agreed on and the new procedures, it was going to make touring much easier and even a little more family friendly for the band members. With more time between shows, being better prepared for emergencies and having breaks scheduled in the duration of the tour, they could see their families and everyone including the crew could have some much-needed down time.

Tana, Carla, Sheryl, and Donna all stayed in the kitchen while the meeting had been going on and were putting together a late lunch for the guys. They overheard some of the topics and concerns that were brought up. When Ben had asked for some of the pyro to be moved back away from his kit, especially if they were playing in an open-roof arena, so the wind wouldn't blow the flames so close, Carla looked relieved and Tana knew exactly how she felt.

After hearing laughter and regular conversations coming from the dining room, Tana and Carla carried trays of sub sandwiches, napkins, and muffins into the guys while Sheryl and Donna followed with cases of beer, pop, and some glasses. As the women entered the room with food and drinks in hand, every single person turned to look at them.

Before Ryder had gotten married, they would have just ordered in food then gone downstairs to the bar for drinks. The crew members had to admit they liked the change.

"You're going to spoil everyone if you keep doing that." Ryder teased as he pulled Tana over to his lap after she set down another tray of subs.

Swinging her arm around his neck, Tana sat on Ryder's lap and kissed him. "What? I can't do something nice for the people that help keep your ass in line when I'm not around?"

Ryder swatted her backside playfully when she stood back up and Ben, Matt, and Chris all thanked their wives for their help while everyone dug into the food. All four ladies left the room to go back to the kitchen, leaving the band and crew managers to finish up. Nikki and Ian were keeping an eye on all the children in the back yard with the dogs and they didn't want to leave them too long.

Chapter 23

Tana was sitting in the waiting room of Langley Memorial Hospital neurology unit nervously tapping her heel as she waited for Nikki to return from her tests. Dan had given his final report to her doctor saying he felt she was fully recovered, so the head neurologist was now examining her.

"If you keep doing that, you're going to jack hammer a hole in the floor." Ryder said to her as he walked back to the door and looked through the glass for signs of Nikki or the doctor.

Tana harrumphed and narrowed her eyes at him. "Oh, and like you're any better. You're pacing between your chair and that door every ten seconds."

Ryder looked at her sheepishly and sat back down. When Tana's heel started tapping again, he put his hand on her knee stopping its movement. Looking at each other, they laughed.

"I think we're both a bit nervous for her." Ryder admitted.

"I just want her to be okay. I know that means she'll be going back to Sherwood Park, but I'd rather miss her knowing she's okay and just living in Edmonton than her to have to prolong starting her own life any longer than she has because of an asshole drunk."

"I know. I'm going to miss her like crazy too." Ryder put his arm around her shoulders and pulled her over to him.

They sat waiting for another half an hour before Nikki and the doctor finally came in looking pleased. Tana and Ryder both stood up shaking hands with the doctor as he went over Nikki's test results.

There were no visible abnormalities in any of her results and even her final scans were clear, showing no permanent damage. He pronounced her fully recovered and told her to avoid any contact sports for at least six more months and encouraged her to check in with her regular family doctor if there were any concerns or setbacks.

"Can she drive a standard again?" Ryder asked, hoping that the car she had gotten was still going to be usable for her.

"Of course. But you should probably practice a little before jumping right back in to make sure those memory patterns and reflexes are still working." The doctor said.

Ryder promised to take her out a few times to give her a refresher before she went back to Sherwood Park. The doctor shook Tana and Ryder's hands again and said he was going to close Nikki's file.

Tana gave her daughter a big hug and Nikki was all smiles.

"Please don't think I don't love you guys, or that I'm not grateful for everything that you've done, but I can't wait to go back home!" She was hopping around with excitement and Tana laughed.

"No. We understand Sweetheart. You have your own life to get back to with friends and of course, Brad." Tana said as Ryder held the door open for them and the trio walked down the hall to the elevators.

They made their way to Ryder's truck and back home with Nikki texting her friends and Brad the whole time. She planned to start packing and moving as soon as Jess and Brad could arrange a few days from work to help her settle in.

Brad and Jess had gotten a nice apartment already. Everything except Nikki's car had been moved out of storage into the apartment. Thanks to Tana, the three of them had a really nice place and hardly needed to spend any money at all to get it set up.

As soon as they got home, Nikki was off making the necessary arrangements to move back to Edmonton. She even called her boss to tell him she could go back on the schedule. Ryder already told her he was going to have a plane ready for whenever Jess and Brad could pick her up. Tana had offered to fly back with her and help her settle in, but Nikki reassured her mom it was okay, that she could handle it with Brad.

Tana was changing the bandage on Ryder's leg when Nikki came flying into the living room talking a mile a minute. Ryder laughed and asked her to slow down to first gear so they could understand her. Nikki took a deep breath to calm down and explained that Brad and Jess were both off on the eleventh, so she wanted to fly back then.

"I can start work again as soon as the sixteenth. I'll be settled in in no time. So, if you can arrange the flight, I'll be out of your guys' hair in two days!" Nikki was thrilled to able to get back to her original plans.

She already told her mother she had registered for Graphics Design and was starting classes in the winter semester. She was planning to work full time until she started school then go back to part time, so she could focus on her studies. Tana was finishing up with Ryder's bandage as Ryder addressed Nikki.

"I'm sure we can get you a flight for the eleventh. That means we need to get you back in the Camaro right away."

Nikki agreed, so she and Ryder made plans to go out the next day then she took back off to her room.

Tana was gathering up all of the supplies from changing Ryder's bandage and she told him his burn was looking really good. His leg was healing beautifully. He gave credit for that to his wife's loving care as he got up to go and arrange a flight for Nikki.

Tana cleaned and dressed the burn three times every day and it was starting to itch which Ryder took as a good sign of healing. He had been off the crutches completely for a while now and was even walking normally again.

~~

Nikki was preoccupied with packing and brushing up on her driving skills during her last two days in Langley. She was a little rusty, but Ryder got her back to her earlier skill level in no time. Tana spent hours helping her pack and get things ready to go as much as she could. She even told her about the money from the auction. It wasn't a huge amount, but it was enough to give her a safety net if she needed one.

Nikki thanked her mother and hugged her tight. "I'm really going to miss you, Mom."

Tana fought back tears as she held her daughter. "I'm going to miss you too, Sweetheart. Promise you'll call and text lots. And if you need anything, just ask."

It was mid-afternoon on the tenth and Ryder planned a surprise farewell dinner for Nikki seeing it was her last night at home. He reserved the Club Room at the Gotham Steakhouse and invited all the other band members with their wives and children to join them.

Tana and Ryder were in their room getting ready for when Ryder noticed she was unusually quiet. Knowing this was bittersweet for her, especially after Nikki's accident, Ryder stopped her as she was brushing out her hair and pulled her into a hug.

"You don't have to say anything, Baby. I know this is tough. You love her so much and the two of you are so close. I get it." He kissed her and when she looked up at him with tears in her eyes, he caressed her face, wiping them away as they spilled over.

"I'm so happy for her. Especially seeing the past few months, but God. It's hard to believe she's already grown up and ready to be on her own. It seems like last week that she was a little toddler still hiding behind me when someone would say hi to her." Tana buried her face in Ryder's chest for a moment and took a few deep breaths to compose herself.

"You've done an amazing job raising her. She's strong and capable. She's also one of the brightest kids I've seen. But then again, she's your child and so much like you, I wouldn't expect her to be anything but a success."

Tana smiled up at Ryder, thanking him for the compliment and for being there for her.

"I wouldn't have it any other way." He assured her.

"This party you're giving her. Thank you for that too. She's going to love it. Plus, all the kids will get to say goodbye to her."

"It's my pleasure. And it's not goodbye. We can visit her anytime and have her come out here to visit too. I think if we didn't have her back every once in a while, Becky, Mia, and Paige would never forgive us. They adore Nikki."

Tana agreed as she finished brushing out her hair and got herself ready to go for dinner. She changed from her jeans into dark gray figure-hugging dress pants with a lime green and black sleeveless blouse and added a pair of black suede ankle boots.

When she appeared from the closet, Ryder arched a brow at her. "Very nice, Mrs. Evans. For someone who claims to be such a simple person, you sure know how to turn heads."

Tana waved him off smiling at him. "Ha Ha. I just wear what I like and what I find comfortable. I don't bother with trends, or the latest fashion must haves."

"What you don't realize is because of that, you draw more attention to yourself. You're very beautiful. Your style and demeanor show a strong, confident woman. And that is very sexy."

Tana smiled and walked over to him. Reaching up to hold his face in her hands, she kissed him passionately.

"Thank you. Even if I think you're crazy."

Ryder narrowed his eyes at her and pursed his lips. "Crazy for you. You're incredibly beautiful and very sexy. So much, so I can't get enough of you."

He snaked his arms around her waist letting his hands caress down her hips and over her bottom. "Tana, I've never had a connection with anyone like I do with you. It goes far beyond sex. You're part of me, my heart, my mind, my spirit, and my soul. Don't get me wrong, my body craves you constantly but so does every part of me. You are the most beautiful, amazing person I have ever met. Inside and out."

Ryder leaned down and kissed her, parting her lips with his tongue as he searched for hers. He kissed her gently and with a passion that Tana could feel reaching right to her very core. Her heart fluttered at the feelings he awoke in her, the same feelings he felt for her. He shared this with her, drawing her to him even more than before solidifying their bond forever. They were both breathless when Ryder broke their kiss, their gaze locked to one another.

Holding her close, he placed a gentle hand on her neck, caressing her cheek with his thumb. "I never want to be without you, Tana. Life would be unbearable."

She looked up at him with everything she felt in her heart visible in those vibrant green eyes. "You have no worries. I'm not going anywhere. You're my best friend, my partner, my lover, my soul mate, my husband, and my light."

Ryder looked down at her with a loving smile. "Good. Let's get moving. We have a party to get to."

Giving her bottom a squeeze, Ryder headed out of their room and down to the front entrance with Tana following behind. Ian was kenneling the dogs in the laundry room while Nikki was putting the finishing touches on her make-up.

There were still a few scars on her face and forehead that hadn't faded as much as she would've liked and it took a little longer to blend them in with make-up. They were up by her hairline, so they were easily hidden with her bangs too. Tana kept reassuring her that they would fade in time.

When she did emerge from her room finally ready to go, she looked happy and healthy. No one would ever know from looking at her that twelve weeks ago she had almost died. Ryder smiled at her as he held the door to the waiting car open and everyone piled in.

Ever since Nikki had been hit by a drunk driver, Ryder was less willing to have a few drinks and get behind the wheel. He would rather have a car come and pick them up than risk being the one to cause the kind of pain that they had to endure to anyone.

The family talked and laughed all the way to the restaurant and everyone was in good spirits as they were led to the private room. Ryder had been at a party there many years ago but none of the others had. He knew from the texts he had received while they were still driving, that everyone else was there and waiting. So far, Nikki didn't suspect a thing.

The hostess led them to the door of the Club Room and ushered them inside. Tana noticed the sign on the door that said, *'Private Party in Progress'* and glanced at Nikki. She noticed it too and frowned, but before she could ask what was going on, she saw Becky running for her. Bending down, she scooped the raven haired four-year old up in her arms and looked into the private room.

The entire Severe State family was there socializing with their wives while the children ran around playing.

"Oh my God. You're all here to say goodbye to me?" Nikki asked looking near tears.

"Of course we are. You're family. We couldn't let you go off on your own without a proper party. That's not our style." Matt said coming up and giving her a hug.

One by one everybody gave Nikki hugs, wishing her well with her big move. Even the kids gave her hugs and kisses telling her that they were happy she was all better now to have a big party. Laughing at the children's innocence, their parents led them to the group of tables off to one side in the room.

Taking their seats at the tables that were arranged in a big U shape the waitresses came in and took their drink orders while the conversations flowed easily. Ian was asked if he was settling in well and he admitted he missed his old friends, but had already made a few new ones while out quadding.

As the guys interacted with each other, they drew Ian into their discussion topics covering the latest football scores and the upcoming hockey season. The women all discussed Nikki's recovery, her move the next day and even mentioned Tana and Ryder's upcoming honeymoon. Meals were ordered, drinks were had and everyone was having a good time.

No one was driving home. Everyone had done the same as Ryder by calling a car and driver, so it was a great evening with all of them just hanging out and having an incredible meal. Nikki even had a few drinks but was still being careful not to overdo it. Ian was allowed to have one too, but Tana had to sneak it to him without the servers noticing.

After dinner, all the younger children, and Tana's two older ones wandered off to the open space where Nikki got them playing games. They played *Ring Around the Rosy, Duck Duck Goose, Red Light Green Light* and *What Time is it Mr. Wolf* while the adults visited and watched all the kids playing.

At one point, Ian was Mr. Wolf. He was telling the kids what time it was, and they were taking the appropriate number of steps toward him. Ben motioned for the other band members to quietly get behind all the little kids. Everyone knew what he was up to and the next time the kids asked Ian *"What time is it, Mr. Wolf,"* Ben, Matt, Chris, and Ryder all yelled and growled *"Lunch Time!"* as all the adults chased the little kids around the room, causing them to screech and laugh.

In all, it was a great evening and one that Tana knew Nikki would treasure.

At the end of the evening as they all sat back in the car relaxing on the drive back home, each of them was smiling. It had been the perfect going away party for Nikki. The little kids got a chance to play with her once more and everyone got to see how well she was doing before she headed back to Sherwood Park.

Back at home, Nikki and Ian said goodnight to their mother and Ryder. When Nikki gave Ryder a hug, she said a special thank you to him for the going away party.

"It was the best. Thank you so much, Ryder."

He squeezed her back and told her it was the least he could do. Nikki stood up on tiptoe and planted an adoring kiss on his cheek then was off to her room for her last night at home. Ryder smiled at her retreating back then folded Tana into his arms.

"Well, that was fun. I'm glad it worked out so well." Ryder said as he held his wife.

"*Mmmm*... me too. It was perfect. Thank you." Tana looked up at him and kissed him as she stood on tiptoe before turning and leading him by the hand up to their bedroom.

Once in the privacy of their own room, Tana let go of his hand and went to lift her shirt over her head when Ryder stopped her.

"Don't." He rasped to her as he sided up behind her and placing his hands over hers.

Brushing her hair over one shoulder, he exposed her neck before leaning down to graze his teeth from her ear down to the point where her neck and shoulder met. Ryder's hands left hers as he kissed his way up and down her neck. He went from front to back and across to the other side as he slowly lifted the hem of her shirt up. Shivering, Tana moaned out softly, writhing against his body as he took his time undressing her.

Continuing to torment her, Ryder ran his hands over her stomach up to her breasts, still cradled in her bra and over her now bare shoulders then down her back. Feeling like her skin was electrically charged, Tana's breathing quickened. She reached her hands up and behind her head, fisting them into Ryder's hair as he lowered his mouth to hers.

Their lips met and parted, tongues attacking each other with heated desire. Ryder let his fingertips trail lightly down her sides to the clasp of her dress pants. Without pulling back from their kiss, he undid her pants letting them slide to the floor.

Tana moaned into his mouth as he slid a hand underneath her lacy thong, his fingertips searching her folds. She pulled him closer, her body pressing against his as her hips moved in time with his fingers and his erection pressed into her back.

When Ryder finally released her mouth, he was completely breathless and Tana was shaking. She rocked her bottom and hips back pressing against him enticingly, making Ryder groan through his teeth. Removing his hand from her panties, he turned her to face him. Unclipping her bra, he slipped it off and threw it to the floor where the rest of her clothing already lay.

Tana stood in front of her husband with nothing on, but a tiny wisp of red lace covering her sex. Looking up at him, her eyes begged him to touch her, to please her, and to make her come.

Ryder placed a finger against his lips as if he was deciding what to do with her. His hazel eyes smoldering into her, making her heart beat even faster with anticipation.

"You're gorgeous." He murmured from behind his finger.

Tana tossed her hair over her shoulder and placed her hands on her hips meeting his hot gaze with her own.

"I want to be inside of you." His voice had that deep huskiness to it that drove her wild.

Reaching out she unbuckled his belt then unfastened his jeans, pushing them down with his boxers. Ryder stepped out of his jeans, leaving them in a pile on the floor as he grabbed the hem of his shirt and quickly ripped it over his head, tossing it to the side. He took Tana around her hips and picked her up, carrying her over to the bed where he deposited her.

Placing a knee and hand on one side of her, Ryder gracefully lifted his body up onto the bed and settled himself between Tana's parted thighs. He braced his weight on his elbows and leaned down to kiss Tana lovingly. When she caressed his tongue with her own, his desire escalated even further and he took the kiss deeper, possessing her.

Tana hooked one leg over his hip and simultaneously pulled his pelvis down closer to hers as she lifted hers up to meet him, rotating her hips. Her signals weren't lost on Ryder, but he was in no rush either. Tearing his lips from hers he slid down her body just far enough to draw one perked nipple into his mouth.

"Ahhh..." Tana cried out as she grabbed handfuls of Ryder's hair.

Ryder worked her nipple, teasing it with his tongue and teeth until Tana was hissing at him as she fisted his hair. He released the now rock-hard bud and switched to her other one working it over as he had the first one. Tana's nails were digging into his scalp and neck while her hips bucked under him. She had been ramped up so high that when Ryder reached down to find her clit with his fingertips she almost came on the spot.

"Whoa, Baby, *Shhh…*" Ryder soothed her, trying to calm her down. "Not yet."

He caressed her face and sides, avoiding any of her intense erogenous zones, trying to help pull her back from the edge. Tana tried to help by taking deep breaths to regain control of her body as Ryder calmed her.

"Goddamn it, Ryder. See what you do to me?" She met his eyes and he could see the intensity still there under a thin veil of control.

He knew it wouldn't take much for her to lose that little bit she managed to regain. Even though his intentions were to prolong this for both of their pleasure, Ryder was tempted to take her now just to feel her come hard all around him.

"I'm barely hanging on myself, Tana." He growled at her. "It's taking everything I've got to keep myself from burying my cock as deep inside of you so I can feel you come."

Tana grabbed his hands and brought them high over her head, lacing her fingers with his and clamping them tight.

"Then do it!" She demanded, planting her heels into the mattress and lifting her hips up to entice him.

Ryder saw the aggression in her face and gave her a slow smile, so hot that her sex clenched even more, aching for him. Tightening his hands down on hers, he lifted his body up and with a swivel of his hips, positioned himself at her entrance. Her eyes daring him to take her, Tana locked her gaze to him, her chest heaving with every hot breath.

Ryder's lips curled back showing his clenched teeth and rocked his hips forward hard, slamming into Tana's tight sex. She screamed out in pleasure, as his eyes rolled back in his head, gasping as her heat surrounded him.

"Oh fuck yeah." Ryder moaned in her ear as he slowly withdrew then rocked back in.

"Baby, you feel incredible." Ryder murmured tightening his grip on her hands above her head.

Every stroke Ryder made heightened Tana's passion driving her closer to climax. Raising her knees up higher, she locked her ankles behind Ryder's back and her head pressed back into the mattress as he began to move faster.

"Yes, Ryder! So good." She cried out as he could feel her body tense.

She was on the edge and Ryder pressed forward hard, tipping her over. Arching her back and gripping his hands hard with her own Tana's voice rang out sharply, the cords in her neck straining at the force of her orgasm. An intense heat surrounded him as he continued thrusting hard and moments later, his own passion intensified as he released deep within his wife.

Collapsing, his body covered hers on the bed, their hands locked together with her legs still wrapped tightly around him. Tana placed small pecks along his collarbone and neck while he caught his breath. It took him a few minutes before he could raise himself up onto his elbows and look down at the incredible woman beneath him.

"I love how aggressive you can get." He rasped leaning down to give her a kiss.

"Do you now?" Tana pulled her hands free from Ryder's and ran them down his sides, grasping his firm buttocks in her hands.

"Yeah, I do. I can be romantic with you when we want. But I like that I don't have to worry about you being offended if I'm a little rough or creative in bed."

Ryder kissed her then lifted himself up a bit to allow Tana to slip out from under him. She settled in beside him and he wrapped his arms around her spooning up against her back.

"Well then, I guess I'll have to do some creative thinking for our honeymoon to keep you on your toes." Tana smirked.

She could feel the deep rumble of his chuckle in her chest and his lips press down on the top of her head. "I highly doubt you're running out of ideas. And I'm not complaining either."

Tana rolled to face him. "You better not be, or we have a real big problem."

Ryder crushed his lips down on hers silencing her.

"No complaints. Promise. Now go to sleep." He ordered and kissed her again.

She lay her head down on her husband's chest listening to his heart as her fingers caressed his abs. She could feel him relax and sink into the mattress, his breathing becoming deeper and more rhythmic as he drifted off to sleep.

Tana lay awake for a while longer listening to him breathe and relishing in the feel of his arms around her. Never had she felt so safe, so completely loved and understood by anyone. And never did she expect to find such happiness as she had with this incredible man. This Rockstar. Her Rockstar. It was something that only happened in dreams, yet she was living it. As a content smile curled her lips, Tana kissed her husband's chest.

"You're my everything, Ryder Evans. I love you." She whispered.

Ryder sighed in his sleep and tightened his arms around her as Tana closed her eyes and listened to him breathe.

Chapter 24

The next morning after Tana had gone for her run, she and Ryder showered then the two of them headed down to the kitchen to make a nice breakfast. Ryder wanted to make pancakes and bacon for the kids. Both of them were busy cooking together when Ian came into the kitchen to get himself some milk asking if they needed any help. Tana got him to set the table then go see if Nikki was up.

Ian poured himself a glass of milk then set the table as Tana finished up the pancakes and Ryder pulled the bacon out of the pan. They were just putting the food on the table when Ian went to go get his sister.

While they waited for the kids, Ryder poured himself a coffee and Tana made herself a tea. Both of them had just sat down when Nikki and Ian came into the kitchen. Nikki detoured straight to the coffee pot to get herself a cup before joining the rest of the family at the table.

"What time do we have to leave for the airport?" Nikki asked as she settled into her seat.

Ian was already digging into the food and Tana chastised him to make sure he left some for everyone else too.

"Your flight leaves at four thirty, so if we leave here about two that should give us plenty of time to get you through security and all of your stuff checked in." Ryder told her as he handed her the plate of pancakes.

Nikki took a couple of pancakes and some bacon then handed the plates back to Ryder. "Okay. That should give me enough time to get cleaned up and to finish packing."

Tana glanced at the clock and was shocked to see it was already after eleven. "Are you going to miss us?"

Nikki stuffed a forkful of pancake in her mouth and nodded. After she swallowed and took a sip of her coffee. "Of course I'm going to miss you guys. I love you all, but it's time for me to live my life."

Tana smiled sadly. She had spent the last eighteen years raising her daughter to be strong and independent and today was the day where all her sacrifices and teachings came back to bite her in the ass. She knew she had to let her daughter go, but it didn't make this any easier. She and Nikki had a very special bond and Tana was really going to miss having her around.

For the rest of the meal, they avoided the topic of Nikki leaving and both kids asked about Tana and Ryder's upcoming honeymoon. With everything that had gone on since the wedding, Tana had barely thought about it. She had no clue what Ryder had planned.

"So where exactly are we going?" Tana asked as Nikki and Ian cleaned up the dishes.

Ryder shrugged. "You've been so preoccupied that I've taken over planning the whole thing. I should just keep it as a surprise. Your passport is still valid right?"

Tana nodded and protested at the idea of him keeping it a secret. "How am I supposed to know what to pack if you keep it a secret? Plus, I'd like to know where we are going."

"I can always pack for you. Ian is going to stay with Ben and Carla, so it's not like you need to know in order to tell them in case of an emergency. They already know." Now that the thought had occurred to him to keep it as a surprise, he was really considering it and seeing if he could pull it off.

Tana didn't like his idea, but she wasn't mad either. She took it in good humor and demanded that if he was going to do that, then at the very least promise to pack properly for her.

"*Hmmm*… I think it'll be pretty easy. That hot little number you wore on our wedding night and your bikini should do it. I doubt you'll be wearing much otherwise." Ryder spun her into his arms and leaned down to kiss her neck.

Tana giggled and pushed his head away from her neck playfully as he held her tighter. Both Ian and Nikki groaned.

"Next time wait till we leave the room, please." Ian begged frowning at them.

"Little brother, this is one good reason to move out as soon as you're done school." Nikki looked up at her brother and he agreed with her as they both hurried out of the room.

Ian offered to help Nikki finish packing and load her bags into the truck for her. He was going to miss his sister, but he was also happy for her. Her moving back to Sherwood Park meant she was okay again. To him, he would rather miss her while she lived far away than if she had died. Tana and Ryder stayed behind in the kitchen and watched them go.

"Seriously, Ryder. Where are we going?" Tana laughed as he nuzzled at her neck telling her nothing definite.

"Well, you need a bikini and your passport. Oh. And we're going to have to get there by plane."

"Well, no shit!" Tana smacked his ass hard.

"Ow. What was that for?" Laughing playfully, acting like he was hurt.

"You know damn well what that was for." Tana was giggling.

She turned around pretending to try to get away from him, but Ryder held fast and pulled her back against him, her bottom pressing into his thighs.

"I'm not telling you. I'll help you pack, but I'm not saying anything till we get to the airport. Just trust me. You'll enjoy it."

Ryder's hot breath on the back of her ear sent shivers down her spine. Trying to contain them only magnified the intensity and she could feel him smile against her head. He opened his mouth and nipped her earlobe making her breath catch in her throat.

"Don't start what we can't finish." Tana hissed through her teeth.

"*Hmmm*... oh, we can finish Baby. Just not right now. We have to take Nikki to the airport soon."

Ryder's voice rasped deep and sexy in her ears making her heart beat faster. He placed a splayed palm on her stomach and pressed her to him even tighter as he rocked his hips in a figure eight, moving her body with his. Tana could feel his arousal starting to mount, pressing into her back.

"If you keep that up, we are going to finish here, now." Tana gasped feeling heat pool between her thighs.

Ryder seized her chin and turned her face to him. Pressing his lips down to hers, he forced his way into her mouth and devoured her with his desire.

Tana returned his intensity feeling that familiar charge running through her, heating her blood and sending it rushing through her body.

She melted against him forgetting about the honeymoon, about Nikki's flight and about anything except becoming one with her husband.

Reaching up, Tana thrust her hands into his hair, gasping as they kissed. Ryder's one hand was still pressed to her belly. His other released her chin and caressed down her neck to her breast then made its way down her side.

Ryder pulled away panting and grasped Tana around the thighs. He tossed her over his shoulder in a fireman's carry and stalked through the main floor headed for the stairs to the bedroom.

Giggling, Tana watched his buttocks moving enticingly through his jeans. "Ryder, put me down. We have to go soon."

"No." He continued up the stairs not putting her down.

"We have to get Nikki to the airport." Tana laughed as he kicked the door closed behind him and carried her over to the bed.

"We have time." Ryder un-shouldered her effortlessly. As she flopped onto the mattress, he was already stripping his jeans and boxers off.

Tana was scooting herself up on the bed when he seized her ankles shaking his head.

"Down here." He said pulling her to the edge of the bed and unzipping her jeans, yanking them down.

Tana's heart was racing and her eyes were shining. There was a little smile playing at the corners of her mouth as he removed her thong and positioned her where he wanted. Ryder could see the pulse in her neck and the way her eyes were shining. It made him hard knowing he could turn her on this way.

"Do you like it when I'm aggressive with you?" He asked not wanting to hurt her or scare her. Tana nodded her head without hesitation.

"It's hot. I mean really hot. I don't want you to be an ass or anything, but when you take charge and even get a little dirty, it really gets me going." Tana admitted shamelessly.

Ryder had a sinful smile curling his lips. "Good. We don't have much time, so this will be quick."

Ryder kissed her whispering how much he loved her into her ear, then stood her over the edge of the bed with her feet on the bottom rail.

He positioned himself at her slit then leaned down to kiss her back and whisper in her ear.

"Promise to let me know if this is too much, or if it hurts."

Panting and excited Tana promised then added, "It won't."

Without warning, Ryder thrust forward hard penetrating all the way into her cervix, making Tana cry out in pleasure.

"Yes! God, Ryder."

Ryder grabbed her hips and held her firmly in place as he pummeled into her. They were both highly aroused, making the intense pace feel incredible for them.

Ryder rotated his hips as he slammed his pelvis into her backside, hitting that spot that was always guaranteed to make her come hard. Not being able to deny her that pleasure, Ryder continued until Tana cried out his name and he could feel her wet, hot and tight all around him. Giving a few more hard thrusts, Ryder's own cries mixed with hers as he held onto her hips more for balance as he caught his breath. Tana was still clutching the duvet beneath her when he finally released her hips and gently pulled her up to a standing position. She stepped down from the rail and he rubbed her shoulders.

"You okay?" He asked kissing her.

Tana nodded and ran her hands up his back. "O*ooooh*... yes. That was intense."

"*Mmmm*... yes it was. You're incredible you know that?" Ryder held her close, for a moment before he bent to pick up her thong and jeans. Handing them to her, Ryder then turned to retrieve his own clothes from the floor to get dressed.

Tana pulled her clothes back on and went into the bathroom to quickly brush her hair. Ryder came in behind her and looked at his own. It always looked mussed up, but it was even more so after Tana had stuffed her hands through it. He straightened it out as much as he normally did then leaned down to plant a kiss on the top of Tana's shoulder.

"I'll see you downstairs." He said and left her to finish brushing the tangles out of her hair.

Once back downstairs, Ryder headed down the hall to check on Nikki to see if she was all packed and saw a pile of bags just outside her room door. Stepping over them, he knocked lightly before poking his head in the room.

"How's it going in here?" Ryder looked around.

Nikki had everything packed up and was just checking the room to make sure nothing she wanted was left behind. Ian was sitting on the chair in her room. They had been talking while she finished up.

"Almost done. Just checking for anything I might have missed then we can load up." She was stuffing the last bits and pieces into Tana's luggage set and closing the suitcases.

Ryder told her he was going to start putting everything into the truck and Ian jumped up.

"I'll help."

Both of them grabbed a couple of the bags each and headed to the garage, passing Tana. She was coming to check on Nikki as well.

"Wow. I didn't think she had that much stuff here." Tana said as the guys passed her each hauling two fair sized suitcases each.

"There's more in the hall." Ian called out as he followed Ryder.

Tana continued to Nikki's room where she was just finishing closing the last suitcase.

"Well, I guess I'm going to have to buy myself new luggage before my honeymoon." Tana saw her whole set was on the bedroom floor, filled with the last of Nikki's belongings.

"Uh... yeah, sorry Mom. But I didn't want to take Ryder's and I needed more bags."

"That's all right. I honestly didn't think you had that much here." Tana said looking around.

"Well, there was everything from the hospital and the stuff you brought from the house, plus I still had a bunch of clothes and stuff that I left behind from our last trip out. It kinda just kept getting added to."

There were nine bags in total filled. Four good sized ones and five small carry on sized ones. Tana and Nikki grabbed a suitcase each and were taking them out into the hall when Ryder came back for another load.

"I'll take those." He took the suitcases from the girls and leaned down to kiss Tana.

"Guess we have to go shopping before we leave." He murmured as he headed back up the hall.

Nikki grabbed the last suitcase out of her room and stood there for a moment looking in.

"Forgetting something?" Tana asked.

Nikki shook her head. "No. Just remembering. It may not have been my room officially or for long, but it was really nice. I'm going to miss having my own bathroom though."

She shrugged then headed up the hall and out to the truck. Tana laughed as she followed her.

~~

Tana was holding Nikki close and tears were falling down her cheeks. She was whispering to her daughter to be careful and to stay in touch. The porters had taken her bags to security already and she was now being called through herself. The time had come for Tana to let her daughter go to start her own life.

Ryder gave her one last quick hug, telling her he loved her and that he would miss her. Then Ian stepped up to say goodbye to his sister. She stood on her toes to hug her brother while tears that had been threatening to fall, slid down her cheeks.

"I'm going to miss you little brother. Come see me soon, kay?" Nikki said as she wiped the tears from her cheeks.

Ian nodded keeping his head down fighting back his own tears.

Tana came up and took Nikki into her arms once more. "I love you, Sweetheart. If you need anything at all promise me, you'll call. I don't care what time it is, you call."

"I will Mom. Promise. I love you too." Nikki sniffed as her tears fell freely again.

"You better go. They're waiting for you." Tana let her go and stepped back as Ryder put a comforting arm around her back.

Nikki headed to security and before she was out of sight, she turned and waved to her family. All three waved back as Tana stifled a sob and wiped her eyes with the back of her hand. In moments, Nikki was gone out of sight.

Tana took a deep shuddering breath as she turned and looked at her son. "Well, I guess that is that. Your sister is officially on her own."

Ian nodded again and all of them headed back to the exit to go to the truck. Ryder still held Tana close, comforting her and knowing this was going to be a big adjustment for her.

As they walked through the terminal, Ryder leaned down quietly asking Tana if she was okay. She looked sad. All he could do was hold her and give her time to adjust. He was just glad that in three days they would be leaving on their honeymoon and was hoping that would perk her spirits.

Thank you for reading my book. If you enjoyed it, won't you please take a moment to leave me a review at your favorite retailer?

Tana and Ryder have more to share. Their love story continues with Book 3 of 'A Rockstar & A Runner', Kindred Souls.